THE BOY CAPTIVE IN CANADA

MARY P. WELLS SMITH

THE BOY CAPTIVE IN CANADA

Mary P. Wells Smith

Published by:
Gideon House Books
5518 Flint St. Shawnee KS 66203
www.gideonhousebooks.com

Typesetting & Cover Design: Josh Pritchard

ISBN-13: 978-1-943133-72-7

CONTENTS

PREFACE

THIS book completes the story of the strange adventures of little Stephen Williams, the ten-year-old son of Deerfield's minister, who lived over a year alone among the Indians in Northern Vermont and Canada. A brief resumé of his story, recounted in "The Boy Captive of Old Deerfield," is given as an introduction to the present volume. In reading this true story, we can but wonder afresh what superhuman power enabled a young boy, suddenly dragged from home and friends by savages, to endure and survive such an ordeal, and realize anew that in the religious faith instilled by our Puritan forefathers lay the secret of this power of enduring seemingly unbearable hardships and sorrow, so often manifested by our ancestors in the trying times of the old French and Indian wars.

In writing this story, it has been impossible wholly to ignore the religious differences which played so prominent and vital part in the history of the period. English Puritans and French Catholics were engaged in a life and death struggle for the possession of this great western continent. The modern spirit of tolerance which, while standing stanchly to its own form of belief, can yet appreciate and admire the merits of a differing faith, was then unknown. Puritan and Catholic alike firmly believed that each held the only truth, and that his opponent's soul was doomed to eternal destruction. At all hazards and by any means, he must be won from the error of his ways, and converted to the truth. Religious differences doubly intensified the bitterness of political strife.

The writer, rejoicing in the friendship of several Catholics whose lives beautifully illustrate the words of Jesus, "by their fruits ye shall know them," can little sympathize with the horror of Catholicism felt by Rev. John Williams and his contemporaries. But the truth of history requires that the actual feeling of the period be faithfully depicted.

M. P. W. S.
Greenfield, Mass.,
June 20, 1905.

INTRODUCTION

ON the night of February 29, 1704, a band of two hundred Frenchmen and one hundred and forty Indians from Canada surprised the frontier village of Deerfield, Mass. The assailants burned nearly half the houses in the little settlement, killed forty-nine of the inhabitants, and carried off into captivity one hundred and eleven unfortunate men, women, and children. Among the captives were Rev. John Williams, minister of Deerfield, his wife Eunice, and his five children, two young children having been slain during the assault. Mrs. Williams, the wife and mother, was killed during the second day of the journey, being weak from recent illness and unable to travel. At the mouth of the White River, in Hartford, Vt., the company separated. Mr. Williams, with his sons, Samuel and Warham, and his daughters, Esther and Eunice, were taken to Canada, by that trail so unhappily familiar to English captives, up White River into the Green Mountains, then down the Winooski to Lake Champlain. But Stephen Williams, a boy of but ten, was separated from all his family and friends, and borne off to the north by his captor, Mummumcott or Wattanamon, doomed to live alone among the Indians, and become an Indian, so far as his captor could make him.

With Mummumcott was his nephew Kewakcum, an Indian boy somewhat older than Cosannip, as Stephen was called by the Indians.

A boy friendship having sprung up between Kewakcum and Stephen, Kewakcum persuaded his father, Waneton, to purchase Stephen from his kinsman Mummumcott. Waneton, and his squaw, Heelahdee, were kind, in their way, to Stephen, and Kewakcum trained him in woodcraft. But his cousin, Nunganey, another Indian boy in the camp, of a sly and crafty disposition, delighted in teasing the white captive whenever opportunity offered. Katequa was the little five-year-old daughter of Heelahdee and Waneton.

The party of Indians with whom Stephen lived rambled about, hunting and fishing in Northern Vermont, for two or three months, until spring, and finally summer, came. Near Cowass[1] they were joined by other Indians, with a few white captives, one of whom was Jacob Hix, a soldier captured at Deerfield, well known to Stephen, but now so wasted by hardship and starvation, that he was but a ghost of his old strong, manly self. Towards the last of July, Waneton and his band "set away for Canada," bearing Stephen with them. And here we resume the story of Stephen's adventures.

1 At Newbury, Vt.

1

THE CAMP IN THE MOUNTAINS

THE July sun was pouring its late afternoon rays hotly down into a little valley, high up among the hills of Northern Vermont, shut in by these same hills, which were tumbled wildly in all about it. Through the valley wound a small, clear river, a mountain stream, rippling down over many a fall on its way to Lake Champlain.[2] Dense forest everywhere covered hill and dale, save a small strip of open meadow land along the river's margin, where the ever-changing current and spring freshets had stripped away the trees, and deposited fertile soil. No house, or road, or sign of human occupation was to be seen. All was wild and solitary, the primitive wilderness.

Out of the forest came a doe and her fawn, to crop the tangled wild grass growing rankly almost as high as their heads. The doe stepped down into the river, to drink the cool water. Not a sound broke the intense stillness. Yet suddenly the doe started, lifted her head, looking eastward, as if frightened, sniffed the air and pointed her delicate ears, as if to catch some distant sound audible to her above the murmur of the river. Then away she bounded with long leaps into the forest, her fawn close at her heels.

2 The Winooski, near Montpelier, Vt.

Presently out of the forest to the East appeared the leader of a small band of Indians, his followers straggling after him in Indian file. They were heavily laden, and walked as if weary. The squaws were bent under great burdens, all they could possibly carry, and even the proud warriors deigned to bear packs in addition to their weapons. Nor were the boys exempt; they too must carry all their strength admitted. For this was Waneton's band of Abenakis, returning from the campaign at Deerfield and their summer hunting to their homes at St. Francis in Canada, laden with skins and the spoils brought from Deerfield.

"Make the camp here," commanded Waneton, as the band reached the meadow; and Heelahdee, Eenisken, and the other squaws deftly swung to earth their heavy packs, and set to work, in the edge of the forest, cutting wigwam poles. Heelahdee braced the board, to which was strapped her pappoose, carefully up against the trunk of a huge pine, saying to Katequa,

"Katequa must take care of little Ohopasha while Heelahdee works."

The pappoose was tired and restless, after the long, hot day, and began to wriggle and twist, setting up a plaintive cry.

"Hush, hush, little mouse," said Katequa. "Do not cry. See the pretty plaything Katequa will make for Ohopasha. Cosannip taught her how to make it."

And Katequa fastened a stem of the long grass to a big pine cone, dangling and swinging it before the baby's eyes, as she softly cooed a lullaby.

Old Wees, nose to the ground, was eagerly sniffing along the trail left by the doe and fawn. Seeing this, Waneton and the other hunters seized their weapons and followed the dog, bending over to examine minutely every bent grass stem or dead leaf, for traces of game.

Mahtocheegah thrust the blunt end of an arrow into the faint trail, and taking up a bit of earth, sniffed at it with a wise look.

"Trail fresh," he said. "Deer stepped here but just now."

The Indians eagerly followed the trail, for game had been scarce of late.

"I wish Cosannip would come," said Katequa.

"Ho, Cosannip no good. Him no stronger than Ohopasha. He way back in the forest, stumbling along like a pappoose of two summers," said Nunganey, throwing down a back load of poles.

He and Kewakcum had been pressed into service by their mothers, and were stripping off the leaves and branches from the poles cut by the squaws. Then Kewakcum waded into the river, bringing out large stones, with which he formed a circle on the turf. This was to be the fireplace. On the stones he started a fire, that all might be ready to cook the game, should the hunters have good luck.

Far up the stream, out of the forest now came staggering along alone what seemed a little Indian boy, bent under a pack far too great for his strength, walking as if each step were an effort. As he drew nearer, Katequa called joyously,

"Ho, ho, Ohopasha. Look, Cosannip comes. Cosannip will play with you, and sing a pretty English song to you. Come, Cosannip, come here."

Looking closely at the little boy, one could have seen that his skin, tanned and burned as it was, did not bear the genuine red hue of an Indian's. For this was Stephen Williams, child of Deerfield's minister, who had now been a captive for five weary months. Katequa ran to meet him, trying with her little hands to help him let his burden down to earth from the carrying strap.

"Now Cosannip can play with Katequa," she said.

"No, Katequa," said Stephen, wearily, shaking his head. Dark circles of fatigue were under his eyes, and his face was thin and hollow, making him look older than his years. "Cosannip must go back for his other pack before darkness falls, or Waneton will be angry."

He turned sorrowfully away. He so longed only to throw himself on the ground and rest, after the long, hot day of weary toil up and down hill, over stones and slippery rocks, through bush and brake and tangled forest paths. But Waneton and his band had accumulated such a wealth of skins and spoils, that all had to carry two packs. Their method was to carry one pack for a mile or two, leave it, and return for the other. Retracing the steps thus all day long, trebled the actual distance travelled, and was most wearisome. But Stephen well knew it was useless to rebel or complain. So long as he could walk, he must bear his share. Katequa sat watching him with a disappointed look, as the little boy walked slowly away, lost to sight at last in the forest.

The setting sun sent long, slanting rays in under the edge of the forest, but, as Stephen penetrated farther into its cool depths, fragrant with the resinous odor of pines and hemlocks, the night shadows began to thicken around him. It was dark and gloomy in the silent, solemn woods.

"I must try to hasten, though I feel as if I could not drag myself another step," thought Stephen, "or soon it will be so dark I cannot see the trail, and the wild beasts will begin to prowl."

At that instant, he heard a sound that set his heart beating fast, a sound like a person moaning. Any unusual noise was alarming when one was alone in the forest. Stephen well knew that the panther's cry is often mistaken for that of a human being in distress. He strained his eyes, looking up with head bent back, searching the tree branches in the gathering dusk for the lithe form of the wild beast, lying along a limb, ready to pounce on its prey. Walking thus, suddenly he stumbled over some object in the path, falling prostrate across it. He leaped up. It was the form of a man, lying huddled on the ground, over which he had fallen.

"Is that you, Stephen?" asked a faint voice.

"Oh, Jacob, is it you? What is the matter? Can I help you?"

"I have fallen from sheer weakness," said Jacob Hix, for he it was. "I cannot manage to rise, laden as I am with this pack. I thought to have perished here alone, a prey to wild beasts."

"I am so sorry for you, Jacob," said Stephen. "It is not far now to the spot where the Indians have camped. If you can manage to struggle on a little farther, you can rest there. Perhaps they will find some game, so we can have food, and that will strengthen you."

"I am too far gone. Nothing can help me now," said poor Jacob, in accents of utter despair. "'Tis too late for me."

Stephen tugged and pulled, and Jacob, encouraged by human sympathy and companionship, at last, by a great effort, managed to struggle to his feet.

"Now keep on, Jacob, as well as you can, straight ahead, towards that light place in the forest yonder. I will get my pack, and follow you," said Stephen.

He soon found his other pack, and hurried back, half forgetting his own weariness, in his sympathy for Jacob. Stephen had been with Indians who were hunting, and therefore, until recently, had had meat to eat most of the time. But the band who had captured Jacob and Deacon Hoyt, had settled at Cowass, planting corn, and the captives' only food had been such as they could find for themselves, chiefly roots and bark. Deacon Hoyt had already died from his hardships, and it was evident that Jacob could not much longer endure.

Stephen soon overtook him, and the two white captives struggled slowly on together, coming into camp at last, where the ruddy flames of Kewakcum's fire were blazing brightly in the dusk of the summer evening.

"Ho, ho, Cosannip," called Kewakcum, cheerfully. "Kewakcum has good news for Cosannip."

"Have the hunters brought in game?" asked Stephen, eyeing eagerly the pot hanging from the crotched sticks over the fire, and sniffing the air, for the delicious meaty odor of boiling venison.

"No, Manitou angry with Abenakis," said Kewakcum, shaking his head. "Deer run too fast; hunters shot nothing. But tomorrow Waneton commands that canoes be built. The river is now deep enough. Canoes float, carry packs. Cosannip no carry pack anymore."

"I should say that was good news," said Stephen, his face brightening. Already he felt less tired, for one ray of hope lightening the heart will carry the body far. Waneton and his band had traversed the Green Mountains until they had struck a branch of the Winooski and following it down, had now reached a point where the river, swollen by many tributary brooks from the hills around, was deep enough to float canoes.

Stephen hastened to tell Jacob this good news. The only supper that night was some strips of birch bark boiled down into a broth, a meagre food for half-starved folk. But at least it was good to drop the packs, and stretching the weary body out on the bed of hemlock boughs, to forget all for a time in the heavy sleep of exhaustion.

The next morning Waneton woke in fine spirits, and seeking out old Notoway, the medicine man, said,

"Waneton dreamed a good dream last night. In his dream he saw two men coming from the West, walking on the top of the trees. They smiled upon Waneton and told him he should kill a bear before another sunset."

"It is good," said Notoway. "Notoway will use all his charms to help bring good luck to Waneton's gun."

Waneton was eager to set off at once. But first the canoes must be started; they were to be "dugouts." Waneton and Mahtocheegah found two good canoe trees, great pines that towered on high, giants of the forest, a century or more old. They hacked away at these with their hatchets and the Deerfield axe, the squaws helping. At last the proud tops began to bend and sway, and then with a mighty cracking and groaning, the trees surged over, crashing on the ground. Long sections of the straight trunks were hacked off and drawn near the fire. Waneton and the hunters then departed, confident of success after Waneton's auspicious dream.

The squaws brought coals from the fire and succeeded in kindling a blaze along the top of the logs, which slowly ate its way down into the heart of the timber. When the logs were well charred, they took sharp metal gouges, made from the half of old gun barrels, sharpened at one end for this use. Some used hatchets, and even sharp stones. With these instruments the squaws dug out the charred wood, then renewed the fires to char the logs more deeply. They also hacked and hewed the ends of the logs into canoe shape. It was the hardest kind of work, but when it was ended the Indians had two canoes, heavy and clumsy, but strong; exactly what was needed for the rough work before them.

As soon as the boys were released from helping, Kewakcum seized his bow and arrows, and called to the others,

"Ho, ho, Nunganey, Cosannip! Come to the hunt with Kewakcum."

The boys struck off into the forest, hoping to secure squirrels, birds, birds' eggs, anything eatable. As they neared a tract of fallen timber, where a cyclone had swept over the forest, prostrating trees for a wide space around, suddenly the others noticed that Nunganey had disappeared.

"Why, where is Nunganey? I thought he was right behind us," said Stephen.

"Ho, Nunganey, he much sly," said Kewakcum. "Him go off by himself. Think him have better luck. Get something for himself, eat it all up."

Stephen, in advance, now made a happy discovery.

"Oh, Kewakcum," he cried, "here are red raspberries, ripe! See how thick the bushes are here, in among these fallen trees! Oh, how good they are," said Stephen, his mouth already full.

The boys picked and ate the delicious fruit, with a hunger born of long starvation. But soon Stephen said,

"I wish we could carry some of these berries home, to Jacob, and Katequa and the rest. But I don't see how we can."

The boys were bareheaded, and nearly naked, save for the cloth worn around the loins. They had no hats or pockets, or anything to put berries in. But Kewakcum's ingenuity did not fail him. He picked long stems of the wiry, wild grass, and began stringing berries on them.

"See, Cosannip," he said. "Make necklaces of the berries."

Stephen hastened to imitate Kewakcum, and the boys worked busily, eating and stringing the luscious berries, when from some distance in the wood behind them came a distressed cry, meant to imitate an owl's note.

"Whoo! Whoo!" rang out the call, in unmistakable distress.

"Nunganey calls," said Kewakcum. "Him want help."

The boys went back on their track, looking far and near in the forest for some sign of the missing Nunganey. The cry sounded nearer and nearer.

"Ho, ho, yonder is the sick owl," said Kewakcum at last. "Ho, ho, Nunganey went out for game and was caught in a trap!"

He pointed up, and Stephen now saw Nunganey high in a tree, in a most unfortunate plight. Walking behind the others, his quick eyes searching the forest all around, Nunganey had happened to spy a bluebird flying into the rotten hollow of an old tree trunk, high up above the ground.

Nunganey said nothing, but slipped behind a tree trunk until the other boys were well out of sight. Then, chuckling to himself at his own superior smartness, his mouth watering for birds' eggs, Nunganey, being a skillful climber, had mounted the tree, aided by broken branches protruding here and there from the trunk.

At last he was high enough to reach his hand over into the hollow. It was deeper than he expected, and he strained to reach down to the coveted nest. As he thus bore so hard upon it, the rotten wood beneath had parted under his weight, catching his arm in such a manner that it was impossible to withdraw it. Meantime the mother bird, finding a robber breaking into her house, whirred about his head with angry cries, picking fiercely at his head and eyes.

So here hung poor Nunganey by one arm, twenty feet above the ground, fighting off the mother bird, as well as he could with his free hand, absolutely helpless to release himself. As the other boys came in view, the bit of broken branch supporting his feet gave way, and the strain upon his arm became most painful, the splinters cutting it badly. No wonder there was a note in his owl's call not unlike a sob.

When at last, to his joy, he saw coming the comrades he had been trying to cheat, forgetting all that, he cried,

"Hurry, Kewakcum! Nunganey's arm is pulling off."

Kewakcum and Stephen could not help laughing at Nunganey's plight, feeling that "it served him right." Luckily Kewakcum wore a knife in the sheath at his belt. As soon as he could for laughter, he nimbly ascended the tree, pulled out his knife and cut away the wood, until Nunganey's arm was released.

Nunganey slid to the ground, looked sourly at Stephen, especially when he noticed the long strings of ripe berries in his hand, and then, muttering something about his arm, which he held as if in pain, struck sullenly off to the camp alone.

When, later, the other boys returned to camp with their strings of red berries, a cry of joy went up from the girls and younger children.

"Ho, ho, the brave hunters bring game," they cried.

Stephen hastened to give Jacob some of the berries, but found to his sorrow, that Jacob could hardly eat them. Nunganey, his arm swathed in a bandage by Eenisken, sat in a downcast attitude eying hungrily the berries, which he dared not ask for, expecting a prompt refusal. Stephen could not help pitying him, he knew so well himself what hunger was.

"Here, Nunganey," he said, holding out a string of berries. "Eat! Berries much good!"

Nunganey gave a grunt, which might be interpreted as meant for thanks, and greedily devoured the berries, a little ashamed, in spite of himself, as he remembered his past treatment of the boy captive.

The squaws were delighted to hear of the berry patch, and hastened with their baskets to gather all they could. The discovery of the berry patch proved timely, as Waneton's dream had not come true. No fat bear or deer did the hunters bring in that night; only two woodchucks—barely enough game to save Notoway's reputation as a prophet. But the woodchucks were fat, and every atom being cut up and boiled made a hot soup, of which all had a portion. Stephen considered himself fortunate in having a woodchuck's leg to pick. Like the Indians, he broke open the bone to suck out the marrow, not wasting a bit of what, in his hunger, seemed savory meat.

2

DOWN THE WINOOSKI

THE Indians broke camp early the next morning. Waneton was rich in possessions, and his canoe was so heavily loaded that it floated with difficulty, for the water, none too deep at best, had shrunken low under the summer's sun. Stephen had secretly hoped they might ride in the canoes; but he soon saw that no such good fortune awaited him. He must still walk, but at least it was a great relief to walk unburdened by a pack. The little band filed along the banks of the Winooski, a lovely stream, bright and sparkling, tumbling down with rush and roar in many a waterfall, as it made its way from the mountains to the lake. Jacob Hix was not able to walk, but still tried to drag himself along, far in the rear. Stephen went back to him, saying,

"Lean on my shoulder, Jacob. Perhaps that will help you a little."

"You are the only comfort left to me, Stephen," said Jacob, as he clasped Stephen's naked shoulder with his hot, shaking hand, and leaned his tottering weight on the boy.

"I can say the same of you, Jacob," said Stephen, with a loving smile into his friend's wasted face. "You are the only one from Deerfield still left. You call me 'Stephen,' and I can talk English with you. But for you, I believe I should really turn into a true Indian."

"I was no church-member, in the old days," said Jacob, panting for breath. "Never was called pious. But if these were—my last words—I would say—cling to your God, Stephen—Pray— don't forget—it's the only help."

"I know that right well," said Stephen.

Here Waneton was seen coming back, with frowning face, because Stephen was so far in the rear. Was the captive planning to escape?

"Cosannip go on," he said sternly. "Leave good-for-nought Englishman to himself. English blood white. No strong and brave like Indians. No good. Dog better than Englishman."

Reluctantly Stephen left his poor friend, who almost fell as his support was withdrawn, and went on to join the other Indians far in advance. He found the canoes drawn up on shore at the head of a cascade, where the river for some distance boiled whitely down, over broken rocks. The squaws were unloading the canoes. Then Stephen, like the rest, had a heavy pack lashed on his back. For this was one of the many "carrying places" along the Winooski.

Waneton and Mahtocheega, each taking an end of an empty canoe on his shoulder, strode off with their heavy burden. Stephen toiled on behind the others along the river's edge on the stones, which began to cut through his moccasins in places, hurting his tender feet. Soon he met the chiefs returning for the other canoe. They said nothing, gazing sternly at the white captive, despising his weakness, as Stephen well knew.

Often he looked back, to see if perchance Jacob might be coming in sight. But Jacob did not appear, nor did Stephen ever see him again. Jacob had fallen by the way, and soon perished in his weakness, the Indians troubling themselves no more about a captive, so sick and feeble as to be only a hindrance in their journey.

It was a good mile down the stream, before there was sufficient depth of water to allow the canoes to be launched. As Stephen limped into the group on the bank where the squaws were reloading the canoes, to his surprise Nunganey thrust something into his hand, then turned shamefacedly away. The gift was a few wintergreen leaves, which Nunganey, who had gone on ahead, had happened to find. He had hastened to pick all he could before the others came up, but had had the grace to save a few for Stephen, who had eaten nothing that day, and gladly chewed the spicy leaves.

"Nunganey isn't so bad, after all," he thought.

The canoes pushed on downstream, followed along shore by the Indians, until at night they came almost into the shadow of a great mountain, which had loomed up to the west of them all day.[3] Here they camped.

After the fire was lighted, to Stephen's amazement, the squaws took deerskins from their packs, and broiled pieces on the coals. When these were cooked all gnawed hard at the inside of the skin, trying to extract a little nourishment. At least it was hot, and had a meaty odor. But at best this supper was poor comfort, and Stephen lay down, as he had many a night before, faint with hunger, to dream aggravating dreams of tempting food.

Again he was at home, under the home roof in Deerfield. Parthena piled the table high with bread and meat, and poured porringers of sweet milk. His mother smiled lovingly, saying, "Come, Stephen; supper is ready." Always in the dream Stephen was very hungry. And always before he could begin to eat, something happened. Sometimes the Indians broke in with wild war-whoops and pulled him savagely away. Sometimes he woke, at first with a vague, comfortable feeling of being back in his old home, to realize, as the light of the camp fire shone into his eyes, and the stars gleamed down through the tree tops, that he was many weary miles from Deerfield, alone with the Indians, in the great northern wilderness.

What wonder that he brushed the tears away, and cried out in his heart, "Help me, my Father in heaven, for thou only canst." Then he would turn over and try hard to sleep again, and so forget his troubles for a time. The Indians were travelling a path well known to them, but to Stephen it was all an aimless wandering in the wilderness. lie had not the slightest idea where he was, or how far from home, or where bound, save that Canada was eventually to be his destination.

The next morning he looked about him with a sinking heart. The country was wild and mountainous, for they were now in the region where the Winooski cuts its way through a section of the Green Mountain chain. All around rose great mountains, dark with evergreen forests. Below him the river forced its way down through a rocky defile. From a dead pine high on the mountain cliff a great eagle spread its wings and flapped slowly over, far beyond the reach of the hunters' arrows.

---

3 Camel's Hump.

"Jacob must be dead," thought Stephen. "He has not come into camp. I am alone with the Indians here in this great wilderness. I don't believe I shall ever see white men again, or houses, much less any of my own family, or get back to Deerfield again. I must try not to think about it. Oh, dear Father," he prayed, "help me, and give me strength to bear whatever comes."

This day was but a repetition of that gone before. The Indians found no game. They pushed on faster than ever, seeming impatient to make progress. Stephen knew nothing about their plans. He only knew that he walked that day at least forty miles, often on the river's stony shore, the steep, rocky banks and tangled forest making that the only practicable path. His moccasins were badly worn, and gradually his feet grew very sore, two of his toes, bleeding and torn, seemingly nearly cut off. As, long after the others, Stephen limped feebly into the camp, in an open spot beside the river where the wigwams were already going up, little Katequa, running to her mother, and pulling at her deerskin garment, cried,

"See poor Cosannip. Him much sick. Him hardly walk."

Heelahdee saw that Stephen was really suffering, and needed attention, did the Indians hope to take him to Canada.

"Run, little flower, and stay with Cosannip. When the wigwams are up, mother will care for Cosannip."

Katequa ran to Stephen and led him to the camp fire. The men had gone off hunting, and the other boys were trying to fish in the river. There was no one near the fire, save patient little Ohopasha in his bark cradle, leaning up against a tree, waiting till his mother should have time to give him attention. He cooed and waved his arms, hoping that Stephen and Katequa would play with him. Katequa had been struck by a happy thought. Going to one of the opened packs, she managed to pull out a soft deerskin, which she dragged down to the fire, and spread out, furry side up.

"Cosannip lie down," she said. "Katequa play be medicine man. Come and cure Cosannip."

Stephen gladly threw himself down on the soft skin. Oh, the relief to his sore and bleeding feet, to lie at rest! Even suffering as he was, he could not help smiling at little Katequa's performances. She had put another deerskin over her head, and shaking high a gourd rattle, danced and jumped grotesquely around him in a circle, uttering in her baby voice wild cries, imitating Notoway's incantations over the sick.

"Does Cosannip feel better?" asked Katequa, stopping her dance to regain breath, her black eyes shining with delight in her own performance. Stephen nodded assent, with a smile. At least he appreciated Katequa's interest.

The little girl resumed her medicine dance and howled with even more energy. But now Heelahdee arrived on the scene.

"Bad girl!" she cried, snatching away the rattle and deer-skin, seizing Katequa and shaking her. "Old Notoway be very angry. The Manitou no like it. Katequa very wicked."

Katequa ran away and hid behind one of the wigwams. Heelahdee pulled off Stephen's moccasins, whose soles were literally cut to pieces. She bathed his swollen feet in warm water, and then made a soft poultice of elder leaves, which she bound on Stephen's feet. His relief and comfort were so great that he soon fell asleep. No one woke him to call him to supper, for the excellent reason that there was no supper, hunters and fishermen alike returning empty-handed.

When Stephen woke next morning, he found that, while he slept, Heelahdee had sewed new soles of thick moose hide on his moccasins. His feet were also better, and he could walk with more ease. So altogether he felt in better courage. Katequa took much credit to herself for his improvement. When her mother was busy tying up the packs, she came, slipping a bit of birch bark into Stephen's hand, whispering,

"Katequa glad she cured Cosannip."

"Katequa heap big medicine man," said Stephen, smiling, and little Katequa felt happy.

Towards noon that day, rounding a curve in the river, the Indians came upon a flock of wild ducks floating in a cove. The ducks whirred up in affright, but not before Waneton's swift arrow had brought down one.

"Ho, ho," said Waneton. "Great spirit smile at last. Better luck coming."

The hungry Indians stopped then and there, built a fire, and buried the fat duck under the hot ashes to roast. Hardly was it half done, when feathers and skin were stripped off together, and the fowl divided among the band, a morsel for each. Stephen's part was only some of the entrails, which he broiled on the hot coals, and ate gladly. In his starved condition, they seemed to him "a sweet morsel."

All now pushed on more swiftly. The mountains grew less high, sank into hills, receded, the country became more open. The sun was near its setting when the trail, which had followed the river's bank closely, turned away and came out on a hillside.[4] When Stephen reached the summit, he stared in amazement at the wonderful view spread out below him.

There lay a great, shining lake, extending north and south farther than the eye could reach, its western shore bordered by rugged mountain peaks and chains, behind which the sun was sinking. Below, on the right, was the Winooski, so long their guide, rushing over one more waterfall ere it entered the lake. Behind Stephen were the high mountains, whose valleys he had been traversing, their green summits softened by the yellow radiance of the sun's last rays.

After being for so many weeks shut in closely by dense woods, it was almost like heaven suddenly to come out on this height, into this great, open space, with the wide and lovely view. The sun had now vanished, but the western clouds, radiant with bright hues, were reflected in the lake's shining surface. From the clear afterglow along the western horizon, from the water, gently ruffled by the summer breeze, from the dewy evening air, seemed to breathe a peace not of this world, hint of another life beyond this. Even Stephen's boyish heart felt this influence.

"I suppose it's like that in heaven, where mother and the children are," thought Stephen, helped and comforted by a feeling of the Great Beyond.

"Petonque! Petonque!" the Indians had shouted joyfully, at sight of the lake.

Petonque was the Abenaki name for the lake, meaning, "The waters which lie between," that is, between the Abenakis and those dreaded warriors, the Iroquois. The Iroquois called it, "Cani-aderi-quarante," meaning "The lake that is the gate of the country."

Well might they so call it, for to them it was indeed an open gateway into the country of the French, and the wilderness that is now Vermont and New Hampshire, which was often traversed by their war parties going out against the Abenakis.

---

4 Near the site of Burlington, Vt.

The French name was the "Lac du Iroquois," because this was the chosen route, whether in peace or war, travelled by the Indians of the Long House to Canada. The Dutch and English around Albany called it "Lake Corlear," in memory of one who was drowned in the lake.

But among all these names, and in spite of the many historic incidents connected with this romantic sheet of water, the name of Champlain, the first white man to see and travel upon its waters, has persisted as the lake's true name.

The Indians were jubilant that the worst part of their homeward journey was now over, saying,

"Plenty of fish and game now. Indians eat a heap now." And Stephen was encouraged.

"This great lake must be the Lake Champlain of which I have often heard," he thought. "We shall go in canoes now, and it will be easier."

"Big hunt tomorrow, Cosannip," said Kewakcum. "Cosannip get up early, go out for game with Kewakcum."

So all went to bed that night with cheerful spirits, even if with empty stomachs.

3

BESIDE LAKE CHAMPLAIN

IN the gray dawn of the next morning Stephen awoke and heard shouts and merry laughter outside. Going out, he saw Kewakcum and Nunganey taking an early morning swim in the lake. Running down the hill, Stephen plunged into the cool water with them, for he could now swim well.

The boys splashed each other and swam about, enjoying the reviving sensation of the cool water lapping their bodies. Then they came out and ran up and down on the shore to dry themselves, for towels there were none.

Stephen found that the others were going hunting and ran up the bank for his bow and arrows.

"Katequa make big medicine for Cosannip while he hunts. Cosannip bring back big game," said little Katequa, standing by the fire her mother had just built, clasping in her arms the little roll of deerskin, with a face rudely marked on one end, which served as her doll.

"Thank you, Katequa," said Stephen, smiling back at his little friend, as he ran down to join the others.

The boys stood on the shore, looking off across the lake at a canoe far out from land, in which were two Indians fishing. At first Stephen was alarmed, thinking them enemy Indians. But as the sun rose higher, he recognized Waneton and Mahtocheegah.

"See," said Nunganey. "Notoway gave them big medicine. Heap of luck."

Even at this distance, Stephen saw Waneton pull out a large fish, and land him flopping in the canoe.

"Heap big one. Taste good," said Kewakcum, his eyes sparkling at thought of the coming feast.

Stephen too felt in good spirits. The dewy morning air seemed to breathe of hope, as the boys went along the lake shore towards the mouth of the Winooski. They now ceased to talk, gliding silently along until near the water's edge, when they lay down, and crawling under the tangle of bushes growing thick on the bank, peered cautiously through.

Below them on the placid waters of the river's bay-like mouth, they saw, riding in fancied security, a flock of wild geese, dabbling their bills in the water plunging their heads under, and preening their feathers with a contented "quack, quack."

Down from the bushes sped three sharp arrows, and up and away flew most of the flock, with loud cries of dismay. The boys ran joyously down the bank. But, alas, here was trouble. Kewakcum's arrow had brought down a goose, but two arrows were sticking fast in another goose, Nunganey's and Stephen's!

"Nunganey shot first," said Nunganey. "Nunganey's swift arrow killed the goose. Cosannip shoot a dead goose!"

"I shot just as quick as you did, didn't I, Kewakcum?" cried Stephen.

Kewakcum shook his head sagely.

"Kewakcum no know who shoot first. Old Notoway himself no tell. Both shoot together. The goose belongs to both."

"Nunganey will carry the goose," said Nunganey, seizing the goose and swinging it over his shoulder.

At least Stephen would not please Nunganey by seeming to care. So he said in an off-hand tone,

"Ho, Cosannip him no care. Nunganey is squaw, brings Cosannip's game in. Cosannip big hunter. Him no carry game."

This was true. It was a squaw's business to bring in game when possible, and to bear all burdens. Nunganey threw the goose angrily on the ground.

"Nunganey no want the goose," he said. "Nunganey shoot plenty more for himself. The White Frog can have it."

He turned and went back towards the river by himself. Stephen picked up the goose, a good fat one, that weighed heavily on his back, while Kewakcum, laughing, said,

"Cosannip got long head. Him talk wise talk, like old medicine man."

Katequa spied the boys coming from afar, and ran to the squaws, crying,

"Ho, ho, the big hunters bring game! Now we can eat."

The squaws, all joyful smiles at the welcome sight of food, hastened to put the fowls cooking. Ere long, the canoe was seen making for shore, and the squaws hurried down to bring up the boat load of fish which the braves had caught. A little later, Nunganey came swaggering in with a large duck.

Eenisken ran to meet him, saying,

"My proud hunter brings in game like a warrior."

"Nunganey shot a goose too. Cosannip bring it in for him," explained Nunganey.

"Nunganey is a great brave," said his proud mother.

As the savory odors of roasting fish and fowl rose on the summer air, it was hard for the children to wait their turn to eat. They hung around, hungrily watching Notoway and the warriors filling themselves with food, old Notoway, hungry as he was, not forgetting before eating to raise a portion solemnly to the sky above, as a thank-offering to the sun.

When at last, the turn of the squaws, the children, and the dogs came, and when at last no one could eat another morsel, the squaws filled a long pipe with k'nick k'nick and lighting it, passed it to Notoway. He waved it gravely first to the west, then to the east, the north, and the south, as a propitiatory offering to those powerful deities, the winds, then took a long whiff and passed it on to the others, who sat cross-legged in the shade of a large pine tree.

The warriors did not feel disposed to exert themselves, after such an abundant feast. There was ample food for another day. Why should they stir? So they sat or lay at their ease in the shade, telling stories and drowsing. The dogs lay in the content of utter satiety, sleeping. Even the children were quiet, for once. Only the squaws kept at work, for their labors knew little cessation. They went off into the woods, and by and by came back, bearing long rolls of birch bark, longer than themselves, rising high above their heads. Then they set to work on the shore, sewing these strips of bark together with deer sinews, making canoes. As the rest of the journey was to be on the water, more canoes were needed.

As for Stephen, he strolled off by himself into the edge of the woods and lay down on a soft bed of moss at the foot of a huge old hemlock, crossing his hands under his head, and looking dreamily up through the shifting branches and leaves above, to the glimpse of sky beyond. It was such an inexpressible rest to be satisfied, to have the long cravings of hunger quelled at last. Soon the soothing rustling of the leaves, mingling with his dream, seemed his mother's voice humming a soft lullaby to her baby, as she rocked gently to and fro in the old living room at home. Stephen smiled as he slept.

He had slept some time, when into his peaceful dreams burst a terrible sound, a shrill, fierce war-whoop close in his ear. Stephen sprang up with a cry, staring bewildered around, not knowing at first where he was. Then he saw Nunganey standing near, his hand over his mouth, doubled up with laughter over his success in frightening Stephen.

"Ho, ho," said he, as soon as he could speak.

"Come on to the hunt," said Nunganey, leading the way uphill to the woods. "Maybe get chipmunks."

The other boys took their bows and arrows and followed him. They rambled about in the woods for a while, without getting any game. The sun had set, and the light began to grow dim in the woods. Suddenly Nunganey gave a shrill whoop and ran swiftly towards a hollow tree.

"Whoop! Whoop! The enemy! The paleface! Ho for his scalp! Take his fort!" cried Nunganey.

Kewakcum joined in the war-whoop and rushed on to the attack, as did Stephen also, without knowing who or what the enemy might be. He was not long left in doubt. Nunganey had attacked a nest of wild bees. If lucky, he hoped to secure some wild honey. It was long since he had tasted any sweet, and he so craved the honey that he was willing to run some risk in getting it. Moreover, the spice of danger in the attack lent it a charm for both the Indian boys. Were they not braves? And should braves shrink from any danger? The nest was torn roughly out and thrown on the ground, Kewakcum and Nunganey dancing and stamping on the fragments with loud shouts of victory.

"Kewakcum, Nunganey met the enemy and were not afraid! His fort is theirs! Whoop Whoop!"

Stephen joined in the dance of victory, and like the others seized some of the honeycomb, dripping with delicious sweetness. But, just as the boys' mouths were filled with this delight, the maddened bees, rallying from their first confusion at the fury of the boys' attack, came flying back, an angry swarm.

The boys' naked skins made them an easy prey. Their skins were oiled with bear's grease as a protection against the gnats and mosquitoes that abounded in the woods, but this was no shield from the piercing stings of the enraged bees, who assailed them on every side.

Flight was the only safety. Nunganey, the brave, led the retreat. Never did three boys make better time than Kewakcum, Nunganey and Stephen, as they dashed downhill to the lake, plunging into the water to their eyes, thus finally ridding themselves of their tormentors.

It was some time before they ventured to come forth. Kewakcum, whose cheek was so badly stung that one eye was already nearly closed, said sagely,

"Honey heap good. Nunganey great brave; but enemy too strong for him that time."

"Warriors must take chances," said Nunganey, "Cosannip is no brave. Brave must always be ready for the enemy, night or day, hand on his gun, give war-whoop, ready to fight. Cosannip a squeaking white mouse. Him no brave."

"That's nothing. Anyone would jump to be wakened up from a sound sleep like that," said Stephen.

"No brave, no brave," cried Nunganey tauntingly, as he ran away.

Stephen had already learned that it was an Indian custom thus to discipline their boys, in order to fit them for warriors. More than once had Wane ton wakened Kewakcum from a sound sleep by a shrill war-whoop in his ear, or a gun fired near his head. Wane ton expected Kewakcum to leap up at once with an answering whoop, to seize a weapon and prepare to give instant battle.

At first Kewakcum had shown terror and confusion when thus aroused, and his father, shaking his head sadly, had said,

"Kewakcum a squaw. No fit to go on the war path. Enemy take his scalp before him know it."

But now Kewakcum was learning his lesson. The last time his father had given the alarm, he had sprung to his feet with a shrill "whoop!" before half awake, had seized a long knife which he kept beside him as he slept, and fallen upon his father so fiercely that Waneton, as he struggled to free himself from the grasp of his strong young son, had said proudly,

"Kewakcum a brave now. Go on the war path before many moons."

"White folks must be different from Indians," thought Stephen, witnessing this scene. "I never could get used to it like Kewakcum, I know, not if Waneton screeched in my ear every morning."

He was not in the least grateful to Nunganey for taking his education in hand. But, being now wide awake, he went down to the shore where the squaws were at work on their canoes.

The sun was sinking low over the Adirondacks across the lake. Waneton and Mahtocheegah had roused from their lethargy and seemed to be fitting one of the dugouts for some expedition, sticking boughs of hemlock up in the prow, and placing in the canoe several sticks, with split ends into which were tied rolls of birch bark. Kewakcum and Nunganey were watching them with interest.

"What is Waneton going to do?" asked Stephen.

"Waneton and Mahtocheegah hunt the deer tonight by torchlight," said Kewakcum. "Deer plenty here. Venison taste heap good."

"I should say so!" exclaimed Stephen. "Roast venison indeed! What could be better?"

"Come on to the hunt," said Nunganey, leading the way uphill to the woods. "Maybe get chipmunks."

The other boys took their bows and arrows and followed him. They rambled about in the woods for a while, without getting any game. The sun had set, and the light began to grow dim in the woods. Suddenly Nunganey gave a shrill whoop and ran swiftly towards a hollow tree.

"Whoop! Whoop! The enemy! The pale-face! Ho for his scalp! Take his fort!" cried Nunganey.

Kewakcum joined in the war-whoop and rushed on to the attack, as did Stephen also, without knowing who or what the enemy might be. He was not long left in doubt. Nunganey had attacked a nest of wild bees. If lucky, he hoped to secure some wild honey. It was long since he had tasted any sweet, and he so craved the honey that he was willing to run some risk in getting it. Moreover, the spice of danger in the attack lent it a charm for both the Indian boys. Were they not braves? And should braves shrink from any danger? The nest was torn roughly out and thrown on the ground, Kewakcum and Nunganey dancing and stamping on the fragments with loud shouts of victory.

"Kewakcum, Nunganey met the enemy and were not afraid! His fort is theirs! Whoop! Whoop!"

Stephen joined in the dance of victory, and like the others seized some of the honeycomb, dripping with delicious sweetness. But, just as the boys' mouths were filled with this delight, the maddened bees, rallying from their first confusion at the fury of the boys' attack, came flying back, an angry swarm.

The boys' naked skins made them an easy prey. Their skins were oiled with bear's grease as a protection against the gnats and mosquitoes that abounded in the woods, but this was no shield from the piercing stings of the enraged bees, who assailed them on every side.

Flight was the only safety. Nunganey, the brave, led the retreat. Never did three boys make better time than Kewakcum, Nunganey and Stephen, as they dashed downhill to the lake, plunging into the water to their eyes, thus finally ridding themselves of their tormentors.

It was some time before they ventured to come forth. Kewakcum, whose cheek was so badly stung that one eye was already nearly closed, said sagely,

"Honey heap good. Nunganey great brave; but enemy too strong for him that time."

"Warriors must take chances," said Nunganey, laughing in one-sided fashion, for his face was badly swollen by stings.

Stephen came out, rubbing his arm, which was smarting and swelling, saying,

"Next time Nunganey hunts bees, Cosannip stay home."

"Ho, that's nothing," said Nunganey. "Warriors no mind little thing like that. Nunganey go alone; get fill the honey."

But Stephen well knew that was only Nunganey's boastful way of talking. The boys' attention was now diverted by something they saw to the north. Far up the lake a twinkling light was seen gliding along. It marked the course of the dugout, paddled by Waneton, while Mahtocheegah, gun in hand, stood in the prow, concealed by the green bushes in front. Upright in the bow was stuck a blazing torch of birch bark, sending a bright light streaming out far over the water, as the canoe wound along near the shore, into bay and cove and river mouth.

Some deer coming down to drink, saw from afar this unusual light moving mysteriously on the water, glancing from wave to wave. Their curiosity was excited, and, quite fearless, they drew nearer and nearer, until they reached the water's edge. Then a gun shot rang through the deep silence of the night. With wild leaps the frightened herd bounded away, up the bank and far into the forest, leaving one noble buck bleeding and struggling on the strand.

Joyfully were the hunters received in the camp on their return, for it was long since the Indians had tasted venison. And the deer meant to them, not merely food, but clothing, moccasins, sinews for their snowshoes and for strings; in fact, almost every necessity of their simple lives.

That night, after the feast, the men, sitting on the ground, thumped their heels as they sang, to the time of a skin drum beaten by Notoway, this hunting song, which, like most Indian songs, was also a prayer:

"Ah yah ba wah, ne gah me koo nah nah!
Ah yah wa seeh, ne gah koo nah nah,"

which, translated, is,

"The fattest of the bucks I'll take,
The choicest of all animals I'll take."

This song began in a high key, going down by descending phrases to a very low note. It was a minor strain, pathetic and weird, yet monotonous. The Indians sang it over and over, for at least half an hour, the wild notes ringing out in the silence of the night far over the lake.

The last thing that Stephen heard, as he fell into an unusually sound sleep, with an unwonted sense of comfort and wellbeing after the day's ample feasting, was the dull thump of the drum, and

"Ne gah me koo nah nah!"

4

NORTHWARD

IN a few days more, the camp on the hillside was broken up, and the little fleet of canoes set off northward. Waneton was impatient to be gone, not only to reach Montreal and dispose of his furs, but also fearing lest some wandering band of Iroquois on the lake's western shore, might spy the smoke of his camp, and come stealthily over at night to attack him and secure his wealth. All the skins, the utensils and belongings were packed in the canoes, with plenty of smoked meat and fish. Some of the canoes were paddled by the squaws, some by the warriors. Kewakcum, a large, strong boy, had charge of one canoe, in which were also Nunganey and Stephen, who were to take turns in helping to paddle. Stephen at first displayed all the awkwardness of a beginner, making much sport for Nunganey.

"Ho, see Cosannip! A pappoose paddle better than that! Him tip the canoe over, Kewakcum, you no look out."

And Nunganey slyly tipped the canoe a bit, pretending this to be caused by Stephen's awkwardness.

"I never paddled before. Of course I have to learn," said Stephen. "I guess you were awkward when you first began, Nunganey."

"Ho, Nunganey never learned. Him always paddled," said Nunganey.

This was true enough, for Indian children are so early trained in all matters of woodcraft that it becomes to them second nature, as if inborn.

"Nunganey tip this canoe once more, and Kewakcum throw him into the lake," said Kewakcum, with the air becoming the commander-in-chief.

"Ho, Nunganey him no care," answered the boy.

But Nunganey did care, for although he was a good swimmer, he knew that Kewakcum might keep him in the water longer that he cared to stay. So he contented himself with jibes and sneers at Stephen, who ignored him, bending his whole energies to the work in hand. After a while he was delighted to find himself catching the knack of paddling, to see that he kept fair stroke with Kewakcum, even if by prodigious effort.

"Cosannip learn fast. Paddle alone by another day," said Kewakcum.

"Paddle to bottom of the lake," said Nunganey.

Here Stephen's paddle gave a sort of accidental flirt, sending a dash of water into Nunganey's face. Kewakcum laughed, Nunganey wiped his face and glared fiercely at Stephen to see if he had done it purposely, while Stephen bent his back to the paddle as if he had no other thought.

The scene around was wild and beautiful. The morning sun rising over the Green Mountain ranges to the East, glistened on the lake, where myriads of tiny wavelets danced and shone in its light. On the West rose the grand chains of the Adirondacks. All was wild, and picturesque and solitary; there were no signs of human beings or habitations anywhere, far or near, save in this little flotilla of canoes, leaving long ripples on the lake's surface as they pushed on to the north.

Although Stephen was somewhat diverted by learning to row, his heart was heavy as he realized that every stroke of the paddles took him farther and farther away from home. Soon this great lake would lie between him and Deerfield! How hopeless to imagine he could ever get back! As these dreary thoughts passed through his mind, he winked hard to hide from the other boys the tears which filled his eyes.

But now something happened that effectually diverted Stephen's mind from his troubles. Kewakcum was filled with pride this morning, not only because he was allowed to manage a canoe by himself, but also because, after long entreaty, his father had at last allowed him to have a gun, one of the guns taken at Deerfield. Waneton had hesitated at first. But Heelahdee, as soon as she heard of Kewakcum's plan, had violently opposed it.

"No give Kewakcum gun," she said. "Three boys—a gun loaded—in a canoe. No, no. Kill each other quick. No let him take gun."

This had seemed to decide Waneton.

"Indian boys must learn to handle guns these days, or paleface shoot down Indian quick. Indians tumble like pigeons off their roost," said Waneton, handing Kewakcum the gun.

Kewakcum also begged to take old Wees with him, but even his father thought that a dog might be a dangerous addition to the combination in Kewakcum's canoe. So Wees took passage in Waneton's own canoe, where, lying on a pile of skins, he often looked wistfully back towards his friends the boys.

Kewakcum after a while made Nunganey take his oar, while he loaded the gun, watched with undisguised envy by Nunganey. Then Kewakcum scanned the lake and country round for a victim. Soon his sharp eyes spied a great fish down in the blue depths of the lake, serenely floating, gracefully swaying and bending, as it gave an occasional stroke of its tail.

Stephen and even the brave Nunganey started, as the loud crash of the gun rang in their ears. They had seen no game.

"Kewakcum waste powder. Waneton very angry," said Nunganey.

But Kewakcum pointed triumphantly to the great body of the fish which had risen to the surface and floated lifeless, white belly up. Kewakcum swam out to his prize and brought it proudly on board. The fish was quite as long as Stephen, and Stephen looked upon Kewakcum -with admiring wonder, while Nunganey begged hard to try his luck with the gun.

"No," said Kewakcum. "Waneton gave Kewakcum the gun. Said no one else have it."

Canoeing was certainly a vast improvement on walking all day through the woods, bearing a heavy pack. Still, it was a hard day's pull in the hot sun, and, long ere sundown, Stephen began to realize that paddling, oddly enough, lames not only the arms but the legs of beginners. Unconsciously he had strained every muscle of each limb, in this new business.

The canoes had kept to the eastward of the green islands covered with forests that divided the lake's broad expanse. The long, hot day ended at last, and a refreshing breath of coolness descended on the water, as the sun's last lingering ray vanished behind the Adirondacks.

"Will they never stop?" thought Stephen. "My legs are so cramped sitting in this canoe, I don't believe I can walk, and my arms ache as if they would drop off."

But soon Waneton's canoe was turned in shore, where a small stream entered the lake from the East. Waneton beached his canoe, and was followed by the others.

Stephen was surprised that the squaws did not begin cutting poles for wigwams. But the Indians drew the canoes entirely ashore, emptied them, and carrying them inland, turned them bottom upwards in a sheltered hollow among thick bushes. Under the canoes they hid their paddles, their furs and other possessions. Lame though Stephen was, he had to carry several back-loads up to the shelter of the canoes.

When everything was safely stowed away, the squaws took the long rolls of bark and skin which made the wigwam covers, and humbly trudged on behind the warriors along the bank of the stream, which proved to be one branch or outlet of a large river.[5] As they reached the larger stream, Stephen saw ahead of them on the river's bank lights, moving objects, smoke rising, and heard the confused sound of many voices and the loud barking of dogs.

"Whoop! Whoop!" rang out triumphantly the voices of Waneton and the other warriors, swelled by the shrill cries of the Indian boys.

Loud answering cries were heard from the village ahead, and the rapid firing of a gun, as if in welcome.

They had reached a spot where the Abenakis from St. Francis often encamped, forming an almost permanent village.[6] Here, on the bank of the Missisquoi, stood a large cluster of wigwams. From them trooped men, women and children to greet Waneton and his band with warm welcome. These Indians were part of his own tribe. Among them were cousins, uncles, old friends. So it was a great pleasure for Waneton and his band to reach this familiar spot, after their long wanderings. The squaws put up wigwams in the place assigned them, near the center fire of the camp.

5 The Missisquoi.

6 At Swanton, Vt.

Strange indeed did it seem to Stephen to be among so many people, after his wanderings in the lonely wilderness. As soon as Heelahdee's wigwam was erected, he gladly crept into it, and lay down to sleep. But weary as he was, he could not sleep. There was noise and tumult outside, voices talking, laughing, singing, boys and young men racing about, wrestling, running, jumping After the long months in the silent forest, it seemed like a pandemonium to the tired Stephen, as he tossed and turned, wakened again and again, as he was dropping off, by some loud cry.

The greatest din came from the wigwam of the chief Unongoit nearby, where a great feast was being held in honor of the return of Waneton and his band from battle, bringing with them a white captive and other spoils of war. Waneton and Mahtocheegah, as guests of honor, were seated back in the wigwam, opposite the entrance, at the left of Unongoit.

After all had eaten till they could eat no more, a long calumet was lighted. Unongoit made the customary smokes of reverence to the sky above, the earth beneath, the four winds, and the pipe was then passed to the left, from mouth to mouth around the circle. Then came the speech-making and talking. Waneton and Mahtocheegah were called upon for an account of the sacking of Deerfield. As, with native eloquence, they described the stealthy approach to the doomed village, the leap over the walls of the palisade, the onslaught, the killing and the burning, excitement waxed great. Shrill war-whoops and fierce shouts of joy rent the evening air, echoing wildly out into the woods along the Missisquoi.

When the story was ended, with wild shaking on high of gourd rattles and loud thumping of drums, all joined in dancing the war-dance, and singing the war song, which, translated,[7] ran thus:

"On that day when our heroes lay low, lay low,
On that day when our heroes lay low,
I fought by their side, and thought, ere I died,
Just vengeance to take on the foe, the foe,
Just vengeance to take on the foe.

7 Translated by Col. McKenney.

"On that day when our chieftains lay dead, lay dead,
On that day when our chieftains lay dead,
I fought hand to hand, at the head of my band,
And here, on my breast, have I bled, have I bled,
And here, on my breast, have I bled.

"Our chiefs shall return no more, no more,
Our chiefs shall return no more,
And their brothers in war, who can't show scar for scar,
Like women their fates shall deplore, shall deplore,
Like women their fates shall deplore.

"Five winters in hunting we'll spend, we'll spend,
Five winters in hunting we'll spend,
Then, our youths grown to men, to the war lead again,
And our days like our fathers, we'll end, we'll end,
And our days like our fathers, we'll end."

It being a warm night, the skins covering the wigwam poles were turned up to admit air, and outside on the ground sat a circle of Indian men and boys, listening to the speeches. As now the Indians danced around in a circle, bent half over, hopping stiffly first on one leg, then on the other, to the cadence of the drum and rattle, fierce shouts from the circle of spectators often burst into the song.

The hearts of Kewakcum, Nunganey, and the other Indian boys swelled with pride and longing for the time when they too should go forth on the war path, returning laden with scalps and spoils, and covered with glory. Kewakcum, especially, had received much training in Indian lore and tradition, not only from his father, but from Notoway, whose business it was, as medicine man, to preserve the records of every heroic exploit, and who was rich in wampum belts which told the glories of the Abenakis.

Many a winter evening had Kewakcum sat, listening to old Notoway's stories, and looking at the belts, until his soul had burned within him to begin his career as a warrior, and add to the glorious traditions of his tribe.

Old Notoway tonight observed the boy's kindling eye, and animated look. Coming to him and laying his hand on Kewakcum's shoulder, he said impressively,

"When the sun comes again, Kewakcum must go forth alone, fasting, and seek his dream, make his medicine. The time has come."

Kewakcum looked solemn yet elated. Manhood was really about to begin for him!

5

BERRYING UNDER DIFFICULTIES

THE Indians believe in many gods or powers, besides the Great Spirit who rules all, and the Bad Spirit, against whose evil influence they must ever be on the guard. These lesser powers may be animals or objects, who can intercede for them with the Great Spirit, and aid them in the hunt and in war. They rely much upon dreams. Each has his special helper, a sort of guardian angel, usually revealed in a dream.

Notoway felt that the time had come when Kewakcum, a boy unusually forward for his age, and giving great promise, should seek his dream, should try to dream for power. In the early dawn next morning Kewakcum rose, and grinding a dead ember left in the ashes of yesterday's fire, made charcoal, with which, mixing the dust with bear's oil, he blackened his face. The blackened face was a sign of fasting. Stephen, who wakened in time to catch a glimpse of Kewakcum as he lifted the door flap to go out, the grey dawn showing dimly his blackened face, called out,

"What is the matter, Kewakcum? What are you doing?"

Kewakcum answered not, but dropped the skin flap, and struck off into the forest alone, disappearing as entirely as if he had died.

Stephen's curiosity was naturally much excited by Kewakcum's strange appearance and demeanor, and later he asked Nunganey what it meant.

"Him fast, go away, make medicine, find his dream maybe," said Nunganey.

This explanation did not enlighten Stephen greatly, and as the day passed and no Kewakcum appeared, he felt anxious lest some disaster had befallen him, although he noticed that Waneton and Heelahdee seemed cheerful and unconcerned. He and Nunganey joined a troop of Indian children going out berrying. Several of the dogs in which the village was rich followed their playmates, including Wees, who seemed to have struck up a friendship with a black dog called Anum.

It was now late in July, and the children found several fine patches of raspberry bushes along the edge of the woods, well laden with delicious ripe fruits. The pickers were so many, and the nimble fingers flew so fast, that the bushes were soon stripped. Nawkaw, son of the chief Unongoit, an older boy, who seemed to be a leader among his comrades, and was the only one allowed to carry a gun, said,

"Nawkaw know a heap better place than this. Heap of berries. Plenty for all. Come."

And away he started into the forest, his comrades filing along behind him, faithfully following their leader, as he pushed on through the underbrush, wading brooks, leaping over fallen logs, sliding down mossy rocks, until at last he came to a great stretch of fallen timber, where some bygone fierce storm had swept over the forest, prostrating acres of great trees.

This disaster had apparently occurred years before, as a dense tangle of bushes filled all the space among the logs, which lay, mossy and decaying, on the ground. Berry bushes abounded, great rampant blackberry bushes, their long sprays hanging low with green fruit. Raspberry bushes were also abundant.

The children fell joyfully to work, picking and eating. But presently a shrill scream rose from a group of girls, who ran as fast as their moccasined feet could carry them, out of the cluster of bushes where they had been picking.

"What is it? What did you see?" asked Nawkaw, a little startled, for so far away from camp in the woods, many things might happen to one.

"Askook, the snake!" screamed the girls, pointing to a long black snake lying under the bushes. "Oh, oh! Run, run!"

"Stop your silly screams! Know you nothing, foolish nunqsquaws?" cried Nawkaw. "You will anger Askook, and he will bring evil on us."

The Indians regarded all snakes with reverence, as undoubtedly powerful spirits, able to bring good or evil luck, if pleased or angered.

"Grandfather Askook, mind not the silly squaw pappooses. They know nothing," said Nawkaw, addressing the snake respectfully. "We are your friends. Here are berries for you, grandfather." And Nawkaw laid a handful of ripe berries before the snake as a peace offering. But the snake glided away under an old log, not deigning to accept the offering.

"He is offended," said Nawkaw. "He may send Maqua the bear to attack us. If you see another snake, show no fear. Speak to him with respect. Hunters and warriors know well they must never anger Askook."

The girls resumed their berry picking, though careful to rap and jar stumps and logs to drive out possible snakes underneath ere they again ventured into the bushes. After picking for an hour or so, the children began to straggle off homewards by twos and threes, well able to find their own trail back, marked as it was by trampled grass and leaves, broken twigs and branches. Stephen was about starting to return, when he heard a loud barking from Wees and Anum, not far away.

"Wees smell game," said Nunganey. "Come, Nawkaw, bring gun, shoot fat raccoon, maybe."

The boys turned back, and soon found the two dogs barking furiously at the foot of a huge stump about ten feet high, the tree having been broken off by the tornado. As the boys drew near, the cause of the dogs' excitement was plain, for from the top of the hollow stump they saw protruding first a brown snout, then the head of a big bear.

Stephen and Nunganey, who were unarmed, were not long in deciding that they had seen enough of the bear, and lost no time in running away as fast as their legs could carry them, looking over their shoulders now and then, as they tore through the bushes, to be sure he was not at their heels, for the trampling of their own feet seemed, in their ears, the crashing of the fierce animal through the woods, close on their trail.

Nawkaw, having a gun, waited at a little distance to see the outcome, feeling also that he might be able to cover the retreat of his friends.

The bear crawled clumsily out, and began to back down the stump, as is the fashion of bears in descending trees. He was a big one, and the temptation to shoot was strong, but after taking a good look at him, Nawkaw decided it was wiser not to fire as, if he merely wounded him, he could not escape the infuriated beast. So he called the dogs off, and retreated into the woods, keeping still, hoping that the bear, if not molested, would perhaps go quietly away. But the bear had no such intention. Once on the ground, he began sniffing the air in the direction of the flying children, and then started in pursuit, heading straight for the spot where Nawkaw was holding back the struggling dogs, who, no longer to be restrained, pulled away, and flew at the bear. At the same time, Nawkaw fired, but in his excitement, his aim was not true, and the bullet, instead of piercing the bear's heart, only wounded his side.

There was no time to reload. The bear started in furious pursuit of Nawkaw, who ran for his life, as well he needed. He could not have escaped the furious beast, had not its progress been impeded by the two excited dogs, who chased after it, barking, and seizing its legs from time to time. The bear stopped to snarl and snap at his tormentors, who instantly dodged back, barking in a way that bid fair to split their throats, only to fall upon the enemy again, the moment he resumed his trot on Nawkaw's trail.

In spite of the dogs, the bear was gaining on Nawkaw so fast that the boy looked hurriedly around for a young sapling strong enough to bear his weight. A bear could easily climb a big tree, but not a sapling, as Nawkaw had early been instructed by his father. Nawkaw spied a suitable sapling just ahead, and rushed to it, none too soon, for the bear was so close behind that, when Nawkaw swung himself up into the sapling, the bear's sharp claws pierced the calf of his leg and held him fast till the good dogs came to the rescue. They bit the bear's hind legs so furiously that he was obliged to let go his hold on Nawkaw, and turn to defend himself.

Nawkaw hurriedly pulled himself higher up into the sapling's top, in spite of the bleeding and the pain in his wounded leg. He watched anxiously the battle below. Poor Anum lay lifeless, killed by the bear, who had Wees at great disadvantage, and would soon have made an end of him too. But, to Nawkaw's joy and relief, a shot rang through the woods, and with a groan, the bear fell heavily at the foot of the sapling, pierced through the heart by a ball from the skillfully aimed musket of Unongoit.

Stephen and Nunganey in their flight had met Unongoit, not far from the camp, and that chief had at once hastened to his son's rescue. His arrival was most opportune, for the bleeding so weakened Nawkaw, that he might soon have been obliged to relax his hold.

"Nawkaw no squaw," he said apologetically to his father, as he dropped to the ground beside the dead bear. "Nawkaw no afraid, but him have no time to load again."

"Nawkaw has done well. His name shall be changed to Wounds-the-bear," said his father. "But Nawkaw must remember that when berries plenty, then bears plenty. Bear eat berries, same as Indian. Brother Maqua heap wise. He know when berries ripe, where they grow thick, same as Indian."

"The nunqsquaws angered Askook, the snake, by screaming at him. He glided into his hole, very angry. Askook send the bear," said Nawkaw.

"It may be so. It is never well to anger our brothers, the animals, especially Askook, who is very powerful. But the nunqsquaws know little," said Unongoit.

Now several men and squaws from the village appeared on the scene. They skinned the bear, and one squaw bore the skin on her back to the village, there to dress and cure it. The rest cut up the carcass into large chunks, which were also borne off on their shoulders by the squaws. Bear's meat, and bear's oil, so good for the hair, to oil the body, and as a medicine, would now be plenty, for the bear was large and fat.

Nawkaw was praised by all as a young hero. His mother aided him to her wigwam, carefully to dress his wounds. Notoway was called with his medicine bag and his charms, to aid the medicine man of the village, in healing the wound of Nawkaw. The sound of their drums, and their weird cries and chantings, as they hopped and danced around Nawkaw's bed of boughs, rang through the village. As Nawkaw was the chief's eldest son, giving promise of being a brave warrior, every effort must be used completely to cure him, lest he go lame for life, so badly were the muscles torn by the bear's sharp claws.

"Katequa heap glad Cosannip ran away fast, before the big bear catch him," said little Katequa, as the sound of the medicine men's conjuring rang through the village.

"Cosannip glad too. Katequa and Cosannip no go to the bear's wood for berries tomorrow," said Stephen.

"No, sir," said Katequa, who had been taught some English words by Stephen.

Stephen and Nunganey had gone to the battlefield and had taken turns in bringing faithful old Wees back to their wigwam, where they made him a soft bed, patting him and praising his valor. Wees proceeded in a very sensible way to lick and dress his own wounds, and was not too sick to eat gladly some of the bear meat, which the boys brought him, feeling that he had earned it.

"Kewakcum feel heap bad, see Wees hurt," said Stephen. "It seems so strange no see Kewakcum anywhere. Maybe he is lost."

"No, no," said Nunganey. "Him come home again after one, two, three suns more, all right. Him seek his dream."

But when the shades of night fell, and still Kewakcum had not come, Stephen sought out Heelahdee who was cooking by the fire burning in the center of the camp, saying,

"Cosannip afraid something happen to Kewakcum. Maybe bear catch him. Maybe him lost. Why does not Waneton go find him, bring him home?"

"Kewakcum fast, him seek his dream. No one must speak to him," said Heelahdee, shaking her head impressively. "Old Notoway say right time had come. Him must do it. Great Spirit watch over Kewakcum, and Blessed Virgin too. Her a mother, her knows," said Heelahdee, reverently crossing herself, and glancing up through the tree boughs overhead, where a bright star shining down with "purest ray serene" seemed to her fancy not unlike the pitying eye of the beautiful Mother, whose picture, with the Holy Babe in her arms, she had once seen over the altar in the cathedral at Montreal, and whose memory she had ever since carried in her heart.

Stephen had to be satisfied, although he did not in the least understand what Kewakcum was supposed to be doing. But ere he slept, he added to his nightly prayer a petition that the all-seeing Father would watch over Kewakcum that night and keep him from all harm.

6

KEWAKCUM SEEKS HIS DREAM

THE second night after Kewakcum's disappearance was breathlessly hot. The sun had set in a bank of white thunder-heads, the clouds pushing rapidly up the sky, beginning to hide the stars, which shone but faintly through the thick, hazy air. It was so close and suffocating in the wigwam that Stephen, amid the many noises outside, was unable to sleep.

He rose and went out, rambling idly around the village, coming at last upon a group of Indian boys, who were absorbed in watching a game that was being played on the ground, by the light of a fire before one of the wigwams. Waneton and one Poudash, a young brave of the camp whose bright eyes and proud bearing indicated a youth of spirit, were the players.

They sat cross-legged on the ground, facing each other. Before each on the ground lay two moccasins, and Waneton held a shining black pebble, which he also placed on the ground. He opened first one hand, then the other, showing the empty palms to Poudash, also opening his mouth, Poudash bending forward and looking intently in. All this was done as assurance that Waneton had no other pebble concealed about him, that all was to be fair, no cheating. For this was the favorite gambling game of the Indians. The stakes lay on the ground beside each player. Waneton had wagered a deerskin coat, and beside Poudash lay a bright hatchet, which he must forfeit to Waneton if he lose the game.

Waneton now took up the pebble and began a rapid shifting of his hands from moccasin to moccasin, never looking at his hands, but leaning forward, keeping his eyes fixed on Poudash with a keen, unwavering glance. Poudash, on his part, with vigilant look, scanned every movement of Waneton's hands, which flew with lightning-like rapidity. A drum was incessantly beaten during the game, by some of the onlooking Indians, a circle of whom stood around, eagerly watching the play.

At last Waneton stopped, and held up both hands, empty. Poudash, sharply scrutinizing Waneton's unchanging face, made a feint of picking up now one moccasin, now another. Finally, he lifted one of the moccasins. There was nothing under it!

"Whoop! Hoo, hoo!" cried Waneton and his friends, as he raised the other moccasin, revealing the black pebble beneath.

Poudash, with an unchanged face that expressed no emotion whatever, passed over the hatchet to Waneton, and taking from his belt his deerskin knife-sheath, handsomely embroidered with quills and beads, and trimmed with a fringe of human hair—hair from the head of an enemy slain in battle by Poudash—laid it down as his next stake. He then went on with the game, which was watched with intensest interest by all the spectators.

This time Waneton lost. Gain or loss only whetted the desire of the gamblers to play on. But now, above the thump of the drum, and the excited cries of the Indians, another sound was heard; a deep, solemn roll of thunder reverberating overhead, along the tree-tops, it seemed, so near did it sound.

"Hark!" cried Notoway. "The Thunder Bird comes. I hear the flapping of his wings, I see the flashing of his eyes!"

A great wind roared through the forest, bending and swaying the tall tree-tops almost to the earth. Now a vivid flash of lightning illuminated the awestruck faces of the Indians, the wigwams, the river, the woods around, bringing all to view in a distinct picture, which in another instant was swallowed up in darkness. A louder, longer peal of thunder rolled overhead, and a blinding, zig-zag line of lightning flashed down from the sky into the woods not far away.

"The Great Spirit is angry," said Notoway. "He sends the Thunder Bird to devour his children. We must pray to the Thunder Bird, and offer sacrifices, to please him, and turn away his wrath."

Hardly had he spoken, when a vivid flash of lightning and a tremendous peal of thunder came simultaneously. A tall pine near the village was split and shivered. All tingled with the electric shock. The Indians ran here and there, hurriedly obeying Notoway's orders. At his bidding, the longest, handsomest pipe was filled with k'nick k'nick and tobacco, and its smoke was waved heavenwards, with solemn cries and prayers to the Thunder Bird. Some of the choicest viands in the village, pieces of venison and bear's meat, some of the first ears of new corn, and the last maple sugar left from the sugar making of the previous spring, were hastily brought by the squaws to Notoway, who, after mysterious chanting, and muttering, and waving aloft of these gifts, placed them on the fire as a burnt offering to the Thunder Bird; and, while the Indians stood around in awed silence, he offered this prayer:

"O! Great One, O! Thunder Bird, destroy not thy children in thy wrath. Come not with thy terrible flashing eyes and mighty roar to devour them. Thou art powerful, but thou art good. Send thy rain down, to water the parched trees and grass, swell the dry streams, make the corn grow, make the berries big and sweet, but slay us not. Burn not our wigwams. See, we worship thee, we bring thee sweet offerings. Harm us not."

Stephen looked about him with awe. In this strange scene, amid the thick surrounding darkness, the roaring of the thunder, the vivid flashes of lightning, almost was he, too, tempted to believe like the Indians in some great evil power, lurking in the dark and storm for his undoing. Then a part of the 29th Psalm which, under his father's instructions, he had learned in faraway Deerfield, came into his mind.

> "The voice of the Lord is upon the waters; the God of glory thundereth; the Lord is upon many waters. The voice of the Lord is powerful; the voice of the Lord is full of majesty. The voice of the Lord breaketh the cedars; yea, the Lord breaketh the cedars of Lebanon."

It was long since Stephen had Been a Bible; but now its words returned to comfort and strengthen him.

"It is no thunder bird," he thought. "There is no such thing. I ought not to mind what the Indians say. It is God's voice. It is He who speaks in the thunder."

Stephen, feeling that he was safe in the hands of his only friend and refuge, the Father in heaven, was no longer afraid. He went to Waneton's wigwam, and crawling in under the door flap, lay down on his bed of boughs.

"Cosannip, is that you?" cried a timid little voice. "Katequa so frightened. She think the Thunder Bird burn the world up."

"Katequa must not fear. It is no thunder bird. It is the great Father above who speaks to us," said Stephen, reaching his hand over in the darkness to Katequa, who clutched it tightly in both her trembling little ones, glad of a human helper in her terror.

"Katequa heap glad Cosannip come. Now she not afraid anymore," she said.

Torrents of rain now came pouring down, shaking the wigwam's frail structure and extinguishing the fire where the offerings were smoking. The thunder was less loud, the lightning not so sharp and near.

"See," cried Notoway, as he stood dripping in the rain, "the Thunder Bird accepts the offerings of his children. He sends his rain to help them, and he burns them no more with the terrors of his flashing eyes. He is pleased. He goes away."

True enough, the thunder gradually grew more and more distant, becoming at last only a grand roar far off over the mountains. The rain slackened and finally ceased. The dark clouds rolled away to the East, and in the sky above the stars shone brightly forth. The air was fresh and cool.

"The stars have returned to their wigwams. They will pray to the Great Spirit for us and watch over his children. The Abenakis can sleep sweetly in peace," said Notoway; and he, like the others, now sought his wigwam, well pleased that his arts had been so successful in averting the rage of the Thunder Bird. Stephen thought much of Kewakcum before he went to sleep.

"He has been gone two days and nights now," he thought. "If he is alive, he is out in the woods somewhere, alone, without food or shelter, in this terrible storm. Oh, heavenly Father, wilt thou watch over Kewakcum this night, and bring him safely home again! "

The next morning dawned bright and serene; the sky a deep, clear blue, every bush and tree hanging with prismatic drops that flashed in the sunlight, the air full of fragrance and life.

As Stephen stood outside the wigwam, he saw someone slowly coming through the woods from the East. Could it be Kewakcum? A second look assured Stephen that it was indeed Kewakcum, but walking feebly, as if hardly able to drag himself along. Stephen ran joyfully to meet him, crying,

"Oh, Kewakcum, I am so glad to see you safely back again! But you walk so feebly. Are you sick or hurt?"

"No," said Kewakcum. "Kewakcum weak. Him eat nothing since he went away. But that no matter. Kewakcum no care."

Waneton and Notoway now came to greet the returned wanderer, while Heelahdee also came running from the fire, where she was cooking a savory stew of bear's meat.

"Was my son successful?" asked Waneton. "Did the Great Spirit send him a dream?"

"Notoway knows that Kewakcum found his dream. He sees it in his face," said the old medicine man. "What sign does our young warrior bring?"

Kewakcum handed Notoway an eaglet's feather, which he and Waneton regarded with delight.

"Tell us your dream, my brave son," said Waneton.

"No. Let him first eat. He is fainting from his long fast," said Notoway.

"Come, my young eaglet," said Heelahdee fondly and proudly, as she led Kewakcum to her wigwam, and brought him a bowl full of the hot stew. Yet, tempting as the stew smelled to the famished Kewakcum, he did not omit to hold the bowl aloft before eating, as a thank offering to the sun, the visible manifestation of the Great Spirit. When Kewakcum had been refreshed and revived by food, he told the story of his experiences to his eagerly interested listeners.

"Kewakcum wandered far away, towards the sunrise," he said. "He followed the course of the river through the forest. Always he watched everything, everywhere, above, below, for some sign from the Great Spirit."

"That was right," said Notoway, nodding his head approvingly.

"Kewakcum watch the fish in the river, the beaver in its dam, the partridge drumming in the woods, but no sign come to him. When the sun go away, and the dark come down, Kewakcum very hungry and tired. He come to great patch of berry bushes, but he eat not one berry."

Notoway again nodded his head in approval.

"As it grew darker, Kewakcum found a sheltered place among thick hemlocks. He rubbed his fire-sticks together and built a bright fire, to keep away wild beasts. Then he made a bed of hemlock branches, close to the fire, and lay down. Him almost asleep, when he heard a fierce cry afar in the woods. It sounded like a lost pappoose screaming."

"Ho, Brother Panther smell Kewakcum from afar," said Waneton.

"Kewakcum know that. Him think quick what to do. He climb fast into a tree near the fire, and sat in the crotch high above the ground. Pretty soon, Brother Panther leap out the bushes, give a great miaou, look all around, see Kewakcum up the tree, want him badly, but could not get him."

Waneton laughed at this, and Notoway also smiled, looking approvingly on Kewakcum.

"Kewakcum want to go to sleep, not be bothered all night. Him shot an arrow down into the panther's side. The panther ran off into the woods with the arrow fast in his side and bother Kewakcum no more. Then Kewakcum fix himself to sleep. Think him better stay up in tree. So he fastened his belt around a small limb one side the crotch, so him no fall off, and tried to sleep. But him no sleep much. Wolves barked and howled, owls hoot and make a big noise. Kewakcum thought maybe they no real owls; Iroquois out on the war path."

"Owls' hoot a bad sign, no luck," said Notoway, looking grave.

"Did the Great Spirit send Kewakcum his dream that night?"

"No, Kewakcum dream nothing," said the boy. "The sun come back, all still in the woods, birds singing, Kewakcum climb down and go on. Him ramble about all day. Saw no sign, feel very faint and discouraged. Begin to think no be able to get back to camp. Dream no dream, never be warrior, just lie down and die alone in the woods."

"Ho, ho," said Waneton, "warriors must be braves; no mind little hardships like that."

"Kewakcum know that, so he kept on, but now walked back towards the camp. When night came, he built another fire and lay down. Then he heard the growl and roar of the Thunder Bird, and saw the flashing of his fierce eyes. Kewakcum laid his bow and arrows on the fire as an offering to the Thunder Bird. He had nothing else."

"That was right," said Notoway.

"Kewakcum looked about for shelter from the storm. The blaze of the Thunder Bird's eyes showed an old tree, with a great hollow high up above the ground, not far away. Kewakcum managed to climb up into the hollow. It was soft with rotten wood and dust inside. Kewakcum snug and dry in there. When the Thunder Bird fly away, and the rain come not so hard, Kewakcum go sound asleep. Him so tired and faint, him sleep hard. Then his dream come."

Waneton and Notoway now listened more intently.

"Maybe it no dream. Kewakcum seem really to see it with his eyes," said Kewakcum, looking earnestly at Notoway.

"It was a vision, sent by the Great Spirit," said Notoway.

"Kewakcum saw a strong man coming from the East, walking on the air. His hair was long, and blew out behind him with the swiftness of his coming. His eyes were bright as the Thunder Bird's, his face brave and strong, like a great warrior's. He said, 'Watch this tree,' pointing to a great pine whose head towered above all the forest. He began to sing with a mighty roaring sound, pointing at the pine. It waved its branches violently up and down, then its head waved to and fro. Then the earth about the roots was heaved up by the tree's swaying, and the tree fell on the ground. Then the mighty warrior of the air smiled on Kewakcum and was gone. Kewakcum wake up—look out of his hollow—look all around. No one there."

"A mighty dream," said Waneton, looking anxiously at Notoway for the interpretation.

"The dream is a good omen," said Notoway. "The mighty god of the East Wind visited Kewakcum. He will help him. Did the East Wind give Kewakcum no sign?"

"No. But Kewakcum slept again. Dream another dream. All the animals and the birds come and talk to him. But he could not remember what they said, until, last of all, a great eagle came and circled around in the air over his head."

"An eagle!" exclaimed Waneton and Notoway in delight.

"The eagle said, 'If Kewakcum be brave and fierce like me, he be a mighty warrior, vanquish all enemies. The eagle give him this sign,' and something seemed to drop from its beak, Kewakcum could not see what. But in the early dawn when he woke and climbed down from the hollow, on the ground at the foot of the tree, Kewakcum found this eaglet's feather."

Kewakcum handed Notoway the precious feather. Notoway took it reverently, saying,

"Kewakcum has dreamed great dreams. His dreams denote that he will be a mighty warrior, a chief among the Abenakis, feared even by the Iroquois. The eagle is the emblem of courage. Only the bravest warriors are allowed to wear its feathers on their heads. The eagle's flight overhead, or the east wind blowing will always be signs of good omen for Kewakcum. All go well with him. Notoway make medicine bundle for Kewakcum."

Notoway proceeded to make with great care a little bundle of various sacred objects, part of his medicine for spells and healing, and tied all up in a tight cover of deerskin, to which he attached firmly the eaglet's feather. This charm Kewakcum always wore thereafter, tied to the necklace of wild rose-hips and tiny shells around his neck. This was his "medicine," his helper in all difficulties. Always must he sacredly keep it, and pass it on to his children.

7

DOWN THE RICHELIEU

ERE long, Waneton and his band resumed their journeying. The valuables, stored underneath the canoes, were found unmolested. The squaws drew the canoes down to the water, loaded them, and all embarked. Stephen, as before, was in the canoe with Kewakcum and Nunganey. But he could not help fancying a change in Kewakcum. He seemed older, different, less boyish.

"He seems to feel he is a man," thought Stephen, eyeing the grave face of Kewakcum, as he paddled on, his eye searching the sky as if for omens, the shore for signs of game.

Stephen was right. Kewakcum did feel that he had "put away childish things," and taken the first steps that led to becoming a renowned warrior. Already he was permitted to go to the hunt with the warriors, and Waneton had told him that, after another snow, he would be allowed to go out on the war path. His interests were now different from those of the younger boys. He felt himself immeasurably older than Stephen and Nunganey.

Stephen, who knew nothing of the geography of the region, wondered at the tortuous course of the canoes, which wound about deviously among green islands, first West, then South, finally North again. On one island Stephen caught a glimpse of stone walls through the trees, heard the sound of a drum, and thought he saw men in French uniform.[8]

But Waneton did not stop. He pushed on, to the North, ever to the North now, as Stephen knew by the sun, which set on his left. The lake grew narrower, until at last Stephen found they were travelling on a broad river, that swept on, bearing the waters of Lake Champlain to the St. Lawrence. This was the Richelieu, the stream called by Champlain "Riviere des Yrocois," because, even in his time, it was the favorite road for the Iroquois into the heart of Canada. To protect the French settlements from these Indian invasions, a chain of forts had been built along the Richelieu, of which the most southern was Fort St. Anne.

Kewakcum ordered Nunganey to take the other paddle. Nunganey made a grimace (but behind Kewakcum's back), yet obeyed, for he too felt the new might that seemed to invest Kewakcum, as he sat, or sometimes stood, erect in the prow, his medicine bundle with the eaglet's feather, sign of mysterious power, hanging on his breast. Stephen was free to think, and the old sad thoughts ever haunting him, returned with new force, as every stroke of the paddles bore him farther and farther on into the northern wilderness. He had no means of knowing where he was, or the day of the week, or what month it was, save as the aspect of nature, and the length of the hot days told him it must be midsummer. One day was like another; something to be endured and lived through as patiently as possible. Behind him stretched what seemed years of such days, as he looked back to his old home in Deerfield.

The landscape had changed in character. The land along the river was flat and low, with no near mountains. The woods were chiefly of fir, whose pointed, tapering tops rose closely each side the stream, their dark green, almost black color, giving a somber look to the landscape. No wonder that Stephen's heart sank within him, and that he thought,

"Even if my father and brothers and sisters are still living, how could we ever meet, how find each other, scattered about in such a vast, wild country? It is plain I must always live with the Indians. But, at any rate, I'll try not to be one, as long as I can."

Here his thoughts were interrupted by Nunganey, who said,

"Cosannip's turn to paddle now. Nunganey want to fish."

"I'd like to," said Stephen, glad of any diversion.

---

8 Fort St. Anne, on Isle La Mott.

Nunganey took a sharp fish bone for his hook, attached it to a strong line of deer sinew, and baiting it with a bit of dried meat, cast it overboard. The boys could plainly see fine, large fish floating below in the river's clear water, and it was exciting to watch one which came nearer, swimming cautiously up to the tempting bait, coquetting coyly about it, at last snatching it only to be twitched out by the excited Nunganey, and landed floundering in the bottom of the canoe, where Kewakcum quickly ended its struggles by a deft blow on the head from his paddle.

"Ho, ho, Kewakcum him dream dreams, but Nunganey him mighty fisherman. Fish jump in the canoe, when they see Nunganey coming for them," said Nunganey, forced to sing his own praises, since no one else did. Chanting the fisherman's song, which was really a prayer for success, Nunganey re-baited, and cast his hook in again.

When the grey shades of twilight settled down over the dark river, the Indians landed on an island, in midstream. A fire was built, its ruddy glare shining out picturesquely on the dark river, and into the fir woods beyond.

When Nunganey brought up from the boys' canoe five large fish, he was so much praised, not only by the squaws but even by the warriors, that he strutted about, hardly deigning to speak to the other boys. The fish, roasted in the fire's hot ashes, made an ample supper for all. A summer shower now began to sprinkle down. But the canoes had been drawn ashore, and turned over, back to the wind. Under their shelter all crept for the night. The shower extinguished the sputtering fire, and drove in torrents against the canoe bottoms, but all lay snug and dry beneath.

Stephen was wakened in the early dawn by something brushing across his face. He opened his eyes to see a grey squirrel sitting so near, that his tail had swept over the boy's face. Stephen reached out his hand and patted the soft fur. The terrified squirrel bounded away, up a tree trunk, where from a lofty limb, with fast beating heart and bright eyes of wonder, it watched the strange creatures crawling out from under the canoes. What could these strange animals be? Little Brother Squirrel instinctively feared them, though never before had he seen their like. Something warned him that these strange creatures boded him and his no good. But being luckily out of sight, he escaped this time the swift flying arrow.

The Indians started off downstream in unusually good spirits, in evident haste to get on. Their dipping paddles dimpled the river with wide spreading circles, as they swept on with the current. Towards noon, the broad stream was divided by an island, covered with a growth of large pines. As they rounded this island, Kewakcum said joyfully,

"The Isle of Sainte Therese! Come to fort before many strokes now!"

The river grew wider, roughening into such tumultuous rapids that the Indians landed and carried canoes and contents around this difficult place. A pack too heavy for Stephen's feeble strength was bound on the boy's back, and he toiled painfully along beside the rushing stream, his eyes bent on the ground, as he picked his footing among rocks and stones. Suddenly he heard a joyous shout from Waneton, who was in advance.

"Ho, ho!" cried Waneton, pointing ahead.

Stephen's heart almost stood still with surprise; then bounded high and beat as if it would suffocate him. For there, below, where the river rushed down the last rapid into a broad, lake-like expanse, stood a stone fort! From its tall flag-staff floated the lilies of France, flapping in the summer breeze. Along the coast below the fort, Stephen saw a line of farmhouses, scattered on the river's shore. Smoke rose from their chimneys, curling up to vanish in the blue of the sky. He heard faintly in the distance the mooing of a cow, the crowing of a rooster.

Blessed, home-like sights and sounds! Evidently this was a white settlement. A new light shone in Stephen's eyes, his heart beat joyously, and he stepped off quickly, no longer feeling his burden.

"Shamblee," said Heelahdee, pointing at the fort, and smiling at Stephen, who smiled back to her.

At the foot of the rapids, the Indians reloaded their canoes, and paddled swiftly across Chambly Basin to the point where, amid the surrounding meadows, stood the fort, close to the water's edge. Landing a little above the fort, the Indians drew their canoes well up on shore, and then went directly to the fort's entrance, before which a sentinel in French uniform, gun on shoulder, paced up and down with measured tread.

"Bonjour, Waneton, Mahtocheegah!" said the sentinel, as he lowered his gun, in signal that the Indians were allowed to enter the fort.

"He seems to know them well," thought Stephen in surprise.

Well might the French sentinel know the Abenakis. For this was Fort St. Louis at Chambly, one of the chain of forts built along the Richelieu to protect the Canadian frontier. Sieur Jean Baptiste Hertel, the father of Francois Hertel de Rouville, who had led the attack upon Deerfield, was lord of the seigniory, which included this fort. His family was one of the oldest in New France and had a romantic history. The seigniory of Rouville included the picturesque Mt. Beloeil, just below Chambly Basin, and that lake, the fort, the whole romantic Rougemont valley.

When Governor de Vaudreuil planned a raid on New England settlements, it was natural to call for service on the brave Hertels. Francois, son of Jean Baptiste, was often the leader of such parties, and Fort St. Louis was the rendezvous and starting point for the forces sent on such raids. "Swooping down from his eyrie, Rouville's beak and talons were at the heart of New England, before the approach of a war party was dreamed of."[9]

From this fort the body of French and Indians had set forth the previous winter for its descent upon Deerfield; and ever since early spring the soldiers at the fort had seen small bands of the returning Indians, with their wretched white captives, passing through to the north. Waneton's band was the last to come in.

The sentinel eyed sharply, as he passed timidly by, the little boy who looked so thin and worn, almost naked, his hair cut Indian fashion, long one side, short the other, his face and body tanned a dark red. Still it was evident that he was a white captive. To one of the *habitans* passing out, the soldier said,

"Another captive from Guerfiel has just been brought in by Waneton's band. The poor little fellow looks sorry and pitiful."

"In my opinion, 'tis a cruel shame that our governor and His Majesty, the King, sanction the savages' bloody raids. 'Twill bring the curse of heaven yet on New France," said the *habitant*, but cautiously and in low tones, glancing around to be sure that none overheard.

"Governor de Vaudreuil feels it wise policy to enlist our Indian allies against our foes, the English, and so strengthen our hold on them."

"Aye, true. But it is a policy little to my liking," replied the *habitant*.

---

9 "Picturesque Canada."

8

AT CHAMBLY

IN the little settlement of perhaps fifteen houses that were clustered around Fort St. Louis, events were few, and intercourse with the outside world rare. Therefore, it was soon noised about the little village that another band of Indians had just come in from the raid on Deerfield, bringing a white captive. Some of the women at once hastened to the Indian wigwams not far from the fort, where Stephen was sitting on one of the upturned canoes, looking longingly towards the houses. It was so strange, yet delightful, to see again houses and fences, and white people coming and going. One of the French women said,

"See, that child yonder must be the captive. How forlorn he looks! Poor boy, my heart aches for him."

"Think, were it your Jacques or my little Pierre, thus torn away from home and parents, how we should feel," said the other.

"My boy, you come from Deerfield, is it not so?" they asked. "What is your name? Are you alone? Are your parents living?"

"My name is Stephen Williams," replied the boy. How long since he had pronounced that name!" My father was the minister at Deerfield. He and all my brothers and sisters were taken captive with me, but I know not whether any of them are now alive. My mother and one little brother and my baby sister were slain by the Indians."

Stephen noticed that the women looked much excited as he spoke. Both exclaimed, talking together in their excitement,

"What, know you not that your father is alive? And the brothers and sisters? They passed through here with their captors early in April. And your father was brought here the last of April. But you, poor child, have been a captive alone with the Indians, all these weary months! Truly it is terrible!"

"Are you sure it was my father?" asked Stephen, hardly able to credit the good news. "Was my little brother Warham alive? He was but four years old, and I thought surely he would be killed, or die on the way."

"No, he was in the best condition of any. His Indian master, moved perhaps to tender pity for the little one by the Blessed Virgin, had carried the child in his arms, or drawn him on a sledge most of the way. Your poor father was very thin, and much worn by his sufferings, and dressed in a dirty, ragged, old uniform. Poor man, it was pitiful to see to what a state he was reduced. He was glad to learn here that his other children had reached Canada, but his heart was very heavy with anxiety for his little son Stephen. Would he could know of your safe arrival!"

"Here is some bread I brought for you, poor child," said one of the women. "Eat it, and I will ask my husband to persuade your Indian master to let you visit our house."

Stephen had not tasted bread since he left Deerfield, that is, for six months, it being now August, as he learned from his kind friends. All the more because it tasted so delicious to him did he hasten to share it with Katequa, and little Ohopasha, who, released from his bark cradle, was sprawling on the ground, trying to creep, and who, in his efforts to eat the bread, rubbed his crust first on the ground, than all over his face, until he was well smeared, but none the less happy.

"White people's meat taste heap good," said Katequa, as she ate the last mouthful of the sweet, tender bread.

"I had such bread every day in my own home, Katequa," said Stephen. Somehow the bread stuck in his throat, perhaps because there was a lump there. The taste of the bread made Stephen homesick, with an irrepressible longing for home and friends. Perhaps he should see his father again.

"I am so glad to know that he is alive," he thought. "Yet that was long ago. He looked so feeble. He may have died ere this."

So hope and fear swayed his heart. Towards night, a French soldier came and asked Waneton's permission to take Stephen to the fort. Waneton consented, but said to Kewakcum,

"Kewakcum go too, and keep eye wide open. Watch what white men do and tell Waneton."

As Kewakcum and Stephen neared the fort, Stephen saw a little girl walking beside a French lady. It was Thankful Stebbins, he was certain.

"Thankful!" he called out joyfully.

The little girl turned, gave him a frightened glance, then seized the lady's hand and went on, not seeming to recognize Stephen.

"How strange! I am sure it was Thankful," thought the disappointed Stephen.

At the barracks within the fort, Stephen found his friend of the morning, who had brought him the bread. Now she gave him a good meal of such food as Stephen had not eaten for months.

A portion was also served to Kewakcum, sitting in the corner, watching suspiciously every movement of the white people. Noticing that Stephen limped, the woman examined his feet, the feet that had walked all the weary miles from Deerfield over ice, and rocks, and stones.

"Oh, the poor little Anglois! Behold, Henri, what the child must have suffered!" cried the woman, as she bathed and tenderly dressed with soothing liniment the scarred and swollen feet.

Her little Pierre stood close by, watching with wonder the strange boy, who had no good coat and trousers and leggings like himself, and who, his mother said, had been brought by the Indians from his own home, far, far away among the Bostonnais.

Kewakcum, meantime, was not enjoying himself, lie, the coming warrior, who already wore a sacred bundle, a medicine bag of his own, and an eaglet's feather, sat alone, unnoticed, while the white captive was the center of attention. Night came on, and the soldier took Stephen into an adjoining room. Through the open door Kewakcum saw Stephen laid on a bed, and carefully covered with a quilt. Then the door was gently closed, and the soldier said to his wife,

"Let the poor child rest a while in peace. By the holy saints, it is terrible, what the Indian allies do!"

Kewakcum rose, and glided out the door unnoticed, his soft moccasins making no sound. Stephen lay on the soft bed of pigeons' feathers, looking about at the walls, where pictures of the saints hung, and at the windows of small, diamond-paned glass. The sensation of being in a house again was so novel, that at first he could not sleep, but gradually the sense of comfort and peace overcame him, and he sank into a deep, sweet slumber. The next he knew, someone was shaking him by the shoulder.

"In a minute, mother," murmured Stephen, thinking he was at home.

Then he opened his eyes, bewildered at first to see such strange surroundings, and the French soldier standing over him, who said,

"Alas, my child, your master has come for you, and demands you immediately. In vain I have plead with him to leave you here for the night. He insists you must go with him now. We dare not offend our Indian allies. You are his property. I must let you go. But I pity you from the bottom of my heart."

It was now night. Out in the kitchen Waneton's tall form towered up, the feathers in his hair brushing the low ceiling.

"Cosannip belongs to Waneton. Cosannip come with Waneton," he said sternly.

When the door closed after the little boy limping out into the dark behind the tall, fierce looking savage, whose belt bore both knife and tomahawk, the French woman burst into tears, crying,

"I care not if the King himself hear me! It is a shame, a cruel, burning shame! It will bring a curse on New France!"

Kewakcum had gone back to his father, and reported,

"Frenchman hide Cosannip, cover him up. Kewakcum think him mean to steal Cosannip in the night. Get all the ransom money for himself, Waneton get nothing."

This news confirmed the suspicious jealousy of Waneton, that now he had come among the French, were he not vigilant, he might lose his captive, his chief share of the spoils of Deerfield, and the big ransom he hoped to get for him, should he decide to part with him. Early next morning, he broke camp. As the canoes glided past the fort, Stephen had a glimpse of his kind French friend, waving her hand to him. Downstream they paddled, out of Chambly Basin into the lower river, past Mt. Beloeil where Stephen shuddered to hear the Indians speak with admiring reverence of "the great brave, Hertel de Rouville," as they pointed out his abode. Past many islands covered with great oaks and walnuts they drifted, until at last they reached the mouth of the river, where it empties into that broad expanse of the St. Lawrence known as Lake St. Peter. Here stood Fort Richelieu, and near it had grown up the village of Sorel.

On the way down the river they had stopped for a day or two near a Frenchman's house, about three miles below Chambly. This Frenchman was very kind to Stephen, and begged Waneton to permit the boy to lodge at his house, but Waneton would not suffer it.

"Waneton no pappoose to be fooled by Frenchman. Keep Cosannip with him," he said.

The Indians had not been long at Sorel, when Stephen saw a boat coming across the broad stream, rowed with vigorous strokes by a young Frenchwoman, who, on landing, came directly to him.

"I have heard of you, poor boy," she said, "and my heart is rent with pity for you. In the last war I too lived as a captive among the Indians, and well I know what you endure."

She brought a quantity of nice food with her—bread, and meat, and cakes—above all, a flagon of milk. Ah, how sweet was that drink of milk to Stephen, after so many months! Although he shared these things with the Indians, they were evidently in ill humor. In truth, they were far from pleased with the attention attracted by their young captive since they had reached Canada, and watched jealously everyone approaching him.

Fort Richelieu was only about eighty rods from the village of Sorel, where the Indians had camped. Great was Stephen's surprise the next day, when Waneton said to him, quite graciously,

"Cosannip may go visiting to the fort. But must not stay long."

"I wonder Waneton allows me to go to the fort," thought Stephen, as he trudged on alone towards the stone fort on the river bank. "I guess he thinks the soldiers will give me food, that I will bring home for him and the rest. I will, too."

The appearance of the forlorn child, whose whole aspect told so plainly what he had undergone, excited the same sympathy among the warm-hearted soldiers here, as at the other places visited. One of them urged Stephen to spend the night.

"Certainly your master will not care, for one night only," said the soldier.

The temptation was too great for Stephen to resist. That night, for the first time in six months, he lay again in a soft bed, with white sheets. The next day he was urged to stay and was so kindly treated that he lingered at the fort, with an uneasy feeling that Waneton would be displeased, yet unable to tear himself away from such rare comfort and peace.

"Maybe the soldiers will persuade Waneton to leave me here," he thought. "Perhaps I will not have to live any more among the Indians."

Vain hope! Towards noon, Waneton appeared, very angry, turning a deaf ear to the soldiers' petitions that Stephen be left with them for the present. With frowning face, he seized Stephen's hand, and dragged him along, muttering to himself,

"Waneton no fool. Him no let Frenchmen steal away his captive." Then he added to Stephen, "Cosannip go no more to the houses of the French."

After this, Waneton never allowed Stephen to enter a French house, unless accompanied by an Indian.

Two days more were spent at Sorel, and then Waneton again embarked. So broad was the expanse of Lake St. Peter that Stephen never imagined that he was on a river. The Indians paddled about among the many islands, knowing well this oft travelled course, and at last entered the mouth of another large river, the St. Francis, which here empties into the St. Lawrence.

9

STEPHEN CHANGES MASTERS

THE Indians turned into the river and paddled up it about three miles, past Fort St. Francis, another of the chain of forts that has been mentioned. Wondering much what his next experience was to be, Stephen, looking anxiously ahead up stream, saw by the river side what seemed a large Indian village. The Indians in the canoes were joyful and excited when this village came in view. As they drew nearer, the warriors began giving loud whoops and shouts, the cry of the warrior who returns victorious from battle. Answering shouts were heard from the Indian village, and a throng of Indians flocked down to the shore. Waneton and his band were warmly welcomed. For this village of St. Francis was the chief settlement of the Abenakis, and their permanent home, so far as Indians can be said to have such a home.

The Indians here dwelt in lodges, stronger structures than the wigwams which were used when moving about. These lodges varied in length from fifty to eighty feet. The families belonging to one clan usually occupied a lodge together. A row of fires burned down the center of the long lodge. Bench-like couches or seats ran along the lodge, each side the fire. Covered with soft skins, these made the seats by day, the beds at night. Long poles were stretched across the lodge over each fire, for smoking and drying meat and fish, seasoning wood for bows and arrows, or hanging and drying garments.

A place and a fire awaited Waneton in the lodge of his kinsman, known by the name of Sagamore George of Pennicook, a name given him in years past by the English in Maine, among whom he had wrought great havoc in various raids. Over the entrance to the Sagamore's lodge fluttered from poles ten paleface scalps. Stephen noticed with a shudder that one scalp had long, golden hair, evidently from the head of some white woman. The Sagamore's deerskin shirt and leggings also were fringed with human hair of mingled hues. Evidently he was a noted brave. Sagamore George was a tall, fierce-looking Indian, whose prominent aquiline nose, high cheek bones, and scowling forehead were weather-beaten by the suns and storms of over half a century. Stephen felt afraid of him.

Mahtocheegah and his family were assigned a fire at the farther end of the same lodge. Heelahdee went to work as usual. The canoes were drawn up the bank and turned over, their contents carried to the lodge and stowed away under the beds, and along the sloping edges of the lodge. Stephen was obliged to carry back-loads of skins up to the lodge for Heelahdee. A group of Indian children had gathered, and stood with open-eyed curiosity, watching every motion of this newcomer, this white boy from the far away "Bostonnais" country. Stephen, as he had opportunity, also looked at them with interest, for apparently St. Francis was to be his home, and therefore these children would be his companions. Among them, he noticed some who seemed different from the rest. In spite of paint and sunburn, their skin was lighter hued than that of real Indians. One boy, he was sure, had red hair, although it had been darkened with grease and charcoal till the original color was hard to distinguish. And surely yonder little girl, who looked gentle and delicate, had blue eyes. They too must be English captives! The children were shy, and stood aloof. But at last, as Stephen was following Heelahdee up the bank, bending under a back-load of furs, he passed quite near the little girl, and resolved to speak.

"Are you not English too?" he asked. "I am sure I am not mistaken. And are not some of the others white captives? Oh, I hope so. It will be so pleasant to be able to speak English, and to play with someone who feels as I do."

The little girl shook her head, as if not understanding, and making some reply in the Indian tongue, ran off behind the squaw who accompanied her, who scowled at Stephen, on hearing him address the child in English, saying to the child,

"Come away, Wilootaheeta. Speak not to the English captive."

"I believe she does understand, though she pretends she does not," said Stephen. "I am sure she is English, and that boy too."

Later he tried to talk to the boy with the same result. The boy affected not to understand him. This strange conduct puzzled Stephen.

"I should think they would be glad to see another white person, and to talk English again. I know I shall always. I shall never feel like an Indian, no matter how long I am forced to live among them."

Heelahdee and Eenisken were evidently most happy to be once more at home, their wanderings and hardships over for a while, at least. The squaws at St. Francis had fields of corn, squash, beans and pumpkins under cultivation, and these vegetables, with the meat and fish brought in by the hunters, made food not only plentiful, but more varied and agreeable than usual. As Stephen ate from a wooden bowl with a horn spoon a mixture of corn and beans which the Indians called "succotash," it seemed to him he could almost feel himself growing fat.

The morning after Waneton's arrival, the village presented an animated scene. There was the bustle inseparable from numbers, the barking of dogs, cries and laughter of children, and noises of many sorts. After singing a hunting song, the men set off for the day's hunting, accompanied by Kewakcum and other older boys. Some of the squaws were busy picking corn and beans, preparing them to dry on skins laid in the hot sunshine. When dried, they would store them away in great sacks for use the coming winter. Some were sewing; with an awl made of a sharp bone they pierced holes in the skins, which they sewed with deer sinews into shirts, leggings, and moccasins. Their sewing was so strong, that often the skins would wear out before the seams gave way.

Little Wilootaheeta, Stephen noticed, was being taught by a young squaw to embroider a moccasin with beads. She sat under a tree, one side the village. The squaw soon leaving her, she sat alone, busy with her work, which she seemed to enjoy. Stephen, roaming about to inspect the village, happened to pass near her. To his surprise, he heard her say in a low tone, looking about to be sure that no one heard her,

"Stephen! Stephen Williams!"

"I thought you did not understand English," said Stephen.

"I do, well enough," said Wilootaheeta, "though I have lived with the Indians many months, and seldom hear a word of English. But I well remember my own home, in the eastern country, and my father and mother. They were both killed by the Indians when I was captured, so I have no home now, only with the Indians."

"What is your real name?" asked Stephen.

"Abigail. My father used to call me his 'little Nabby,'" said Wilootaheeta, with a wistful look in her blue eyes.

"Why did you pretend not to understand when I spoke to you yesterday?" asked Stephen.

"Because my Indian mother would be angry. She wants me to forget English, and be a true Indian in every way, and a Catholic too."

"I know one thing. I will never be an Indian, nor a Catholic either," said Stephen stoutly.

"Perhaps you will not be able to help yourself," said Wilootaheeta. "If we must live with the Indians, it is best to try to please them. Then they are kind to us."

"I know I never will," said Stephen, as he walked away.

He noticed as he walked about the village, a small building, whose gable bore a wooden cross. Coming from it, he saw a man wearing along black robe, whom he heard a squaw address as "Father."

"It must be the Roman Catholic priest," thought Stephen, gazing for the first time with mingled curiosity and horror on a teacher of that religion, which he had been trained to regard as dangerous error. He saw the priest talking to Heelahdee, who looked pleased as she listened. She had been to confession, and felt safe and happy now, back under the wing of the church.

Later in the day, when the little chapel bell rang out, its chimes a touching note of civilization and Christian faith amidst the savage surroundings, Heelahdee went to mass, taking Katequa with her, and her pappoose on her back. She beckoned Stephen to follow, saying,

"Cosannip come. Go to mass with Heelahdee. Holy water wash away all his sins. See the pictures of the holy saints. Father talk good talk. Make Cosannip better."

"No," said Stephen, shaking his head firmly. "Cosannip no go."

Heelahdee looked displeased. She would have liked to say, "Heelahdee tell Waneton when he come back. Waneton whip Cosannip." But, alas, Waneton was not of her faith, and though the priest had labored with him, even the evening before, he could not seem to impress Waneton in the least. Heelahdee resolved to redouble her prayers to the Blessed Virgin, that she would soften Waneton's hard heart, and bring him into the true faith.

The hunters returned towards night, having had good success. After the abundant evening meal, the whole village fell to enjoying the long summer twilight. The young men, imitated by the older boys, had wrestling matches, and performed feats of strength and agility, such as seeing who could pitch a stone farthest, who could beat in a running match, who could shoot an arrow highest straight up in the air, and make it fall at a given point. Kewakcum was foremost among the boys. When, in wrestling, he threw down one of the St. Francis boys, larger than himself, from the circle of spectators came loud cries of,

"Ho, ho! Behold Kewakcum, the strong one, the mighty Elk!"

"Ho, that not much," said Nunganey to Stephen. "Nunganey do that easy enough."

"Why don't you do it then?" Stephen could not resist asking.

"Nunganey no care. Him no want to. Come, Cosannip, go see the braves play."

Stephen followed Nunganey over to a group of men deep in the gambling game. Stephen saw that Waneton was pitted against Sagamore George. The two, sitting face to face, glared at each other unflinchingly, like two fighting cocks, as their hands flew to and fro, each trying to outwit the other.

Even the squaws were sitting at ease, after their hard day's toil. Some bore their pappooses on their backs, some had put their children on the ground beside them, where they rolled and sprawled at their ease, as their mothers chatted and gossiped with each other. Some of the squaws were also engaged in a gambling game, which was played by tossing up plum stones marked on one side, catching them in a basket as they fell, wagers being laid as to which side would come uppermost. A party of young squaws wandered out to a spring, at the edge of the forest. Certain young braves strayed forth in the same direction, and ere long, the young people were having a merry time together, with much laughter and play.

Suddenly the peaceful scene was disturbed by angry voices and loud quarrelsome tones, coming from the group of men who were gambling. Sagamore George accused Waneton of cheating. Waneton angrily denied the charge. The dispute grew louder, and when the friends of each chief ranged themselves on his side, bloodshed seemed imminent. Waneton had his hand on the knife in his belt, and the Sagamore was drawing his from the sheath, when, alarmed at the noise, the black robed father appeared on the scene.

Stephen could not understand what he said, but he saw that gradually the excitement subsided. Sagamore seemed to assent to some proposal made by the priest, while Waneton, partly pacified, but still with a lowering, sullen face, walked off to his lodge. The next day Kewakcum sought out Stephen, saying.

"Kewakcum tell Cosannip big news. Waneton goes away today. Him going down Albany way," he added, pointing off to the southwest.

This was most unwelcome news to Stephen. His last lingering hope of rescue vanished, if he must again be dragged far off into the wilderness, away from Canada, where he now knew his father and family to be. So long as he remained in Canada, there was a slight chance at least that he might yet meet with them, perhaps even be redeemed. But once off in the western wilderness, remote from settlements, his chance of rescue would be small indeed. He turned pale, his heart sinking with a sickening feeling of despair, as he exclaimed,

"Oh, Kewakcum, Cosannip very sorry. Why does not Waneton stay here? Food is plenty. This is his home."

"Waneton no like Black Robe Father," said Kewakcum. "Him try heap to make Waneton turn his back on the Great Spirit, the four winds, all Waneton's helpers. And Waneton him quarrel with Sagamore George. The Sagamore cheat Waneton. Waneton no stay. Him go Albany way. Sell skins to Dutchman for heap money. Dutchman no bother Waneton about religion."

"Cosannip very sorry. Him no want to go," said Stephen sorrowfully.

"Ho, Cosannip him no going. Waneton give him to Sagamore George."

This was news indeed, which Stephen heard with mingled feelings. He was relieved to learn that he was to be left at St. Francis, yet it was a hard trial to change masters, to leave Waneton who had been kind to him in Indian fashion, and belong to the fierce Sagamore, whom he feared. Young though he was, Stephen began learning, even now, one of life's lessons; that, while there is rarely a cloud so dark that it has no "silver lining," so also there are few pleasures without some alloy or drawback. Early must one learn to cultivate the habit of looking on the bright side of things and making the best of even undesirable happenings.

"Cosannip sorry to lose his friend Kewakcum," said Stephen.

"Ho, Kewakcum come back again before many moons. Him be big hunter, warrior, take Cosannip to hunt and on the war path with him," said Kewakcum.

Accustomed as he was to the wandering life of the Indians, Kewakcum took to its frequent changes and haphazard ramblings as a matter of course. He expected that Stephen would live at St. Francis, and become an Abenaki, and to St. Francis, the headquarters of the Abenakis, Kewakcum knew that he was sure to return. He regarded the parting as only temporary.

Later in the day Heelahdee, with the patient meekness of the squaw, packed again all her belongings, and stowed them in the canoes. If it was hard for her to break up and start forth again on a wandering and precarious life in the forest, she made no complaints, but did her lord's bidding without a murmur. The good father comforted her as best he could, exhorting her to hold fast to her faith, to remember that God, the Blessed Virgin, the holy saints, could hear her prayers afar in the wilderness, and urging her not to remit her efforts for her husband's conversion. Her faithfulness would yet save his soul. He had blessed and given her a rosary which was a great comfort to her, a visible link with the religion which had appealed so forcibly to her heart.

The two canoes pushed away from St. Francis and set off down the river. Waneton and Kewakcum were in the foremost. Heelahdee followed in the other, with the younger children. A company of children stood on the bank watching the departure.

"Goodbye, Heelahdee. Goodbye, Kewakcum," called Stephen, with a choking sensation in his throat, that made his words broken. "I shall always remember how kind you were to me."

Heelahdee smiled, rather a sad smile, while Kewakcum, dipping his paddle for a stronger stroke, laughed and said,

"Kewakcum be back before many moons. Find Cosannip a big brave then."

Old Wees, sitting in Waneton's canoe, his head coming just above the edge, now discovered Stephen standing on the shore, and evidently thought something was wrong. He stood up, his paws on the edge of the canoe, barking loudly, as if crying in dog language,

"You've left Cosannip behind!"

In his excitement he seemed about to leap over into the water, until Kewakcum took him by the nape of the neck and made him lie down. But still his bright eyes looked back, fixed on Stephen, sure that the stupid human beings, who would not listen to him, had made a mistake. From Heelahdee's canoe came a sound of wailing, the voice of little Katequa, who wept aloud, and refused to be comforted.

"Me want my Cosannip. Cosannip come too. Katequa no leave Cosannip behind."

Tears filled Stephen's eyes, and, in spite of hard winking and swallowing, one coursed down his cheek. Nunganey, who was standing by, was quick to notice this weakness.

"Ho, ho," he shouted, "See the white pappoose. Him cry! Him want Heelahdee carry him on her back. Yah, yah, yah!"

The other Indian boys were quick to follow Nunganey's example and jeer at Stephen, especially the red headed boy, Tododaho, who was loudest of all, shouting,

"See the sick white pappoose! Run tell Kippenoquah come carry him home in bark cradle. Yah! Yah!"

Stephen paid no attention to these jeers; his heart was too heavy to care much, as he stood watching the canoes bearing away the best friends he had known in his captivity until they were lost to sight. Then he turned slowly to face his new life.

The other boys, finding that their persecution made no impression, had gone away, but to Stephen's surprise, Tododaho lingered. Still more to Stephen's surprise, he said,

"You mustn't mind what I say to you before the Indians, Stephen. I have to talk so before them to make them think I am just as much an Indian as they are. I really feel sorry for you. My real name's Ben. Let's call each other Ben and Stephen when we are alone, will you?"

So a little drop of comfort already fell into Stephen's cup.

10

SAGAMORE GEORGE'S BOY

STEPHEN often wondered why Waneton had parted with him to the Sagamore. Perhaps in the wild fury of the gambling game, the white captive had been one of the pledges staked and lost by Waneton; or possibly he had been obliged to give up the white boy, to settle the charges of cheating brought against him by the Sagamore. The priest had probably used his influence thus to settle the quarrel, feeling it better for the boy to remain in the village, where he would come under religious influence, than to ramble the wilderness with the unconverted and obstinate Waneton. At all events, Stephen was now the property of Sagamore George.

The children of the Sagamore and his squaw, Kippenoquah, were grown up, and started in life on their own account. The chief and wife would, therefore, find it useful to have a boy to help them, while they retained Stephen. But the Sagamore was avaricious. He regarded Stephen as a profitable investment. He hoped to receive a large sum for his ransom and meant to be most shrewd in driving a good bargain, securing the utmost possible for the captive's redemption.

Stephen felt forlorn and friendless, left thus with strange Indians, to neither of whom was he much attracted. He missed Heelahdee, and Kewakcum, and his little friend, Katequa, even Ohopasha and old Wees. He had lived with them all so long that they seemed to belong to him. But he tried to conceal his feelings, and make the best of the situation, knowing that to be his only safety. Yet underneath the quiet exterior of the sober little boy was a homesick heart, a heart that only his religious faith kept from utter despair.

It was now September, the "Month of Falling Leaves." Both hunters and squaws worked busily laying in stores of food to help them over the long, cold Canadian winter, close at hand. One morning, almost before Stephen had swallowed his bowl of venison stew, Sagamore George ordered him to follow, as he started off down to the river. Here he embarked in his canoe, motioning Stephen to take one paddle. The Sagamore gave a grunt of satisfaction, when he saw that the white boy handled a paddle not unskillfully. He wasted no words, but sat grim and silent, as the canoe swept on downstream, his eyes keenly scanning earth, water, and sky, with the habitual observation of an Indian, whom no motion escapes. Presently Stephen noticed him eyeing intently what looked, to Stephen's untrained eye, like a dark cloud far away in the sky. But the cloud moved rapidly nearer, and resolved itself into a flock of wild geese, flying in wedge-shaped procession to the South. Faint and high sounded their "konk, ka konk."

The geese, as they drew nearer, sank downwards, finally alighting at a point downstream. Sagamore George was on the alert now, and Stephen too felt excited. Remembering his former success in killing geese, he thought, with vain regret,

"If I had only brought my bow and arrows!"

The geese had alighted below a turn in the river bank. Pulling rapidly on, the Sagamore beached his canoe, and, taking his gun, crept cautiously up the steep bank, whose top would command a view of the cove where the geese had alighted. Creeping stealthily on hands and knees, not even rustling a leaf or stirring a pebble, and followed in like fashion by Stephen, who had learned many Indian ways, the Sagamore reached the summit. Peeping through the leafy screen of the bushes, there, in the quiet cove below, they saw a pretty picture.

The clear water reflected as in a mirror the brilliant tints of the overhanging foliage, the dark green of pines and firs, and the blue sky above, with its white clouds sailing over. Amidst this wealth of color floated the birds, "swimming double, swan and shadow," in perfect quiet and confidence. Some were diving for food, some picking and arranging their feathers in careless ease, but one, who seemed the appointed watchman, stood on the sandy beach opposite, on the lookout for enemies. He was a large gander, who was every instant alert, head up, neck stretched out, watching in every direction. If any of his flock even swam towards the bushy covert of the opposite shore, he gave loud warning cries of alarm.

It was the sentinel himself whom Sagamore George selected for his victim. The loud report of his gun shattered the peace of the scene with a hundred echoing repetitions from hills all around. The startled geese flew up and away, leaving their leader prostrate on the sand. So heavy and fat were the geese, that they rose but slowly, and the Sagamore was able to shoot yet another before they could escape.

His grim face softened with a look of satisfaction as the Sagamore said,

"Cosannip, go bring the game."

"It's lucky I know how to swim." thought Stephen, as he ran down through the bushes to the stream, and went across, sometimes swimming, sometimes wading, and returned bringing first one goose, then the other. It was a heavy load for him to bring the two geese uphill by the legs, but Sagamore George did not offer to help him.

Their voyage downstream was now continued, until they reached the mouth of the St. Francis. Here, as the stream widened to enter Lake St. Peter, were mud flats, where the rich earth brought down from the meadows above, in the spring freshets of many years, had gradually been deposited. This was a favorite spot for eels, as Sagamore George well knew. He selected a good location and threw his line over. Stephen, who supposed the Sagamore in pursuit of ordinary fish, and had never seen an eel, was startled when the Indian hauled out a slippery eel, four feet long, and threw it, squirming and writhing, into the canoe bottom.

"Oh!" cried Stephen involuntarily, drawing up his bare legs. The eel looked altogether too snake-like to be pleasant as a near neighbor.

"Paleface boy a squaw pappoose. Afraid of an eel!" said the Sagamore with infinite contempt, as he dropped his line in again.

As at this season the eels were going downstream towards the salt water, they were abundant. When Sagamore George was tired of fishing for them, he took a long-handled spear, stood in the canoe, and darted his spear down into the bed of mud below, thus bringing up many, for some of the eels had already taken up their winter quarters about a foot down in the mud.

When the Sagamore had secured a heavy canoe load, to Stephen's joy he at last stopped spearing, and set out for home, well pleased with his success. Stephen viewed the canoe load of eels, some still squirming, with disgust.

"I suppose the Indians mean to eat them," he thought. "But nothing will ever induce me to touch a mouthful, no, not even if I am starving."

Stephen's trials were not yet over, for when they reached home, he had to help Kippenoquah carry the eels up to the lodge, and, worse yet, help her skin and dress them, ready to cure on the poles over the fire, where the thick smoke was ever rising. When well smoked, she would store them away for winter use.

Stephen had no objection to another task she set him, which was watching one of the geese that she was roasting on a stick before the fire, turning it around as it browned. Stephen had had nothing to eat since morning, and anticipations of a good supper of roast goose reconciled him to his task, as the goose browned and sizzled before the fire, sending up a most appetizing odor.

The next day Stephen and most of the other children, went out with the squaws for blackberries. The squaws gathered berries in a way new to Stephen. The bushes hung low with their burden of fruit. The squaws spread skins on the ground, broke off the bending branches, and beat them with sticks on the skins, thus gathering great quantities without the slow effort of patient picking.

Later the same day, Stephen was watching a game played by some of the young squaws and big girls. They had a large ball of moose skin, stuffed hard with dried grass and hair. This they kicked about in the open space among the lodges and wigwams. Apparently, no player was allowed to touch the ball, save with her feet. Stephen did not understand the game, but it was a lively scene, with plenty of shouting, laughter, screaming, pushing each other down, and chasing the ball about, and he could not help laughing for sympathy with the fun, as he looked on. As Sagamore George and others of the Indians sat in the shade of a tree nearby, watching the game, an Indian came up to the Sagamore, Stephen noticed, and spoke with some excitement, pointing towards the river. The Sagamore at once arose and went down to the shore, where Stephen now saw a boat making for land, rowed by two white men, while a third satin the stern, a man of stately presence, dressed more richly than his attendants. As this seigneur stepped ashore, Sagamore George received him with much deference, and escorted him respectfully to his lodge, where the guest was given the seat of honor. Roast goose was offered him, and a pipe filled for him to smoke. Stephen wondered who this stranger might be, and what was his business with the Sagamore. His heart yearned towards the white men. He longed to run to them, crying,

"I am not an Indian boy. I too am white. Cannot you get me away from the Indians?"

He was filled with an intense homesick longing, an eagerness which he dared not express outwardly, to make his case known to the white men. But now Tododaho came running to him, looking excited.

"Stephen!" he cried, but in low tone, looking around to be sure no Indians were within hearing. "Stephen, Kippenoquah just told me that yonder noble stranger is Monsieur Hertel, the seigneur of Chambly. And for what do you suppose he has come? To buy you! Kippenoquah said so. She said he had heard about you, and was trying to buy you of Sagamore George!"

"Oh!" cried Stephen, leaping to his feet, and running for the lodge as fast as he could go, closely followed by Tododaho, who was curious to see the outcome. As Stephen ran, his thoughts flew faster than his feet. True, the noble stranger's name was Hertel. But he had a kind face, and Stephen well remembered all the kindness he had received from the French, at the fort. Perhaps Thankful Stebbins had told Hertel De Rouville about him! Could he only get away from the Indians and back to the fort, he should be happy indeed. Such were the hopes animating him as he skimmed over the ground to the lodge, into which he dashed.

There sat Monsieur Hertel, haughty and stately, his two retainers standing behind him. He had heard the pitiful story of the little white boy, son of the Deerfield minister, in wretched captivity among the Indians, and a natural feeling of humanity had prompted him to try and rescue the helpless captive. It was his son who had led the assault on Deerfield. Perhaps this fact made the story of the boy captive come home to him with some twinges of remorse.

The pipe of ceremony having been duly smoked, before which it would have been, as Monsieur Hertel well knew, contrary to Indian etiquette to broach any business, Monsieur Hertel had opened negotiations, mentioning the sum he was willing to offer for the captive's redemption. As Stephen entered, Sagamore George was saying, with lofty scorn,

"Ho, that nothing, nothing at all. Sagamore George him no mean *give* the captive away. Him too wise. Him get heap big money for him in Montreal, Kebec."

"Oh, Sagamore George!" burst in Stephen, his face pale, his eyes big and shining with eagerness and excitement. "Do let me go with the French gentleman! Please, please let me go!"

Sagamore George looked at the eager boy with a stern scowl.

"Cosannip keep still," he said. "No speak another word, or Sagamore George beat him, take the skin off."

Monsieur Hertel, moved by the boy's evident distress, and his forlorn appearance, now raised his offer. But the greedy Sagamore, hoping for yet more, rejected this offer also, contemptuously.

"Monsieur Shamblee, think him buying sick dog. Sell sick dog cheap. Paleface boy worth heap of money. Sagamore George no fool."

Monsieur Hertel had had previous dealings with the Sagamore, and well knew how avaricious and extortionate his demands were apt to be. Not disposed to be over-reached, he reluctantly gave up his humane project, and rose to depart.

"Oh, don't leave me, do take me away!" cried Stephen, frantically, running after the Frenchman.

"My poor boy, it grieves me that I cannot rescue you. But it is impossible, I see," said Monsieur Hertel, as he departed.

Hardly was he gone, when the Indians present seized Stephen, and began berating him because he had shown such a willingness to leave them, and go with the Frenchman. Sagamore George, made doubly furious by rage at his disappointed hopes, drew out his knife and held it at Stephen's throat, crying,

"Sagamore George kill the fool paleface. Him know nothing, good for nothing. Spoil bargain."

Kippenoquah, foreseeing trouble, had run out and now returned with the Jesuit father, whose presence at once stayed the Sagamore's hand and quelled the tumult.

"Cosannip better look out. Sagamore George kill him like a weasel, him try to get away again," muttered the chief, as he replaced his knife in its sheath.

The Jesuit father, looking kindly at the poor little paleface, alone among all these savage Indians—pale indeed he was at that moment—laid his hand on the boy's shoulder, saying,

"What! No love the Indian? Indian save paleface boy's life; bring him to Canada, save his soul. Must love Indians. Indians your friends."

Poor little disappointed Stephen could make no reply. He could not speak. All his efforts were required to restrain his tears, which he knew would only make the Indians more angry. The Indians gradually dispersed, Sagamore George went out, and when Stephen saw an opportunity, he stole out of the lodge into the adjacent forest. Finding a sheltered nook among thick growing firs, he threw himself face down on the ground, and his pent-up grief broke forth in convulsive sobs that shook his prostrate form.

"Oh, God!" his soul cried within him, "Didst Thou not see? Wilt Thou not help get me away? Must I always live with the Indians?"

The first violence of his grief had partly subsided, when he felt something grasp his leg.

"Sagamore George has come to kill me!" he thought, starting in terror.

Lifting his red, tear-stained face, he peeped fearfully around. There stood, not the dreaded Sagamore, but little Wilootaheeta, her blue eyes full of tears.

"I am so sorry for you, Stephen," she said "Tododaho told me all about it. It was too bad. But don't cry any more. The Indians will not like it if they see you have been crying. Come out and see what I have brought you; something very nice."

Wilootaheeta's voice was soft with loving pity, and she held up a little dark brown lump.

Stephen crawled out and took the lump curiously.

"What is it, Nabby?" he asked.

"Maple sugar!" said Wilootaheeta, her face radiant with pleasure. "My mistress was much pleased with me today, because I embroidered such a pretty flower on my moccasin. So she gave me some of the very last sugar she had left from that she made last spring. I saved part to give you, because I felt sorry for you."

"Thank you, Nabby. That was good in you," said Stephen, with a grateful look at the little girl.

It was long since Stephen had tasted a morsel of sweet, and the sugar was a welcome gift. But sweeter still, amidst all the wild, hard surroundings, was the loving sympathy of a friend in misfortune. Stephen bathed his face in a spring nearby, to hide the traces of tears, and, somewhat comforted, walked back toward the lodge.

11

THE SAGAMORE CHEATS

EARLY in October Sagamore George set off on journey of more than usual importance. Stephen had to carry back-loads of skins and furs to the canoe, where Kippenoquah packed them in, till the canoe could carry no more. Then the Sagamore stepped in and paddled away.

"Sagamore go to Montreal. Sell his furs for heap money. Get more money too," said Kippenoquah, as the two stood a moment watching Sagamore George's swift, strong strokes.

Stephen wondered if this last statement was an allusion to an attempt on the Sagamore's part to raise money on his ransom in Montreal. The mere idea made him uneasy and restless. Kippenoquah contrived to keep him busy most of the day, but still he often found time to wonder when the Sagamore would return, and if possibly the chief's return might bring at last his own release.

One afternoon Stephen had a rare time of leisure. Kippenoquah was busy dressing a deerskin, and for the time had no employment for the captive. He roamed about the village, with some of the Indian boys, in search of amusement. The boys had their bows and arrows, ready for any small game that chance might throw in their way. Orono, one of the boys, drawing an arrow from his quiver, gave an exclamation of disgust. The point was broken off.

"Come to Kahbeewahbekokay, the Spear Maker," said another boy. "Speak softly to him. Him make Orono new arrow head."

This proposal pleased Orono, and the boys turned their steps towards the wigwam, where old Kahbeewahbekokay plied his trade. Stephen had often wondered how the Indians made arrow heads, so he followed the others with lively interest.

Old Kahbeewahbekokay was sitting outside his wigwam in the shade of a tree, hard at work with a small stone hammer, knocking chips of flint from a block held firmly between his knees. He wielded the hammer with the deftness born of many years' practice. At the base of the stone lay a pile of broken and useless chips, not large or perfect enough for use. The good chips were laid carefully one side, in a pile by themselves.

The boys did not venture to interrupt Kahbeewahbekokay, but stood in a circle, watching him in respectful silence, the old Indian apparently paying no attention to them, and not seeming to see Orono standing with his broken arrow head in hand. After a while, Kahbeewahbekokay laid down his hammer, and drawing on some buckskin pads, arranged to protect his hands from the sharp-edged stones, began shaping the flint chips into perfect arrow and spear heads. For this purpose, he used a tool made of a straight, sharp piece of deer-horn. Holding one of the smaller flints firmly in his hand, he pressed the sharp point of the tool against it, breaking off tiny fragments of the stone. In this way he worked along one edge until it was straight; then beginning on the other side, he worked with great caution, as he approached the point.

But this time his caution was in vain, for unluckily the flint had some secret flaw that had escaped even the old spear-maker's sharp eyes, and suddenly the point snapped off, and all his labor was lost.

"What a shame!" exclaimed Stephen.

The Indian boys said nothing, and Kahbeewahbekokay with unmoved dignity tossed the useless point into the rubbish heap and began work on another flint. He worked so quickly that, ere long a perfect little arrow head lay in his hand, at which Orono cast covetous eyes. Ere he could speak, Kahbeewahbekokay handed the arrow head to him, saying,

"The hawk lend his eye to Orono, that he may see game from afar."

"Orono's grandfather makes Orono's heart sing for joy," said the pleased boy. "If Orono's sharp arrow brings down a squirrel, Orono will bring it to his grandfather as a thank-offering."

Kahbeewahbekokay was no relation to Orono, but it was customary among the Indians, to address an elder as "Uncle" or "Grandfather," and an older woman as "Grandmother." Friends and equals were addressed as brothers, younger folk as sons, or nephews.

Orono tied the new arrow head tightly into his shaft, with deer sinew wound around and around; and then the boy sallied forth into the woods.

"Orono's new arrow a charm, bring good luck," said Orono, as he picked up his third squirrel.

When the boys returned at night, he presented a fine large grey squirrel to the old arrow maker, saying,

"Kahbeewahbekokay's sharp arrow has eyes. Sees king of squirrels afar; flies to kill him."

Kahbeewahbekokay received the offering graciously, for he liked roast squirrel, saying,

"The Sun, the stars, and the four winds will smile on Orono, and speed his arrow, because he treats the aged with respect, and does not forget to be thankful."

As the boys were turning to leave, Orono called to Stephen,

"Look, Cosannip. Yonder comes from Montreal the canoe of Sagamore George!"

Stephen's heart gave a great bound, as he strained his eyes towards the distant canoe, which Orono's quick eyes had discerned to be his master's. He dared not run down to the shore, as he longed to do, to meet the Sagamore and ask if he had seen or heard aught of his father or had succeeded in effecting his ransom. Too great eagerness on either point was sure to anger the Sagamore. But he ran to the lodge and said to Kippenoquah,

"Sagamore George comes! His canoe close by! Cosannip make big fire, so Kippenoquah can cook meat for the Sagamore."

Kippenoquah went down to the shore, to draw up the canoe, and bring up any bundles which might be there. Sagamore George strode majestically up the bank, bearing his gun, followed by Kippenoquah bringing the paddles, and a bundle containing the goods for which Sagamore George had exchanged part of his furs with the French traders at Montreal. For part he had taken money, and part, alas, he had exchanged for brandy, the "firewater" of the palefaces, so much craved by the Indians.

The Jesuits, seeing the terrible effects of the brandy traffic on their converts, had prevailed on the French government to pass most stringent laws against it; imprisonment, and even death, being at one time the penalty for selling brandy to the Indians. But the traders, greedy to make good bargains in furs, were constantly violating this law by stealth, and rare was the Indian, going to Montreal rich in furs, who could not secure the coveted drink.

It had been Sagamore George's good fortune, as he felt, to secure enough brandy to make him gloriously drunk at Montreal. He had been for a short time a happy Indian, howling and dancing in "La Place du Marche," waving his tomahawk above his head with fierce whoops, pleased and proud to see people fleeing on all sides in terror, for a drunken Indian was well known to be capable of any atrocity.

"Whoop! Hoo, Hoo! The great warrior, Sagamore George speaks, and the earth trembles!" cried the chief, swinging his tomahawk right and left.

But suddenly he felt a grip from behind, and his tomahawk was snatched away. Two French soldiers had tight hold of him, and Sagamore George had an opportunity to cool and calm himself in a dungeon cell. When released, he had hastened to his canoe and started for home. He was now suffering from headache and ill temper. He glared savagely at Stephen, as the boy appeared with a back-load of wood. He eagerly scanned the Indian's face, as he threw down the wood, and replenished the fire.

"Heap money," Stephen heard him say boastfully to Kippenoquah, touching an otter-skin pouch that hung from his belt, still bearing the head and paws of the otter, and gay with embroidery of beads and quills.

But he said nothing indicating any change in Stephen's prospects, and the boy dare not ask him questions. Yet, on this very trip, Sagamore George had reported to the governor that he had in his possession the son of Deerfield's minister, young Stephen Williams. Mr. Williams was then in Montreal, and the news that his little son was living and in Canada, filled his heart with joy. He sought Gov. de Vaudreuil and implored his aid. The governor had placed a handsome sum of money in the greedy hand of Sagamore George towards the redemption of Stephen, saying,

"Bring the boy to Montreal at once, and you shall have full satisfaction."

Sagamore George grunted, apparently in assent, as he grasped the money. But he had not the slightest intention of letting the captive go, until he had extorted the last penny possible to obtain for him. This money received was clear gain, as he would simply keep it, and await further offers.

The light of hope gradually faded from Stephen's heart, as days passed, and nothing was said about his redemption. The future stretched before him, dreary and almost hopeless.

"Perhaps," he thought, "I shall soon grow like Ben and Nabby. They seem to have settled down to be real Indians. But I will not until I must. Perhaps I can get a chance to run away sometime."

The Jesuit priest tried to have the Sagamore and Kippenoquah bring Stephen to mass, and make efforts for his conversion, but, as these Indians, though nominally Catholics, were not very zealous in their devotions, they did not exert themselves to convert Stephen. They asked him once or twice to go to mass, but, on his refusing, did not trouble themselves further in the matter.

It was now October, the "Deer Moon," when the deer were at their fattest and their skins in the best condition. The Sagamore devoted himself to hunting, sometimes taking Stephen out with him. Much as Stephen disliked the Sagamore, he could but admire the wonderful skill with which he traced a deer's track on the fallen leaves, and the sure aim with which, when the branching head was seen afar through the trees, he sent a bullet straight to the creature's heart. The Sagamore made little of bringing home a whole deer on his back.

One dark, cloudy night, when not even one star illumined the darkness, Sagamore George took Stephen out in his canoe to hold aloft a blazing torch of pitch pine. Stephen was ordered to sit in the bow, holding up the torch.

"Cosannip make no noise, speak not, stir not," were the Sagamore's orders, as he took his paddle and set off up the St. Francis.

Stephen felt far from sleepy. The scene was so strange. All around was the dark night, save as the reflection of his torch flashed and glimmered for a short distance on the river's ripples, and sent a bright stream of light into the dense woods along the shore, illuminating mossy tree-trunks and bending branches with its red light. There was no sound but the river rippling over rocks, the faint plash of the paddle, and the east wind sighing through the evergreens.

For some time they paddled on, seeing nothing. But presently Sagamore George sent the canoe in nearer the right bank, and Stephen felt rather than heard him, so noiseless were the Sagamore's motions, lay down his paddle and pick up his gun. In an instant more, Stephen saw the deer, whose tread Sagamore George's quick ear had detected. It came out of the forest and stood on the river's bank with uplifted head and great wondering eyes, gazing at this strange light, which had excited its curiosity, and brought it down to the shore to investigate.

"Bang!" went the gun. The deer gave a great spring and fell wounded, its life to be quickly finished by Sagamore George's knife. Whatever the Sagamore's faults, he was a skillful hunter, and Kippenoquah was kept busy these autumn days, dressing and preparing deerskins, smoking and drying all venison not used for her winter stores.

Bears were also plenty, and very desirable at this season. One day a party of Indians went forth from the village on a bear hunt. Several of the older boys were taken on this hunt, their fathers wishing to begin early their training as hunters. Nunganey accompanied Mahtocheegah, and Ben, or Tododaho, was also taken out by Wiwurna, his Indian father.

Having adopted the boy as his son, Wiwurna wished to instruct him in all wild-wood lore. Sagamore George did not take Stephen to the bear hunt, because some accident might happen to the captive, who was too valuable an investment for the Sagamore to be lightly risked.

Nunganey was allowed for the first time to carry a gun. He felt so proud, that his skin coat could hardly contain him.

"Ho, ho," he said to Stephen, who stood watching the hunters set off, "Nunganey big hunter. Go hunting with the warriors. Cosannip wait. Before the sun set, him see Nunganey come back with bear's claws. Make fine necklace, finer than Kewakcum's."

"Good luck to you, Nunganey," said Stephen, who, now that Nunganey was his oldest acquaintance in the village, and associated in his mind with Kewakcum, felt kindly towards him, unless Nunganey treated him too badly. Stephen saw Ben, his red hair carefully smeared with bear's grease and charcoal, his face daubed with paint, in all outward aspect a genuine Indian boy, marching off on the trail of the hunters, a gun over his shoulder. Ben turned and smiled triumphantly at Stephen, pointing at the gun, which he carried by the barrel, the butt over his shoulder.

"Ben's so pleased because Wiwurna lets him carry a gun," thought Stephen, almost with a twinge of envy, for he too would have enjoyed being trusted with a gun. "Wiwurna only does it to make him love the Indian life, make him a real Indian."

Ben was destined to have more experience that day than he expected, when he set off so happily to the hunt. He followed the hunters as they trod in single file far on into the forest, in a direction in which some of them had seen signs of bears. As these signs thickened, it was decided to scatter, each going in different directions, to drive the bears out.

"Tododaho stand here, keep his eyes wide open. See if bear come this way," said Wiwurna, as he strode away, leaving Ben stationed at the foot of a rocky hill in the woods.

To tell the truth, Ben did not wholly enjoy being thus left alone, though he dared not object. His heart beat so loudly and fast in his ears that he could not hear other noises plainly. He had come out hunting bears, yet the real dread down deep in his heart was,

"What if I should really see a bear coming!"

He gazed around him, rather fearfully. Not an Indian was to be seen. Apparently, Ben was alone in the woods. Every time the leaves rustled in the wind, or a dead branch fell, or branches rubbed against each other with a creaking sound, Ben was sure a bear was coming. At last he heard a crashing noise on the hill above. Lo, his worst fears were realized! A large bear was coining, running down the hill through the woods directly at Ben, as it seemed to him. Ben jumped behind a tree. On came the big, clumsy creature, crashing and tumbling along through the thick undergrowth and over rocks and logs. When the bear was within a few feet, Ben suddenly remembered that he had a gun. He sprang out, pointing the weapon somewhere in the direction of the bear, and shot blindly. The bear fell, and so did Ben, from the recoil of his weapon, and because he chanced not to be standing any too firmly on the hillside. Bear and boy sprawled side by side. Ben, who every instant expected the bear to attack him, scrambled up and ran for his life. When at safe distance, he ventured to halt behind a large tree trunk, and peep around it. There lay the bear where he had fallen. Could it be that Ben had really killed him? Very cautiously did Ben at last venture back, going slowly nearer and nearer. Still the bear stirred not. Then Ben found a long pole, and with fast beating heart, poked it into the bear's soft fur. Still he did not move.

"He may be pretending," thought Ben, not disposed to venture too near. "Wiwurna says bears know a great deal, are very wise, almost as wise as Indians."

To his relief, he now saw Wiwurna's head appear above a bush, and others of the Indians returned, having heard the report of the gun.

The bear was really dead. Ben's shot had by good fortune happened to hit his heart. Wiwurna was very proud of his adopted son, and said,

"Wiwurna will take Tododaho, the Bear Hunter, on the war path against the palefaces down the Long River, before many snows."

When Nunganey appeared on the scene of battle, he declared loudly,

"Nunganey saw the bear first and scare him. Bear run away from Nunganey, right on Tododaho's gun. Tododaho shot Nunganey's bear."

"Brother Maqua him no stand still, wait for Indian to shoot him," said Mahtocheegah. "If Nunganey means to be big hunter, must learn to shoot quick, quicker than bear runs."

Ben walked proudly back to the village, there to be the envy of all the other boys. He gave Stephen a full account of his adventure, only somehow, in telling the story, Ben did not dwell much on his fright, and his aim at the bear had grown cool and deliberate. He wound up the tale by saying,

"It's great fun hunting bears, Stephen. You ought to get Sagamore George to take you out sometime."

12

HOPES AND FEARS

THE weeks passed away, and still Stephen was a captive. Sagamore George and the other hunters spent the late fall chiefly in hunting beavers, this being the season when beavers were the fattest and their fur the finest. At this time beaver-skins brought the highest prices in the fur markets of Montreal and Quebec. Winter set in early. It was now December, the "Snow-Shoe Moon." The snow already lay deep on the ground, and the cold was more intense than Stephen had ever known.

Kippenoquah, seeing how greatly the white boy felt the cold, made him a shirt of bear-skin, the fur inside, with a sort of hood that pulled up over his head; also warm leggings, and moccasins such as the Indians wore in winter, with high flaps which they tied up over their leggings, both for warmth, and to keep out the snow. Thus attired, Stephen was better able to endure the cold, but his life was far from comfortable or pleasant. It was simply a matter of patient endurance.

He had learned to be quite at home on snowshoes. Kippenoquah took him almost daily into the woods, to help bring home back-loads of wood, to feed the fires which blazed high along the center of the lodge, day and night. Sometimes in the night, Stephen would waken because he was so cold, even under the thick bear-skin which made his cover-lid. Looking up, he would see the stars shining bright, clear, and cold, down through the smoke hole, and outside he would hear the great trees snapping and the river's ice cracking from the cold, with loud reports like pistol shots. The fire was nearly extinct, having died down to a few coals, and the cold intense.

At last, Kippenoquah or Sagamore George, also awakened by the cold, would stagger sleepily up, and throw fresh logs on the coals. Again, the fire blazed high, shedding warmth around, and Stephen could sleep.

The hardest nights were when a fierce snowstorm was raging. The smoke, unable to escape, and beaten back by the storm, would fill the interior of the lodge to suffocation. Stephen then found himself obliged to imitate the Indians, and lie on his face, with his nose towards the lower edge of the lodge, where some fresh air forced itself under. Only in this way was it possible to breathe.

Events to break the monotony of the dreary life were few, therefore all the Indians were much stirred, one day, by the arrival of a visitor from the outside world. Stephen was, with some of the children, coasting down a steep bank out on the river's thick ice. They had made a slippery track down the bank. An old deerskin served them for a sled. Sitting on the furry side, and gathering the ends up tightly in front, a boy standing behind gave the laughing load a push, and away they went, screaming and shouting, down the slippery incline, and far out on the ice. Stephen's attention was first attracted to the visitor's arrival by Nunganey, who said,

"Ho, ho, Frenchman come from Montreal. Come to look after Cosannip, maybe."

Looking where Nunganey pointed, Stephen saw a young Frenchman coming up the river on the ice, wearing over his other heavy garments a "capeau," a long, hooded blanket coat, belted in with a sash, a knit cap with long tassel pulled well over his ears, two pair of heavy woolen hose under his moccasins, ribbed leggings outside all, and his hands encased in two pair of warm mittens. He carried on his back a pair of stout snow-shoes to use when needed.

Stephen was full of anxiety. He watched, and saw that the stranger, after inquiries, made his way to Sagamore George's lodge. Stephen longed to run to the lodge, to ask the Frenchman if his father were in Montreal, or if he knew aught of him, and above all, to beg to be taken away. But he remembered too well his former experience and dared not risk angering the Sagamore again.

"I must wait here," he thought. "They will send for me, if I am to go away with the Frenchman. Oh, how I hope he has come for me!"

Unable longer to divert himself by sliding, Stephen stood at the top of the hill, pushing the others off in an absent-minded fashion, not turning his back for an instant on the Sagamore's lodge, whence the thick, blue smoke curling up from the smoke hole, showed that a feast was being offered the visitor.

At last, Stephen saw the Frenchman come out, followed by Sagamore George. The messenger turned and seemed to speak again earnestly to the Sagamore as if making one last effort, but the Sagamore shook his head, decidedly. With sinking heart, Stephen saw the Frenchman go down to the river and away, striding swiftly along, his face towards Montreal. As he vanished, all Stephen's hopes vanished with him, and he felt in despair. Ere long, he went to the lodge. He asked no questions, but, the Sagamore being out, Kippenoquah said,

"Onontio at Montreal send Frenchman here, try to buy Cosannip. But him no give big enough money. Sagamore George say no, no, no. Him must have more money."

"Oh! Kippenoquah," said Stephen, "cannot you persuade Sagamore George to let me go? Perhaps the governor will never send again! A little money is better than none at all."

Kippenoquah shook her head.

"Kippenoquah think that too. But Sagamore George like big rock. Kippenoquah's talk like wind blowing on rock. Him no feel it, no care, no good."

"Do you know, Kippenoquah, if my father is alive? Did the Frenchman say anything about him?"

"Kippenoquah think so, but knows not surely."

This meagre possibility was some comfort to Stephen. Surely, if his father were alive, he would exert himself to the utmost for his son's redemption.

"I will try to have patience, and trust in God that he will yet bring about my redemption," thought the boy.

In truth, the messenger's coming was owing to Mr. Williams's entreaties. Moved by the father's grief and appeals, Governor de Vaudreuil had dispatched this special messenger, to negotiate with

Sagamore George for the boy's release. The messenger was instructed to offer thirty crowns, an ample price for what had cost Sagamore George nothing. But the Sagamore scorned the offer and sent back word that only forty crowns would induce him to part with Stephen.

As the winter went on, game grew more scarce around the village, and the Indians were obliged to take longer hunting excursions. Now too they were often obliged to fall back on the stores of smoked or frozen meat and vegetables. The squaws, as the weather grew cold, had frozen quantities of meat, fish, and vegetables, storing them in holes dug in the ground, covered first with fir branches, then with earth. Into these rude cellars, "Indian barns," as the white settlers were wont to call them, the squaws now dug, bringing forth their treasures.

The time came when Stephen found that he could eat smoked eel. It tasted much like other fish. Often Kippenoquah boiled it with a little corn. At home, Stephen would certainly not have considered this an appetizing dish, but—it was vastly better than nothing! The sharp cold gave hunger a keener edge, and often Stephen was glad to still its cravings even with eel stew.

Before many weeks, another Frenchman arrived, like the first a messenger from the governor, seeking to effect Stephen's release. His efforts met with no better success than those of his predecessor. The governor offered thirty crowns, and the avaricious Sagamore stood stiffly out for forty. Mr. Williams was unwearied in his exertions to induce the governor to secure his son's release, and messengers were sent, again and again, during December and early January. Stephen was kept in a fever of alternating hope and despair. One day, when another messenger from the governor appeared, and there had been the usual fruitless wrangle and dispute, Sagamore George deter-mined to settle the matter once for all. He asked Stephen,

"Can Cosannip talk paleface talk on paper, make black marks, tell story?"

He moved his hand along as if writing, and Stephen understood.

"Yes, Cosannip can write," he said eagerly.

What was the Sagamore's plan now, he wondered?

"Cosannip wait. Sit still here, till Sagamore George come back." said the Sagamore, as he strode out of the wigwam, soon returning, bringing an ink-horn, a quill, and a sheet of paper, which he had obtained from the Jesuit father, and accompanied by Notoway.

"Now Cosannip talk on paper for the Sagamore to the English priest, Cosannip's father. The English priest great man. Onontio gives him two hundred pounds a year. Great man. Notoway tell Cosannip the words to say to his father."

Stephen learned by this that his father was living, and in or near Montreal, and that the Sagamore believed him to be enjoying an ample income. His heart was glad within him to be assured at last that his father was alive, and so near. He took the pen, awkwardly and stiffly, for he had not touched one since those days in Master John Richards' school, which now seemed so far, far away. He began scratching his name, "Stephen Williams," on the paper's margin, to see if he had forgotten how to write. Then he wrote the heading, "Honored Father," ready to begin. His heart warmed with love as he wrote those words and knew that soon his father's eyes would rest on them.

Sagamore George had brought old Notoway to dictate the letter, as Notoway knew English quite well.

"Now Cosannip put down Sagamore George's words, just as Notoway talk them," commanded the Sagamore.

Stephen conscientiously obeyed. The Sagamore ordered him to tell his father that, if he were not ransomed before spring, after that time nothing would induce the Sagamore to part with the boy. And that the price demanded was forty crowns. Not a crown less would the Sagamore take.

Stephen longed, yet dared not, entreat his father to use every effort for his rescue. Nor did he venture to say anything about his present life among the Indians. He only wrote what Notoway dictated, and then added in his boyish handwriting,

"Your loving son till death,
"Stephen Williams."

The Sagamore and Notoway, resolved to assure themselves that Stephen had written as ordered, took the letter to the Jesuit priest, who knew enough English to be able to read the letter aloud to them. Finding thus that Stephen had obeyed orders, they returned well pleased, and the Sagamore gave the letter to the French messenger, saying,

"Tell Onontio and the English priest Sagamore George speaks no more. All his words are on the paper. They talk for him."

Sagamore George, like the other Indians, was about setting off for his long winter hunt. During the winter hunting season, but few Indians remained at St. Francis. In the spring they came in, usually laden with furs, which they dis-posed of at the great annual fair, which had been established by the order of the French king at Montreal. Parkman thus describes it:

"There every summer a host of savages came down from the lakes in their bark canoes. A place was assigned them at a little distance from the town. They landed, drew up their canoes in a line on the bank, took out their packs of beaver skins, set up their wigwams, slung their kettles, and encamped for the night. On the next day there was a grand council on the common, between St. Paul Street and the river. Speeches of compliment were made, amid a solemn smoking of pipes. The governor general was usually present, seated in an armchair, while the visitors formed a ring about him, ranged in the order of their tribes. On the next day, the trade began in the same place. Merchants of high and low degree brought up their goods from Quebec, and every inhabitant of Montreal, of any substance, sought a share in the profit. Their booths were set along the palisades of the town.

"Here was a throng of Indians armed with bows and arrows, war-clubs, or the cheap guns of the trade ; some of them completely naked except for the feathers in their heads, and the paint on their faces; merchants and *habitans* in their coarse and plain attire, and the grave priests of St. Sulpice robed in black. Order and sobriety were their watchwords, but the wild gathering was beyond their control. The prohibition to sell brandy could rarely be enforced, and the fair ended at times in a pandemonium of drunken frenzy."

Never were the Abenakis of St. Francis happier than when fortune had smiled, and they returned with the spring rich in furs, which enabled them to enjoy the gains, the delights and excitements, of the great fur fair at Montreal.

Sagamore George would have taken Stephen with him on the winter hunt, but, having sent a letter to the governor that Stephen must be bought before spring, if at all, he dared not take him away into the wilderness, lest the boy be sent for in his absence. Kippenoquah usually went with the Sagamore to the hunt, to do the work; carry and dress the game, cook the food, erect the wigwam, make and paddle canoes; but she too must be left behind, to take charge of the captive. Sagamore George gave her many injunctions.

"Kippenoquah keep both eyes wide open, all the time. No lose captive; no let anything happen to him; no whip him; no let Onontio steal him; no sell him to Onontio but for forty crowns."

"Sagamore George have no fears. Kippenoquah will have eyes like the hawk's by day, see far; like the owl's at night, see in the dark. Onontio will be stronger and wiser than Brother Maqua if he steal Cosannip away from under Kippenoquah's wing."

Stephen was glad when he saw the back of his stern master disappearing in the woods to the South, and knew that he was to be left for some time in the sole charge of Kippenoquah. Kippenoquah was an Indian, with Indian ideas and ways; but, like most squaws, she was disposed to be kind to children, and Stephen did not fear her as he did the frowning Sagamore.

13

UNDER KIPPENOQUAH'S WING

IT was now nearly a year since Stephen's capture. In order to understand his subsequent experiences, it is necessary to return to Deerfield, and briefly note the happenings there during this year. After the capture and partial destruction of the town, February 29, 1704, and the loss of over half the population by death or capture, the terrified remnant left in the devastated hamlet resolved to abandon the seemingly hopeless effort to maintain a settlement in this exposed place on the northern frontier. But the Connecticut Colony well knew the vital necessity, for her own protection, of keeping this frontier far from her own boundaries. The post at Deerfield must be maintained. The General Court of Connecticut sent sixty men up to Deerfield, for scouting and garrison duty, and took other action towards holding the place. On March 2, Colonel Partridge of Hatfield, military commander of Hampshire County, impressed all the able-bodied men left in Deerfield, as soldiers in the service of her Majesty Queen Anne.

The women and children took refuge among friends in the towns below. The men, doing duty as soldiers, were able to work but little on their land, and were constantly exposed to attacks from small bodies of Indians lurking in the woods around. Alarms were frequent. On May 11 occurred the attack on the Allens at the Bars, previously related. In July, Deacon John Sheldon, discovering tracks of Indians near the fort, went with a party of men in pursuit. They came in sight of a band of Indians and exchanged shots with them. The Indians retreating along the west side of the river to the North, killed Thomas Russell. About the same time, Sergeant John Hawks, riding to Hatfield, was fired upon by a band of Indians in ambush, and wounded. Later, in July, Thomas Battis, travelling post to Boston, was shot and killed, east of Hadley.

There could be no cessation of vigilance. Scouting was kept up constantly, armed scouts riding out into the woods to the North, with every sense alert for any traces of the enemy. But even amid such harassing cares and distractions, the thoughts of those Deerfield settlers still left in the fort turned constantly to the friends who had vanished from their sight, on that terrible night in February. Who among them were dead, who living, no one knew. But all longed to rescue the survivors if possible.

Governor Dudley, of the Massachusetts Bay Colony, who held one hundred and fifty French prisoners, including the notorious Captain Baptiste, had been dispatching letters to Governor de Vaudreuil by way of Albany, seeking to affect an exchange of prisoners, but without avail. It was so vitally necessary for de Vaudreuil to retain the good will of his Indian allies, that he must proceed most cautiously in any measures depriving them of their captives, whom they considered the legitimate reward of the services in war rendered by them to the King of France.

Receiving no answer to his letters to Governor de Vaudreuil, Governor Dudley decided that possibly his letters had failed to reach Canada and had therefore proposed to his council to dispatch a special messenger there, to arrange, if possible, an exchange of captives. At this opportune moment two Deerfield men appeared in Boston, urgent to be licensed to make this trip. These were Deacon John Sheldon and young John Wells, who had ridden on horseback down to Springfield and thence by the Bay Path through the woods, to Boston. This was a perilous trip, for the almost unbroken woods along the path might anywhere conceal Indians in ambush. But Deacon Sheldon and young Wells were so strongly impelled by love for their friends and relatives in captivity, by a sense of their probable sufferings and an intense desire to rescue them, that they were ready to brave any peril or hardship. Deacon Sheldon's three children, Mary, a girl of sixteen, two boys, Ebenezer and Remembrance, aged eleven and twelve, and his daughter-in-law, Hannah, the young bride, were among the captives, as well as Mrs. Belding, the mother of John Wells. The cruel death of his mother was as yet unknown to John, and it was a son's devotion that impelled him to this hazardous undertaking.

Sheldon and Wells reached Boston about December 12, 1704. Soon after, by great good fortune, Captain Livingstone of Albany also arrived in Boston. He had travelled the route from Albany to Quebec several times and offered to act as escort for Sheldon and Wells for one hundred pounds and his expenses. The governor had expected to charter a vessel to convey Sheldon and Wells to Quebec with the dispatches to the French governor, and gladly embraced this less expensive method for their embassy, the more so because he felt great confidence in Captain Livingstone's experience and ability. Sheldon and Wells rode back as they had come, stopping in Hatfield to be properly equipped by Colonel Partridge for their difficult and dangerous journey.

In Hatfield, where events were few, more than one busy housewife noted the two men riding in at the palisade's southern gate and halting at Colonel Partridge's. When it was noised about the little settlement who these men were, and what was their errand, great was the interest and excitement.

There were many still living who well remembered the wonderful journey of Benjamin Waite and Stephen Jennings, in pursuit of the Hatfield captives in 1677. Many an old man shook his head dubiously, saying,

"Deacon Sheldon and young Wells little know what they are undertaking. It is a terrible task to go on foot through the snow, three hundred miles to Canada, with the woods full of Indians. The chances are they will never live to get through. I remember,"—and then followed the painful reminiscences of some Hatfield captive.

In Hatfield, as in the other neighboring settlements, were a number of Deerfield fugitives, abiding with relatives and friends. These sought out Sheldon and Wells, begging them to make every possible effort to find and redeem the child, the wife, the brother, or sister who had been carried away captive, and, with tear-filled eyes, they prayed for God's blessing on the two devoted travelers as they rode away.

Sheldon and Wells returned first to Deerfield, to report the success of their mission to the anxious men there, and then started on their perilous journey West and North, taking what was then, and for nearly a century later, the regular Albany road, striking it at Northampton. Thence there was a fair bridle path to Westfield. From Westfield a rude bridle path followed the old Indian trail, up the Westfield river, through the region where are now Blandford and Sheffield, crossed Hoosac Mountain, and ran down into the valley of the Hudson, through the Dutch settlement of Kinderhook to Albany.

At Albany the travelers were joined by Captain Livingstone. The journey thence was probably pursued on foot, on snowshoes, by way of Lakes George and Champlain, down the Richelieu and St. Lawrence, to Quebec, where they arrived safely, probably in February, not far from a year after the sacking of Deerfield.

Rev. John Williams, who was then living at Chateau Richer, twenty miles below Quebec, was allowed to visit Quebec for a few weeks, to see these friends. Great was Mr. Williams's joy to meet again these two parishioners from Deerfield, and to hear directly from that place. His hopes of redemption were much raised by their arrival, as were those of all the poor, unhappy captives. Of them, Mr. Williams says in his narrative: "The hearts of some were ready to be discouraged and sink, saying they were out of sight and so out of mind. I endeavored to persuade them that we were not forgotten; that undoubtedly many prayers were going up to heaven for us. Not long after came Captain Livingstone and Mr. Sheldon, with letters from his Excellency our Governor to the Governor of Canada, about the exchange of prisoners, which gave a revival to many, and raised expectation of a return."

Eagerly did Mr. Sheldon and John Wells question Mr. Williams about the fate of their friends, and gently did the pastor break to young John the sad fate of his dear mother, comforting him as best he could with words of religious faith. Deacon Sheldon learned that all his children were living; that his daughter Mary and daughter-in-law, Hannah, though arriving in Canada very lame and exhausted after their terrible journey, had recovered, and were now near Montreal, Hannah with a French family in that city, Mary adopted by an Indian squaw. Remembrance and Ebenezer were living with Indians, one near Quebec, the other with the Caughnawagas, but both were now off on the winter hunt with their masters, somewhere in the vast northern wilderness.

There were no telegraphs, telephones, railroads, or even regular mails to bear the news; yet somehow the tidings soon spread all over Canada, that envoys from Deerfield had arrived to affect an exchange of prisoners. Ere long the tidings reached even the scattered, outlying Indian hamlets. On March 29, Mr. Sheldon had the pleasure of receiving a letter from his daughter-in-law, Hannah, written from Montreal, where she had heard of his arrival.

To return to Stephen, who was yet quite unaware of these events, so full of interest to him. As Sagamore George had taken with him the larger part of Kippenoquah's store of food, she was obliged to exert herself to get such small game as she could, to eke out the scanty supply left. One morning she surprised Stephen by saying,

"Cosannip come, help Kippenoquah catch fish."

"Fish!" exclaimed Stephen, looking out on the deep snow, and the ice-bound river, also buried in snow. Had Kippenoquah lost her mind?

"Fresh fish taste heap good," added Kippenoquah.

Stephen heartily agreed with this, for he was so tired of smoked eels and meat, that only actual hunger enabled him to force down enough to sustain life. So he willingly followed Kippenoquah down the trampled path to the river, curious to see what she meant to do. She carried in her hand a tool, made of a strong stick, to whose end was tightly bound with deer's sinews, a sharp, stout deer horn. The sinews were put on wet, tightening as they dried. First she made Stephen help her clear the snow from the surface of the ice for a space, each using a snowshoe as a shovel. Then she tied deer-sinew strings to two poles, about four feet long, which she had cut on the way down. Sharp, crooked little bones answered for hooks, which she baited with bits of dried meat. Pounding hard with her pronged tool, at last she succeeded in breaking a hole through the ice. Handing one pole to Stephen, she said,

"Cosannip be spry as weasel. Pull line out quick, if fish bite."

Kippenoquah began breaking another hole for herself, while Stephen bent his whole energies to watching his line. There! He certainly felt a slight twitch ' Up came Stephen's line with such a jerk that it landed the big gray trout attached far out on the snow.

"Look! look, Kippenoquah! I've caught one already! See what a big one it is!" cried Stephen.

Kippenoquah gave a grunt of approval and cast in her own line. Stephen needed all his interest in fishing to keep him from noticing his discomfort, for it was bitterly cold. His moccasins stuck to the ice, pulling up with a ripping sound as he walked; his nostrils clung together, and the fur around his face and neck hung thick with icicles. While securing his fish, he dropped his line on the ice. When he returned to it, the line was frozen fast to the ice, and a thin skim of ice already coated the hole.

Stephen broke it away, tore his line up from the ice, and cast it in again. Ere long he pulled out two more fine trout. Kippenoquah had equally good success at her post. At last the hands of both were so cold that it was absolutely impossible to stay out longer. They returned to the lodge, where Kippenoquah soon had some of the fish roasting in the ashes. Stephen, as he smelt the appetizing odor, was hardly able to wait till the meal was cooked.

Orono had not been fishing. He was amusing himself by his mother's fire, at the other end of the lodge, with a lasso which he had made from a long strip of deerskin. He threw it with considerable skill, succeeding at last in lassoing a little child who was playing around the next fire. Loud wails rose from the terrified youngster, as he felt the noose tighten around his neck.

"Evil one! Son of a snake!" cried the child's mother, flying to her little one's rescue. Diving for Orono's hair, she gave it one good pull before Orono squirmed, eel-like, away.

"Come not near here again, or Ounsokis will cut a hole in the river's ice, and duck Orono under!" cried the enraged mother.

Orono, with the cheerful grin of one well pleased with himself, scampered away. Nearing Kippenoquah's fire, he again took aim, and succeeded in throwing his lasso over the head of Shunko, an old dog whom Sagamore George had left behind with his wife. Shunko was sitting sedately by the fire, sniffing the tempting odor of the fish, and waiting patiently for the share he knew his friend Stephen would surely give him. Already Stephen had thrown him one sweet mouthful, which Shunko had caught with a snap and swallowed whole. With erect ears, and eager eyes, he watched intently Stephen's every motion. Suddenly his happy expectations were rudely disturbed. The lasso slipped around his neck, and he was jerked over backward. With loud yelps he struggled up. Orono laughed as Stephen ran to release Shunko, who, growling at Orono, took refuge the other side of the lodge.

"What did you want to do that for?" asked Stephen. "Shunko was not hurting you. I don't see what good that did you."

"Nothing to do. Must do something," said Orono. "New lasso. Wanted to try how it works. Lasso fine, works well. Cosannip make him lasso. Then Orono and Cosannip go out in the woods for game. Maybe lasso Brother Rabbit."

"I will make one, if Kippenoquah has any leather for it," said Stephen, glad of any diversion. "But you must let old Shunko alone."

"Orono hungry. Fish smell good," said Orono, sniffing the air.

"Orono come and eat," said Stephen in Indian fashion, as he gave Orono a piece of fish, which Orono ate eagerly, not omitting to throw a generous bit as a peace offering to Shunko. The dog accepted it affably and seemed to regard Orono more favorably. Kippenoquah, meantime, had been called out of the lodge by a squaw, who said, as she beckoned her out,

"Big news. Kippenoquah come."

She soon returned, looking rather excited, and astonished Stephen by saying,

"After another sleep, Kippenoquah and Cosannip go far away; go far into the forest."

Stephen was much disturbed at this news. Any change in this condition was quite sure to be for the worst, rather than the better. Here he was in a well-known Indian village, on the river, the highway of the region, where he could easily be found. Governor de Vaudreuil and his father knew where he was. But if carried away into the wilderness, his chances for rescue would be faint indeed.

"Why does Kippenoquah move?" he cried. "Cosannip want to stay here, with Orono," he added, looking at the Indian boy, as if he might possibly help him.

Orono, having finished his fish, was wiping his greasy hands on Shunko's hair.

"Ho, that nothing. Orono follow on Kippenoquah's trail. Find Cosannip easy enough, anywhere in woods," he said, as he picked up his lasso and departed.

"Cosannip say nothing. No good. Kippenoquah goes away with the sunrise," said the squaw firmly.

An Indian messenger had come to her lodge bringing word that some "Bostonnais" were in Quebec, come to affect an exchange of prisoners with the French, and warning Kippenoquah to be on her guard, lest her captive be taken away from her by the French without any ransom. Kippenoquah was filled with alarm. What would Sagamore George say and do, rather what would he *not* say and do, should he return to find that his much-prized captive had slipped through her fingers, leaving no ransom to show for him? She resolved by prompt action to avert such a catastrophe.

14

THE WIGWAM IN THE WOODS

EARLY the next morning, Kippenoquah kept her words good. She packed up the little food left, her cooking utensils, skins, and other possessions, and struck off towards the Southeast, into the thick fir woods. Stephen followed her, his back, like hers, bent under a big pack. In the trail left by their snow-shoes trudged old Shunko, faithful to his friends wherever their fortunes might take them.

Stephen felt unhappy and forlorn. He took refuge in his only comfort and help, a silent prayer to his Father in heaven, that he would watch over him. The thought of this Friend, who saw everywhere, who was as near and as able to help in the wild forest solitude as in Deerfield's palisade, was Stephen's abiding comfort. After walking for a while in silence, they reached an opening in the dark forest, a knoll near an open spot, which seemed to be the snow-covered surface of a small pond. Kippenoquah dropped her pack, looked around, gave a grunt of satisfaction, and said,

"Kippenoquah make camp here."

Stephen judged this spot to be not over half a mile inland from the river. Greatly relieved to know that he was not to be carried farther away, he too dropped his pack. Almost cheerfully he imitated Kippenoquah in using the convenient snow-shoe as a shovel, to dig away the snow from a circular space, until at last they reached bare ground. Around this space Kippenoquah set up her wigwam poles, covering them with large pieces of bark, throwing skins over the bark for greater warmth. The banking of snow thrown up around the wigwam outside, also added to its warmth. When she had kindled a fire on the ground in the center, and stowed away her possessions under its sloping edge, Kippenoquah was quite settled, ready to keep house. She kept Stephen busy carrying in the fragrant branches of balsam fir, which she cut for beds from the trees around.

When this work was done, Kippenoquah, now satisfied, and feeling that Stephen was safely hid from any Frenchmen or "Bostonnais" designing to steal him, proceeded to cook breakfast. She cut a hole in the pond, filled her kettle, and boiled some smoked eel, with a handful of dried corn. As they ate, Shunko showed signs of uneasiness, finally going outside, and barking loudly. Kippenoquah looked disturbed, saying,

"Someone comes."

"Ho, ho," came a shout from the distance, and Kippenoquah's face cleared.

"Orono comes," she said.

Down the aisle of the dark forest, Stephen saw Orono wading along on his snow-shoes, lasso in hand, and bow and arrows on his back.

"Orono follow trail, just as he said," said the boy. "Glad Cosannip no go far. Cosannip make lasso; go hunting with Orono."

Kippenoquah, who hoped Stephen might possibly bring in some small game, willingly cut off a long, narrow strip from a deerskin which she had cured for garments. Stephen, under Orono's directions, made it into a lasso that slipped easily, and the two boys sallied forth, accompanied by Shunko, who, however, was careful to keep at a respectful distance, eyeing the lassos askance.

The boys on their snow-shoes were able to walk over the drifts lying deep in the forest, and to penetrate its wild, solitary depths. Often they found the tracks of little wild creatures, zigzagging over the snow. Once they came to the track of some heavy animal, who had sunk deeper into the drifts than the squirrels and rabbits. These tracks ended abruptly at the base of a tall pine tree.

Orono at once changed his course, circling far out around the pine, at whose base Shunko was barking loudly, saying,

"Brother Wild Cat up in that tree now, maybe. Him pounce on Orono and Cosannip as quick as the thunder bird shoots his fiery arrows, no look out."

The boys walked on in the silence becoming hunters, who know that the sound of voices in the silent forest will frighten the shy wild creatures. At last, far in advance among the tree trunks, Orono's quick eye perceived moving objects. He nudged Stephen, pointing ahead, and whispering that he should stand still and hold Shunko. To keep him quiet was a difficult task, as Shunko was quivering with excitement.

In an opening in the wood ahead, two deer, a buck and a doe, with two little fawns, were feeding, gnawing the bark from some young trees, and stripping the green twigs of the firs. The noise made by their own gnawing helped to cover Orono's approach as he crept stealthily nearer, from the shelter of one tree trunk to another. But the deer, like all wild animals, were always on the alert for enemies. Every few moments they stopped, erecting their delicate, pointed ears to listen intently, and sniffing the air. At such moments the sly Orono lay still behind a tree trunk, as motionless as the tree itself.

In this way, he had succeeded in approaching quite near, when suddenly the buck gave a wild sniff, then, startled, threw back his head and leaped away through the woods, the others bounding after him. Orono sprang forth, throwing his lasso at the fawn who was hindmost. His practice on the dogs and pappooses at home had not been in vain. The lasso fell over the fawn's head, checking its speed so suddenly that it was thrown to the ground, the jerk also throwing Orono down.

The fawn, with a shrill cry of terror, leaped up and bounded wildly, pulling Orono, who clung stoutly to the strap, headfirst through bush and brier, scratching his face, and bumping his head against a stump. Still Orono hung manfully to the strap. But, luckily for the poor fawn, the leather had a weak spot, and suddenly it broke, near her neck. Away bounded the terrified fawn, the bit of strap dangling from her neck.

Stephen and Shunko now ran up, Shunko rushing off into the woods on the trail of the deer. Orono sat on the ground, rubbing his head, his face scratched and bleeding.

"It's too bad. Cosannip sorry," said Stephen.

"Ho, Orono, him no care much. Bad spirit got in lasso. Have strong lasso next time. Orona him catch deer whenever he wish."

In fact, the knowledge that he had actually been able to lasso a fawn, largely compensated Orono for its loss, and for his scratches and bruises. Having already the true Indian spirit, which taught him to ignore personal suffering, he made light of his injuries, and bravely went on. Stephen loaned him his own lasso, but not again did such a chance to display his skill come in Orono's way.

The boys rambled on. Orono shot two squirrels, and Stephen was pleased when his arrow brought down another. Then Orono called Stephen's attention to certain tracks in the snow, running from one big pine to another. Shunko sniffed eagerly at the tracks.

"Brother Marten has his lodge not far away. Orono and Cosannip make trap, catch him," said Orono, pointing with his arrow to the marks of the marten's feet, and the trail left on the snow by his long, bushy tail. The boys constructed a trap of logs and branches, so skillfully arranged that a heavy log would fall on the marten's neck, should he venture in after the tempting bit of squirrel flesh, that Orono cut off for bait.

The short winter's day was now beginning to wane. The sun, circling low around in the southern half of the sky, was already near its setting, and the cold grew more intense.

"Bo-oo, my feet are freezing, I believe," said Stephen, stamping his ice-cold feet to warm them. There was a suspicious white spot on his cheek, numb to the touch, but that he did not know. Orono, hardened by the life of exposure of the Indian, was not so sensitive to the cold. But he said,

"Orono hungry. Go home now, roast our squirrels. Taste heap good."

Stephen agreed, and the boys walked as rapidly as their snow-shoes allowed, back to Kippenoquah's wigwam in the woods. To Stephen's surprise, as he was about entering the wigwam, Kippenoquah seized him, and dragging him outdoors, began rubbing his face vigorously with snow. Stephen struggled, and tried to resist, but in vain. Kippenoquah's sinewy arms held him firmly, as she rubbed yet more snow on his face, none too gently, saying,

"Cosannip froze cheek. Kippenoquah cure him."

Then, for the first time, Stephen realized that the squaw's seeming roughness was real kindness. His cheek tingled smartly when at last he was released and allowed to go in to the fire, where Orono already had the squirrels roasting in the ashes, superintended by Shunko. The old dog, like his young masters, had a sharp appetite after his ramble in the woods. His patience was rewarded with the remains of the squirrels, when the boys and Kippenoquah had finished their supper. Already night had fallen, the long, northern night.

"Can Orono find his way?" asked Stephen, as he raised the skin flap over the entrance to let his friend out.

"Ho, Orono find it in the dark. But the Great Spirit kindles his fires tonight to light Orono on his way," said the Indian boy, pointing upward.

The northern sky was a wonderful and beautiful sight; the brilliant rays of the Aurora Borealis streamed high, even to the zenith, flashing, quivering, changing, as if indeed alive with a conscious spirit. The snow-covered ground was reddened by the glow of the sky above. Kippenoquah, looking over Stephen's shoulder, crossed herself at the awe-inspiring sight, and muttered a prayer.

The boys started for their trap early the next morning, Shunko running ahead. His loud barkings proclaimed success, for when the boys reached their trap, they found fast in it the frozen body of a fine pine marten, clad in his winter fur, dark, thick, shining, at its very best. Orono, delighted, said,

"Marten's skin bring heap money in Montreal. Orono keep skin, Cosannip take marten home to eat."

This division was entirely satisfactory to Stephen. But when he went home, Kippenoquah was not pleased, and told Stephen that he must bring the skin of the next marten caught to her.

One morning Stephen woke to find a dreary outlook. The sun shone faintly, a dimly seen grey ball through the dense clouds shrouding the sky. A piercing wind howled and moaned through the firs and pines, and the deadly chill of the air seemed to penetrate even to the bones. A little smoked meat made the meagre breakfast. To Stephen's surprise, Kippenoquah announced her intention of going over to the fort of St. Francis, near the Indian village. She knew a Frenchwoman living near the fort, who she thought would probably give her some food. Taking a pair of moccasins, which she had lately em-broidered prettily with beads, as an offering to this friend, Kippenoquah departed, first saying to Stephen,

"Cosannip must work today, while Kippenoquah is gone. Bring wood from the forest all day. Kippenoquah want heap of wood to burn."

Kippenoquah departed, and Stephen was left alone in the great surrounding forest. How still it was, how solemn, as the wind moaned through the dark trees! Stephen felt awed and lonely. Nor did he exactly like to venture forth alone into the woods.

"A wild cat or some other creature may pounce on me, when I am there all alone," thought the little boy, as he stood before the wigwam, looking out into the dark depths of the wild forest around, and hesitating whether he should obey Kippenoquah, and set forth for wood as she had ordered. But now a few snowflakes came floating down, soon increasing to a furious, driving storm. It was impossible to see far through the mist of thickly driving flakes. Stephen looking about, saw that Kippenoquah had almost half a cart load of wood piled up outside the wigwam. This was an unusual quantity of wood for an Indian to have on hand.

"I know she will not expect me to go out for wood in such a driving storm as this, especially when she has so much on hand," thought Stephen, glad enough to be relieved by the storm from setting forth. He went back into the wigwam and busied himself for some time in repairing his snow-shoes, which were broken in places. Then he tried to make an arrow, using for the head a sharp bit of iron, that Orono had given him.

"There, old fellow," he said to Shunko, who lay by the fire. "I guess that will do the work."

Old Shunko was a great comfort to him. He could talk to the dog, and Shunko seemed to understand, answering with a loving look and thumps of his tail. Even the sound of his own voice in the solitude was less dreary to Stephen then the echoing silence. The wigwam was filled with smoke, and snowflakes drove in at the smoke-hole overhead, sputtering in the fire. Altogether, it was a long, dreary day, and Stephen was really glad to greet Kippenoquah, when she came plodding heavily through the snow, late in the afternoon.

But Kippenoquah's face wore no pleasant answering smile. Her trip had not been as successful as she expected, and she was tired, cold, and cross. When she found that Stephen had disobeyed her, and brought in no wood, she was furious, glad of any excuse to vent her ill temper.

"Lazy, good for nothing paleface!" she cried. "Kippenoquah would whip you till blood run, but Sagamore George him say no; no whip Cosannip, no matter what happen. But the Jesuit Father come soon.

Kippenoquah ask him to beat Cosannip. Teach Cosannip to mind Kippenoquah."

Stephen had to go supperless to bed that night. Old Shunko, as if feeling sorry for him, came and curled up beside him. Stephen threw a corner of the bearskin over Shunko, and snuggling closely up to his dog friend, fell asleep, for a time forgetting his troubles.

15

A NEW EXPERIENCE

THE storm was followed by brilliant days, the sun gleaming from the pure, new fallen snow with dazzling brightness. The second day after the storm, as Stephen was coming from the forest, bent under a back-load of wood (for Kippenoquah now kept him busy at the slighted task), his heart sank within him. Through the tree trunks he saw approaching the tall, slight form of the Jesuit priest, clad in the long black robe, which gave the Jesuits their Indian name of the "Black Robes."

"I don't believe Kippenoquah really will ask him to whip me," thought Stephen, trying to keep up his courage. "I guess she only said that to scare me."

But Kippenoquah had been entirely in earnest. The Jesuit, faithful in the care of his wild flock, and following them so far as possible, even to their scattered abodes in the outlying wilderness, had come here to look after Kippenoquah, to see if she were true to her religious duties, to speak good words to her that should strengthen her faith, and help uplift her poor life a little above its ordinary dreary level. But he found Kippenoquah full of her grievance against the captive boy. He had flatly disobeyed her. Her husband had left the boy with her, forbidding her to whip him. Soon she should be able to do nothing with him, unless he were punished for disobedience. The Jesuit father must whip him for her.

It must be remembered that whipping was the custom of the times. In New France, as well as in New England, both children and servants were no strangers to the rod. At home and at school it was freely plied. Stephen well knew what it meant to be whipped soundly. Both his father and Master Richards had been faithful to what they considered their duty towards him, in season, and also out of season, as Stephen sometimes thought.

The Jesuit felt the squaw's complaints to be entirely reasonable. A disobedient boy must, of course, be whipped. He regarded Stephen as standing in the place of a son to Kippenoquah. He had flagrantly disobeyed her, therefore he must be whipped. As her husband had forbidden her to whip the boy, it fell to her priestly father to perform this duty for her. He had with him a scourge, possibly one used to flagellate his own flesh in penance, a rod with six knotted cords attached. He took Stephen out behind the wigwam, and applied the scourge, saying, when he released the boy,

"Now remember. Cosannip must be a good boy and mind the squaw. Kippenoquah is good to him. She feeds him, cares for him. Cosannip must never disobey her again. Bad boys are always taught obedience by the rod."

The sulky Stephen made no reply but plunged off into the woods. To say that he did not love the Jesuit father, would be stating his feelings mildly. His heart burned within him. Worse than the pain, was the rankling thought that he was an object of persecution. He, the minister's son of Deerfield, had been whipped by a Jesuit priest! What would his father say, could he know of this? Because this chastisement had been given by the priest of a faith upon which he had been taught to look with horror, Stephen felt it a case of religious persecution, and as such, indeed, it has gone into history. On the contrary, as has been stated, the priest simply acted in accordance with the custom of the times.

Far from growing accustomed to his life as a captive, and gradually sinking contentedly into Indian life and ways, as was often the case with young white captives, Stephen felt his captivity grow daily harder and more unendurable. This was perhaps in part because he was kept secretly restless, by the knowledge that his father was alive, and making efforts for his rescue. His only happy moments were when he and

Orono, with Shunko at their heels, were allowed to go off for a day's hunting. The boys made more traps to catch marten, and also spring traps for rabbits and foxes, by bending down a slender sapling and so fastening it that when some small creature of the wood ventured to nibble at the bait attached to the noose, up sprang the sapling, taking the victim of the boys' ingenuity with it. Happy were the boys when Shunko ran ahead barking wildly, and they saw rabbit or fox, dangling in the air, high above the reach of prowling bear or wolf.

A few days after Stephen's whipping, he was on the pond, trying to break the ice to get water that Kippenoquah might stew a rabbit which he had brought in, when, to his dismay, he again saw coming through the forest the slender, black-robed figure of the Jesuit priest. He turned his back and pretended not to see him, but the Jesuit came directly down to the pond, his face wearing the pleasant smile of one innocent of offense.

"Good morning, my son. I rejoice to see you at work, helping good Kippenoquah. That is right. I bring you good news. Behold a letter which I come to bring you!"

A letter for him here afar in the wilderness! From whom could it be? Stephen's clouded face brightened, and he had the grace to say "Thank you," as he eagerly took the letter. It was addressed, in his father's handwriting,

"For Master Stephen Williams, these."

The lonely, homesick, little captive read the letter from his father with a joy hard to describe. This bit of the old familiar home-love shone into his dreary, forlorn life, like a veritable ray of bright sunshine, transforming everything. Mr. Williams exhorted Stephen to be patient, saying he was sure that Governor Dudley of Massachusetts would soon "take care that we be redeemed." The letter earnestly exhorted Stephen to stand fast in his religious faith. "My heart is heavy with sorrow and anxiety for you and your brothers and sisters, in captivity, and exposed to fatal snares of false doctrines, but my trust is in God. His grace is sufficient for us. He is able to do exceeding abundantly, above all we can ask or think. I long to speak with you. I hope God will appear for us before it be long. My prayers are daily to God for you, my son, and for all my children and fellow prisoners. I am your afflicted but loving father, John Williams."

Stephen kept this precious letter tucked inside his fur shirt, next his skin, reading and re-reading it, until the worn folds began to drop apart. From it he learned that his father, too, was still held a captive. He spoke of this to Kippenoquah.

"English father captive all same as Cosannip, but no with the Indians; with the French," she said.

In what part of Canada his father was, Stephen did not know. Far from dreading the coming of the Jesuit priest, Stephen now watched for his return, hoping that he might bring another letter, or word that his father's efforts for his release had been successful. But the days crawled along with incredible slowness to Stephen's impatience, and no further message came to cheer his hopes.

The days, meantime, as they passed, grew perceptibly longer, the sun warmer and brighter, ushering in the month of March, well called by the Indians "the Month of Snow Blindness," for the sunlight was reflected from the sparkling crust that now covered the snow, with a dazzling brightness most painful to the eyes. Stephen and Orono had some sport, sliding downhill over the slippery crust, on strips of bark for sleds, Shunko bounding after them in such excitement that sometimes he lost his footing and actually slipped up, greatly to the boys' delight.

But Kippenoquah kept the useful captive at work whenever possible, and with spring found new tasks for him. She took him into the woods to help her cut down trees, whose trunks were about a foot in diameter. These trunks she chopped into sections about two feet long, which Stephen carried to the wigwam, until Kippenoquah had a pile of twenty of the logs. On these she worked hard, aided by Stephen, burning and chipping out the center, until she had fashioned them into wide troughs. One fine morning, when the bright sun and balmy, spring-like air made Stephen feel more hopeful, though he knew not why, Kippenoquah said,

"Cosannip take load of troughs, all he can carry. Come with Kippenoquah."

Stephen wondered where Kippenoquah was going, though he obeyed, taking a load of troughs, and following Kippenoquah, who bore a still larger load. They walked over the crust some distance, until they reached a fine grove of sugar maples, on one side of which stood a long, rude bark structure. Indians were coming and going about it, mostly the old men, women and children left behind in the village of St. Francis by the hunters. Stephen recognized several of them, and as they drew nearer, Orono came out, with friendly hail.

"Ho, ho, Cosannip. Welcome. Cosannip help make maple sugar."

This then was the Indian sugar camp. Stephen was rejoiced at this agreeable change in his labors and was quite ready to begin sugaring off at once. But there was plenty of work to be done first. Kippenoquah made him help her bring many back-loads of wood to pile up near her fire, that she might have a supply on hand when she began to boil the sap. She also, like the other squaws, made large shallow vessels of bark, water-tight, to hold the sap when gathered. Then with a hatchet she cut notches in the maple trees allotted for her use. In these notches she stuck chips, to conduct the sap down into the little troughs, one of which Stephen set under each tree as she tapped it.

The first day, towards noon, Stephen went out to examine the trees tapped in the morning. Yes, the sap was running freely, dripping off the chips into the troughs. Stephen took the end of a chip in his mouth, and much to his delight had a good drink of the sweet sap.

Night and morning, Stephen and Kippenoquah visited each tree, gathering the sap and emptying the troughs into the big bark vessel. Here it froze during the night. In the morning, to Stephen's surprise, Kippenoquah broke up the ice thus formed on the surface and threw it away.

"Kippenoquah throw away sugar!" cried Stephen.

"No, Kippenoquah throw away water," said the squaw. "Make sap sweeter. No have to boil so long."

Stephen, unconvinced, tasted the ice, and found that it was indeed watery, with little sweetness.

Kippenoquah was rich in owning a big copper kettle, which Sagamore George had brought home from a raid on some eastern settlement. This she hung over her fire in the sugar house, and Stephen had to tend it, while Kippenoquah was busy elsewhere. Orono's mother was the first squaw to sugar off, a great event for all the children. She had set Orono to tend the sugar. He called to Stephen:

"Cosannip come and help Orono."

Stephen went quite willingly. Several other small boys wanted to "help" Orono, but he drove them away, saying, "Eat sugar all up."

Orono, as the boiling sap slowly began to thicken and bubble, frequently filled a small wooden bowl and spread some of the syrup on the snow crust to harden, saying wisely,

"Must try sugar. See if him done."

Stephen was as faithful as Orono in this duty of testing the sugar, and the sap in the kettle was no doubt lowered somewhat, by the boys' industry. But Orono's mother was good natured, and well knew that the boys would soon become sated, when her sugar making could proceed with less "leakage."

After Stephen's long living on coarse Indian fare, chiefly smoked meat and eels, or flesh roasted without salt or relish, the maple wax melting in his mouth seemed indescribably delicious, and he did willingly all the drudgery required of him by Kippenoquah in this new business for the sake of the sweet mouthfuls she now and then allowed him to have.

She pounded up most of her sugar when hard and stored it in sacks made of deerskin. But some she poured into molds made of bark, in which it hardened into little cakes. She hoped to make enough to last her nearly a year. The Indians' habit was to use the sugar, not daily, but as an occasional luxury, or for high feasts. Sometimes it was melted in bear's fat, into which they dipped the roast venison, or bear's meat, as they ate. Sometimes they boiled corn, or other vegetables, with it. Now and then, as a great treat, a child was made happy with a small lump to eat, this being the nearest approach to candy known to the Indian children.

Kippenoquah slept in her wigwam nights, going in the early morning to the sugar camp to gather her sap, and spend the whole day boiling it down and sugaring off. One day, having sugared off all the syrup she had on hand, Kippenoquah returned home earlier than usual, consenting to leave Stephen a little longer, to aid Orono in the critical business of "testing" some sugar nearly done. When, later, in the waning sunlight, Stephen walked back along the now well marked path to the wigwam, as he drew near, to his surprise he heard voices in the wigwam. Who could be with Kippenoquah? Was it the priest, with good news for him?

Alas, no, for now he recognized the voice of Sagamore George, who had returned from the hunt that day, with several other braves, rich in skins and furs. He told Kippenoquah she must go with him the next day and help bring his wealth home. The Sagamore was so -well pleased with Kippenoquah for her carefulness in removing into the woods, for the greater security of his captive, and to find Stephen safe and well, that he was in an unusually gracious mood. But Stephen liked him no better than formerly, and was sorry to see him back.

While Kippenoquah was absent next day, Stephen was left in sole charge of the sugar making, gathering all the sap so faithfully that he had collected a large quantity ready to boil by night. He was very tired after his hard day's work, and as soon as he had eaten, he went to his bed of boughs. He was about to drop upon it, ready to fall asleep as soon as he should touch it, when Kippenoquah seized him, pulling him towards the entrance.

"Cosannip must work tonight," she said. "Kippenoquah goes to Sorel tomorrow. Cosannip must go to sugar camp, stay all night, boil all the sap into sugar before sunrise, so Kippenoquah can go away early."

This was unwelcome news to Stephen. But, unable to help himself, he walked back again to the camp, built up a good fire under the kettle and managed to keep it boiling hard all night. Often did the little boy nod drowsily, and drop off into a dreamy half sleep, soothed by the crackling of the fire, and the wind sighing through the bare branches, the solemn stillness around intensifying his feeling of loneliness. But every time he roused himself with an effort and threw more wood on the fire.

He had never before had the entire responsibility of "sugaring off," and was not aware that, as the syrup neared the sugaring point, it needed constant stirring. So, when Kippenoquah came over with the earliest dawn, hoping to find a fine kettle full of sugar, lo, it was all scorched and spoiled.

She and Sagamore George were both unreasonably angry, making no allowances for the boy's lack of experience. They scolded Stephen as harshly as if he had ruined the sugar purposely. Kippenoquah cooked that morning some venison which the Sagamore had brought in. Stephen, weak and faint after his night watch, so hard for one of his age, watched the venison roasting by the fire, with eager expectation. It was long since he had tasted venison, and it smelled so delicious!

"It smells good, doesn't it, old fellow?" he said to Shunko, who also sat watching the roast with lively interest.

When the venison was done, Kippenoquah filled Sagamore George's wooden bowl with tempting pieces, then her own, but said to the hungry Stephen, with frowning face and harsh tone,

"Cosannip get nothing to eat this morning. Him burn sugar all up for Kippenoquah. Him know better next time. Not burn sugar next time, lazy good-for-naught."

16

AT LAST!

SAGAMORE George having returned, it was no longer necessary to continue to live in hiding, and he and Kippenoquah decided to move back to the Indian village at St. Francis, the headquarters of the Abenakis. Kippenoquah stripped the wigwam poles, and again gathered all her possessions into packs. She walked away, bent under one huge pack, and Stephen, weak as he was, after his sleepless night and breakfastless morning, was obliged to carry a pack far beyond his strength. Anyone who had chanced to see Sagamore George that morning, striding along, cumbered only by his gun and other weapons, and followed by his squaw and captive, bent under their burdens, would have felt him abundantly able to care for his own interests, and defend his own rights. The first person whom Stephen saw, after he had dropped his pack at Kippenoquah's old place in the lodge, was Nunganey, who cried in friendly tones,

"Ho, ho, netop. Nunganey come back from the hunt with the warriors. Him shoot a moose with his gun. Nunganey big hunter."

"Halloo, Nunganey," said Stephen, really glad to see again the familiar face of his old tormentor, "Has Kewakcum come back?"

"No. Him no come back yet. Eenisken cook some of Nunganey's moose. Cosannip come and eat."

This was a peculiarly welcome invitation to the famished Stephen, and he hastened away to Mahtocheegah's lodge. Nunganey was so filled with pride, because he had actually shot a moose, and Eenisken was so pleased with her boy's success, that they pressed the choicest morsels of roast moose upon Stephen, until he could eat no more. Nunganey, while Stephen ate, entertained him with stories of his wonderful adventures as a hunter. Stephen felt cheered and comforted when, with a friendlier feeling than he had ever before been able to cherish towards Nunganey, he bade that valiant young hunter Goodbye, returning to his own lodge. He was none too soon, for the Sagamore and Kippenoquah were about going down to their boat. Orono seeing him in the distance, came running after him, calling,

"Cosannip stop. See Orono's new bow."

"Cosannip must go now. See bow when he comes back," said Stephen with a cheerful smile.

Stephen did not feel it necessary to mention to the Sagamore his nice breakfast of roast moose. But, oh, what a different world this looked to him, now that his hunger was relieved. The sun shone with spring-like warmth, the snow banks were melting and running off in streams over the soaked ground, which already showed many bare, brown patches. The branches of the willows by the river side were gray with soft, downy "pussies," which some of the little Indian girls were picking, not for any use, but only because they were pretty, and they loved to stroke them, and tickle each other's faces with the downy sprays. High overhead flew a line of wild geese, headed for their summer homes in the far north. Something in this bright, balmy morning whispered hope to Stephen, as he sat in the canoe, swiftly paddled down the St. Francis by the strong strokes of the two Indians.

"I don't believe I shall have to spend another winter among the Indians," he thought. "I feel that I shall yet be redeemed. I cannot see how, but God can. He knows, and he will bring it about, I believe!"

The Indians paddled down to the mouth of the St. Francis, into Yamaska Bay, and thence into that wide expanse of the St. Lawrence known as Lake St. Peter. Winding among the Islands they went about fourteen miles upstream, in a southwest direction, reaching at last Sorel, at the mouth of the Richelieu. The wide mouth of this river afforded a fine harbor, and several canoes and small vessels were moored there. Stephen recognized the place, and remembering the

Frenchwoman who had been so kind to him during his previous visit to Sorel in August, keenly scanned the opposite shore and the country round about as he landed.

"I wish my friend could know that I have come back again," he thought. "But perhaps she would not remember me now, even if she saw me."

He had to help Kippenoquah carry her possessions ashore, to the spot where she proceeded to erect her wigwam. Stephen was busy helping her, when he heard a friendly voice close by say,

"Bon jour, mon pauvre petit."

The sun, low in the west, shone in Stephen's eyes, so that at first he could hardly see the face of the woman who had drawn near while he was busily at work. But there was no mistaking the sweet, kind voice. It was his friend, the young Frenchwoman. It did her heart good to see how radiant Stephen's sorry, downcast face grew, as he recognized her, and eagerly seized her hand. Even to see a white face again meant much to him, and when that face was young, and sweet, and full of loving pity for him, it is little wonder it seemed beautiful to Stephen.

The Frenchwoman gave Kippenoquah a present of a few raisins, a rarity much prized by the Indians. This gift so pleased Kippenoquah that, when the Frenchwoman asked permission to take Stephen to the fort, not far away, she graciously consented.

"Cosannip no run away. Sagamore George close by. Kill Cosannip if he try to run away," said Kippenoquah in a threatening tone to Stephen as he departed. As she spoke she slipped a raisin into her mouth. Stephen's forlorn appearance after his hard winter among the Indians excited much sympathy among the kind-hearted French soldiers and their wives, at the fort. They gave him abundant food and urged him to sleep at the fort.

"At least, poor child, you can stay here and be comfortably housed while your Indian master tarries nearby," urged his friends.

"I dare not stop, without asking Sagamore George," said Stephen, wistfully. He so longed to stay but remembered too well Waneton's wrath during his former visit, when he had ventured to stay overnight at the fort, without permission.

"Wait a moment," said one of his friends. "I will send some food to your master, which may soften his heart, and incline him to let you stay."

Stephen was given a loaf of bread, some cakes, and meat. When he carried these welcome gifts to Kippenoquah, the Sagamore gladly consented to allow Stephen to sleep at the fort, hoping that further donations might thus reach him. The Sagamore stayed a fortnight at Sorel, and every night during that time Stephen slept at the fort. He was careful to visit the wigwam every day and as he often brought food to them, the Sagamore and Kippenoquah felt the plan to be a successful stroke of policy on their part.

"Huh! Sagamore George no fool. Him know how to please the French, get big presents," said the Sagamore, as he munched the bread Stephen had just brought in.

"Ho, yes, but Sagamore George keep his eye wide open all the time, all the same," said the cautious Kippenoquah. "Frenchman sly. Steal captive away and hide him some night."

"Frenchman no dare do that," said the Sagamore, with a fierce scowl, grasping the handle of his tomahawk.

To undress and lie down in a civilized way each night, between white sheets, on a soft bed and pillows of pigeon feathers, was a great luxury and rest to Stephen. He had almost forgotten how it felt to go to bed in the old way, so long had he been obliged to follow the Indian custom of throwing himself down to sleep as dressed for the day, on the pile of fir boughs, covered with skins. The first night, it was long ere he could sleep, from the novelty of the situation, and because he was so strongly reminded of home, his old home in Deerfield, which began to seem almost unreal, like a dim, long ago dream.

The French officers and soldiers pitied Stephen so much that they would gladly have ransomed him but were unable to pay the sum demanded by the Sagamore. Their evident interest in Stephen, combined with Kippenoquah's constant warnings and suspicions, began at last to make the Sagamore uneasy, lest somehow he lose his captive, without getting any ransom money. Moreover, it was now well on in April. Spring had come forward with unusual rapidity, and the planting season was drawing near. So one fine morning the Sagamore re-embarked, and Stephen was again obliged to turn his back on the brief glimpse he had enjoyed of civilized life and comforts, and return to the Indian village. But the kind Frenchwoman, who spoke English but brokenly, made him understand that his friends at Sorel would spare no efforts to induce the Governor to redeem him.

"Have hope, Stephen, have much hope," said his friend, as with tears in her eyes, she pressed his hand in farewell. "The Blessed Virgin knows. She sees. She will help the little boy."

So Stephen was paddled back to St. Francis, his heart heavy within him, at what seemed to him this hopeless return to Indian life. Orono gave him a joyous welcome, and even Nunganey condescended to be pleased to see him again, though chiefly because he could inflict upon the captive long stories of his own prowess, which the older Indian boys received with scant faith and open jeers.

Tododaho and Wilootaheetah, who had been off on the winter hunt with their Indian parents, were also now back in camp, apparently quite contented and happy. Stephen often wondered at them.

"I do not see," he thought, "how Ben and Nabby can settle down, satisfied to be Indians. It must be because their father and mother are dead, and they have no hope of getting away, and no homes to go to if they should escape. I could never feel so, I know, if I lived with the Indians forty years."

The squaws were making preparations for planting corn. Kippenoquah was one of the first to begin, ordering Stephen to help her, because he was a captive. Tododaho, being the adopted son of a chief, and a future warrior, was not allowed to demean himself by labor fit only for squaws. But Wilootaheetah being a growing young squaw, must help her Indian mother.

One fine May morning, when the air was sweet with the odor of new grass and fresh earth, and the birds were filling the world with rapturous melody, Stephen and Wilootaheetah were working in the cornfield near together. Stephen had an Indian hoe, a sharp stone fastened to a stick for handle. He hoed the ground as well as he could with this awkward tool, and Kippenoquah (who had carefully saved some seed corn, even under the pressure of acute hunger during the winter) dropped into each hill a few kernels of corn, from the skin pouch hanging at her belt. Stephen covered the seed, and then went on to the next hill.

Wilootaheetah's mother did the harder work of hoeing and let Wilootaheetah drop in the corn. Stephen was bent over, hard at work, when Wilootaheetah called,

"Cosannip! Cosannip! Look! See what comes!"

She pointed towards the river. Stephen, straightening himself, and looking where Wilootaheetah pointed, saw coming up the river a batteau of unusual size, rowed by French soldiers in bright uniforms. Seated in state in the stern was a dignified and commanding figure, his face shaded by a plumed hat. As this distinguished company were seen approaching the landing, great excitement prevailed throughout the Indian

"It is Onontio! Onontio comes to visit his children!" cried one to another.

"Oh! Cosannip," cried Wilootaheetah, when she learned that it was the governor, "I wonder if the governor has come for you! I believe he has!"

"He has come to arrange something about the fur trade, I guess," said Stephen. "It cannot be he has come for me."

Kippenoquah was much excited, especially when Governor de Vaudreuil was seen to direct his steps towards the lodge where Sagamore George stood outside, eagerly awaiting the coming of the governor. Kippenoquah hardly knew what to do. At first, she seized Stephen, and was about starting for the lodge with him. Then a second thought struck her.

"No, no. Maybe Onontio take Cosannip away, no pay Sagamore George any money for captive. Kippenoquah be ready to hide the captive in the woods. No give him up without much money no, not even to Onontio."

Accordingly, she took Stephen over to the edge of the thick woods, some distance from the lodge, where she stood, intently watching the lodge for some signal from the Sagamore, that should direct her action.

Mr. Williams had found a friend in Quebec as kind hearted as he was influential. He was Captain De Beauville, brother of the Lord Intendant. Mr. Williams says of this gentleman: "He was a good friend to me, and very courteous to all the captives; he lent me an English Bible, and when he went to France gave it me."

Mr. Williams had implored Captain De Beauville to use all his influence with the governor for the redemption of his oldest daughter, Esther, and for the purchase of Stephen from the Indians. De Beauville's efforts had not been in vain, for the haughty Governor de Vaudreuil, finding all his attempts unsuccessful to negotiate with Sagamore George, through various messengers sent, had now taken the trouble to come in person to try to redeem the captive boy. Stephen, his heart agitated with surging hopes and fears, watched anxiously the distant lodge, to learn any indications of his fate. The parley was long, for the Sagamore obstinately stood out for his forty crowns, and not a shilling less. At last Stephen saw Sagamore George step out of the lodge and scan the country round, as if looking for someone. Orono, who with a cluster of other Indian children, had stood outside the lodge, filled with curiosity to know the outcome of the parley, was seen to run up to the Sagamore, speaking eagerly, and pointing across to the woods. Sagamore George nodded his head, and disappeared within the lodge, while Orono, with the speed of a fawn, came running towards the wood, calling as soon as within hearing distance,

"Cosannip! Cosannip! Come! Come fast! Onontio buy Cosannip! Him go away with Onontio!"

Stephen stood stock still, so stunned by this good news, that he was unable at first to credit it. But he was pulled along fast enough by the elated Kippenoquah who exclaimed, as she ran towards the lodge, dragging Stephen along,

"Ho, Sagamore George, him know much. Him beat Onontio. Onontio only a pappoose to Sagamore George!"

Governor de Vaudreuil did not repent his action, when the captive boy was dragged into his presence, thin and wasted in body, his face wearing an anxious, careworn look pitiful to see in a child, and wholly naked, save for a cloth around his loins.

"Pauvre garcon!" muttered the governor to himself. Then he beckoned Stephen to follow him to the batteau.

Stephen's departure was not delayed by any packing of baggage, for he had no clothing, no earthly possession but his bow and arrow. As he stepped into the batteau, he was regarded with much interest by the soldiers. "'Tis well the governor has redeemed the poor boy," said one to another in low tones.

Orono, Nunganey, Tododaho, and Wilootaheetah, with the other Indian children, stood on the bank, watching Stephen's departure.

"Goodbye, Cosannip," called Wilootaheetah, not without a touch of wistfulness in her voice.

"Cosannip better come back," called Nunganey. "Nunganey take him out with him, teach him to be great hunter, like Nunganey."

Stephen was so excited, as he took his seat in the batteau, that he could hardly say Goodbye. Was it really true? Should he soon see again his father, his brothers and sisters, perhaps even go back to live in Deerfield? Looking back from down the stream, he saw Kippenoquah and Sagamore George standing outside their lodge, eagerly counting over the money paid them by the governor. A commotion had arisen among the children on the shore. Nunganey had thrown a lasso over the neck of Orono, a younger and smaller boy than himself, laughing in great glee at his struggles. Tododaho was evidently fighting Orono's battle for him, pouncing on Nunganey like a fierce panther, while old Shunko bounded around the young warriors, barking furiously and helping all he could in the struggle against Nunganey's mastery.

On the river's bank still stood one solitary little figure, watching the batteau as long as it was in sight, the form of Wilootaheetah. Who can tell what feelings struggled in the child's breast, what vague rebellions against fate, what dim longings for the old home, and the father to whom she had been the tenderly loved "little Nabby," what wishes that she too, like Stephen, were going back to that old life which already seemed to her a remote dream?

The batteau, swept rapidly on by the current and the strong strokes of the rowers, rounded a curve, and Stephen saw no more of St. Francis. He had turned his back on the Indian life forever.

17

A HAPPY MEETING

THE batteau glided swiftly down the current of the St. Francis. In the stern sat Governor de Vaudreuil, an imposing presence. High up in the bow, as the boat cleft the water, sat the captive boy, a wretched little figure, thin and worn and sunburned, his hair cut Indian fashion—short on one side, long on the other, and darkened by smoke and charcoal.

The governor, having accomplished his mission, gave the matter little further thought, but sat in dignified silence, his mind so absorbed in perplexing cares of state, that he hardly noticed the lovely landscape around him. Little did he dream that his connection with the helpless English captives would furnish his chief title to fame's remembrance!

Though Stephen looked outwardly so pitiful, within his heart sang for joy. Indeed, he could have cried, he was so glad; for great joy, like great sorrow, softens the heart with a tenderness from which tears lie not far away. The warm May sunshine, the birds soaring and dipping in the soft air as they poured out their happiness in a chorus of song, the rippling waters glancing in the sunlight, the tender green of the foliage along shore, all the beauty around him, seemed but the echo, the fitting accompaniment of the joy radiating from Stephen's young heart.

"I am free," he kept telling himself. "I shall never go back to be an Indian slave again. Soon I may see my father, my brothers and sisters. I wonder if we shall ever get back to Deerfield again, and live there together, just as we used to—only mother—"

And here tears did fill Stephen's eyes, to be quickly brushed away, from force of the long habit which he had been obliged to practice among the Indians, of repressing outward signs of grief. Stephen's heart sang praises to God, as he glided on. "Oh, I thank thee, my Father in heaven," was the undercurrent of his thought.

The batteau put in at last at Sorel, and Stephen was left at the fort for the present, while the governor returned to Quebec. The soldiers gave Stephen a glad welcome, rejoicing in his release, and his faithful friend, the young Frenchwoman, was full of joy at his rescue.

"It is the Blessed Virgin!" she exclaimed. "Behold her work! I knew her tender heart, so full of compassion, would feel for thee. I told thee she would not fail to make intercession for thee. Come, my poor child, and pay thy gratitude and thanks to the Blessed Mother, for all her loving kindness towards thee."

Stephen did not understand his friend's words, as she spoke French. But the genuine loving interest shining in her face and softening her tone, went straight to his heart, and he willingly followed her, as she motioned him to do, though where she went, he knew not. But when she turned in towards a small building, whose gable uplifted a cross, and from whose open door floated out the sweet, solemn sound of chanting voices, Stephen drew back, shaking his head decidedly, as his friend urged him to enter the chapel.

"No, no, I cannot," he said. "It is wicked. My father would be filled with sorrow should I go into a Romish chapel to worship."

His friend could not understand his words, but his attitude of refusal was unmistakable.

"Wilt thou then not come to render thanks for thy deliverance?" she asked, sorrowfully.

Stephen again shook his head, turning and walking quickly away. He was sorry to grieve his kind friend but felt that he must stand firm in the faith in which he had been reared.

"Ah, the hard hearts of these poor heretics!" murmured his friend to herself. "That even a child should be so obstinate! 'Tis greatly to be hoped he may yet be brought to the truth, even if by added sorrows. 'Twill enter and beseech the Blessed Virgin even now for his conversion."

As Stephen was walking back to the fort he saw a man coming, whom he instantly recognized as an Englishman. The stranger regarded Stephen closely, as they drew near each other, and finally said,

"Can it be that you are young Stephen Williams, son of the Deerfield minister?"

"Yes, I am he," said Stephen eagerly, looking up into the strong, kind face of the speaker.

"Well met, boy. I was looking for you, having just heard of your redemption and arrival at Sorel. I am Capt. John Livingstone of Albany. I have been sent to Canada, as you may have heard, with Deacon John Sheldon and another of Deerfield, to discover and rescue as many as possible of the unhappy captives taken from that settlement."

"Oh, I am so glad to see you, Captain Livingstone," cried Stephen. "Have you seen my father? Is he going home with you and Deacon Sheldon?"

"I cannot answer yet for your father. The French government will not lightly part with so prominent a captive as he. They hope, by holding him, to force Governor Dudley to render up in exchange for your father, one Captain Baptiste, a notorious spy and renegade whom Governor Dudley holds prisoner. It will require further negotiations to secure his release. But I will surely take you back to Boston with me, my poor lad. 'Tis plain to be seen what a sorry time you have had with your Indian masters. You will not have to wait long, for I start in a day or two."

Stephen's heart was filled with joy to hear that he should so soon be going home. On reaching the fort, he heard that Captain Livingstone had brought there several white captives, whom he and Deacon Sheldon were about taking home, by way of Lake Champlain and Albany.

"I shall see someone I know from Deerfield!" thought Stephen, joyfully, as he hurried to the place where the redeemed captives were. The first person he met there was his sister Esther I Brother and sister had last seen each other on the dreary march through the snows of northern Vermont. Joyous yet strange was their meeting here, in faraway Canada, after all their weary months of captivity and hard, strange experiences. Esther listened to Stephen's story of his life among the Indians, hardly able to believe that her little brother could have endured such hardships and yet be living.

"You and poor little Eunice have had the hardest lot of any of us," she said. "Eunice is still with the Indians, down at a settlement of theirs called Caughnawaga, nine miles below Montreal. Her master and mistress are kind to her, my father told me the last time I saw him, when he was suffered to be at Montreal for a short time. But they seem to regard her as their own child. Father will spare no effort for her redemption, of that you may be sure. Through his kind friend Captain De Beauville, he has secured my release, and I hope he can also get Eunice, with the Captain's aid."

"Oh, I hope he can get poor little Eunice away from the Indians," said Stephen. "I know too well what it means to live with them. But tell me what happened to you, Esther."

"Monsieur the governor was really most kind to me," said Esther. "I was so lame when the Indians brought me into Montreal, that I could hardly walk, and so weak and exhausted for lack of food, that I thought I should die."

"Yes, I know how you felt," said Stephen.

"The governor redeemed me out of the hands of the Indians, and sent me to the hospital of Hotel Dieu. The Black Nuns, as the nuns of that hospital are called, were most pitiful and kind to me. I never can forget their kindness. They carefully nursed me until my lameness was cured, and I was strong again, and then the governor placed me with a French gentlewoman, who also treated me with great kindness. 'Twas hard to be in a strange land, among people of foreign language and habits, separated from all my family, not knowing what they might be suffering, or even if they were all living. But my sufferings were little, when compared with yours, poor Stephen."

"Do you know anything about our brothers?" asked Stephen, who felt as if he could hardly wait to hear all Esther had to tell, of such deep interest to him.

"Yes, they are both in Montreal, in French families. A French gentlewoman happened to see poor little Warham, in the hands of the Indians, as they passed her home. Her heart was so rent with pity for the helpless child that she had no rest till she had bought him from his masters. Afterwards the Indians repented of giving Warham up. I suppose they thought that he was so young they could make a true Indian of him. They came back and offered the gentlewoman a captive man who understood weaving, in exchange for Warham, saying that the man would be much more useful to her. But God, I believe, kept her firm, for she would hear nought to them, but cherishes little Warham as her own son, I am told."

"I am so glad for dear little Warham. I have thought so much about him, and even feared he was dead before this. And Samuel, do you know anything about him?"

"Yes. He too has been fortunate. After he had been in Montreal with the Indians six weeks, and begun to feel in despair about ever escaping from them, a Montreal merchant, one of the richest in the city, after long negotiations with the savages, at last succeeded in redeeming Samuel from them, and took him to his own home, where Samuel now lives. But I know nothing more about him."

"I have had a hard time," said Stephen, "but I think I am so fortunate now, to be actually going back home, and with you too, Esther."

"I am so glad too, Stephen," said Esther.

The next day Deacon Sheldon joined the party, after further fruitless attempts to find his two boys, who were still off somewhere in the wilderness, hunting with their Indian master. He and Captain Livingstone had succeeded in redeeming only five captives in all; Esther Williams, Hannah Sheldon, Mary, the daughter of Deacon Sheldon, and two others. These were the first of the captives from Deerfield to be returned.

Stephen's hopes were doomed to cruel disappointment. Governor de Vaudreuil changed his mind and refused to allow Stephen to return with the others. The next day Stephen stood sorrowfully on the shore of the Richelieu, watching the little fleet of canoes push off. The fleet carried not only Deacon Sheldon and Captain Livingstone, with the five happy returning captives, but also Captain Courtemanche, a French officer, with eight French soldiers, sent by Governor de Vaudreuil nominally as an honorable escort to the company. But Captain Livingstone looked upon this courtesy with scant gratitude, saying aside to Deacon Sheldon,

"If the truth were known, I believe they are sent to spy out the country, and for naught else."

"Goodbye, Stephen," called Esther, as the canoe in which she sat glided off up the broad river to the South. She was sorry for her disappointed little brother, yet she could not help a note of gladness in her voice. Was she not going home?" Keep up your heart, Stephen. Do not despair. I believe you and our father will be coming soon."

"Goodbye, Esther," said Stephen, dejectedly.

He could not share Esther's hopefulness. He had known so many bitter disappointments and hard buffetings of fate, that he was easily disheartened. This last disappointment was indeed hard to bear.

"It's easy for Esther to be cheerful, for she's going home. But I don't believe I shall ever get back," he thought, as he stood gloomily watching the canoes disappearing in the distance.

But the very next day brought a new turn in his eventful life. The Lord Intendant of Canada appeared at Sorel, with orders to take Stephen to Quebec. So Stephen, after a loving farewell to his French friend, whom he loved for all her kindness, even if he could not gratify her by adopting her religious faith, again embarked in a large batteau, manned by soldiers. The Lord Intendant was second only in dignity and power to Governor de Vaudreuil himself, and, in truth, often felt himself quite the equal, if not the superior, of that dignitary. Therefore, he assumed all the state permissible, and carried himself loftily.

Again was Stephen perched in the bow, looking small and insignificant compared with the magnificent Lord Intendant and his soldiers in their uniforms. He gazed about him in wonder, as, leaving the islands in Lake St. Peter behind, the batteau swept into the main stream of the St. Lawrence. So broad and ocean-like was this majestic river, that the batteau seemed lost, a mere leaf tossing aimlessly on that mighty flood, ever sweeping down from the great lakes to the Atlantic. Stephen was almost terrified as he looked about.

"It seems most hazardous to venture out on a great, strong river like this, in such a small boat," he thought.

But the French soldiers were at home on the St. Lawrence, for it was the highway for all the Canadian settlers between Montreal and Cap Tourmente. They traveled it with canoes in summer, and on sleds when winter froze its broad surface solid. It was the chief channel of communication between the settlements that bordered its stream, the grand highway of the country.

The distance between Sorel and Quebec is about one hundred miles. As the current was with them, the soldiers made good time, sweeping swiftly on, past many a little log house set beside the river, its long, narrow strip of clearing running back into the vast primeval forest which covered Canada, except for the line of settlements along the river. They passed the square palisade which enclosed the fur-trading hamlet of Three Rivers. Often the batteau was the only boat to be seen on the wide stream. Occasionally they saw a canoe pushing off from one of the log houses, rowed by a *habitant* bound for Quebec, or for a neighboring hamlet, who stared long and hard at the batteau, with its crew of soldiers. Once they met a canoe-load of Indians paddling upstream, who cried out in shrill greeting, at sight of the soldiers,

"Ho, ho, netop!"

Stephen shrank back, turning his face away. What if Waneton should chance to be among those Indians, should recognize him, and claim him as his own again? Once, too, they met a black-robed Jesuit priest, bearing the sacred vessels of his office, paddled upstream by the strong arms of a young French novice, in training for the priesthood. He was going, perhaps, to the far away Ottawa, or perhaps to the fur posts on the great lakes. The good father was bound somewhere in the wilderness to minister to groups of Indian converts, or scattered Frenchmen, on far outposts. Both the Lord Intendant and the soldiers gave the priest respectful, even reverent, greeting, as they met and passed.

All was new to Stephen, and he gazed about with lively interest and curiosity at these novel surroundings. The wild nature of the country, its strangeness, the vast river, the feeling of being borne farther and farther away from home, would all have filled him with sore homesickness, but for one comforting thought, to which the boy's heart clung as almost his only hope.

"Perhaps I shall see my father soon!"

This was the secret thought buoying up Stephen's courage. Late in the afternoon of the second day, he noticed the soldiers pointing with interest downstream. He turned to look down the river and saw, looming up above the river's surface, a bold promontory. Then one of the soldiers said,

"Quebec!"

So, this was where he was bound. Stephen gazed with intense interest, until finally the high, steep cliff of Cape Diamond loomed up far above the little batteau, the cliff crowned with great buildings, which looked most imposing to the little boy born in the frontier settlement of Deerfield, who hitherto had seen no other town save the tiny clusters of houses around the forts at Chambly and Sorel. Nestled under the high cliff was the big magazine of the French fur company, with two round towers, and two long wings. In this building large business was done, for here all the furs brought into or gathered in the colony, were assorted and packed to be shipped to France.

At a landing near this magazine the batteau put in. The Lord Intendant stepped ashore, and escorted by some of the soldiers, walked up the steep pathway leading from the river's level to the heights of the promontory. He passed the sentinels, who with guns on their shoulders, paced up and down before the stately structure, and entered the Chateau St. Louis, the fortified residence of the governors of Canada. Stephen followed timidly behind the Lord Intendant, as that dignitary had motioned him to do. The soldiers in the two guardhouses, with mansard roofs each side the gate, said to each other, as they saw the neglected-looking, almost naked child, an Indian in all but his skin, following the Lord Intendant,

"Voila, le pauvre petit Anglois! Un autre captif de Guerfiel, peut-etre."

18

MORE FRIENDS

GOVERNOR DE VAUDREUIL had not yet decided on Stephen's disposal. For the present he was assigned quarters in a tiny room, high up under the mansard roof, located within the servants' portion of the chateau. This room resembled a cell, so narrow and dark was it, lighted only by one window, high up in the stone wall. But when Stephen climbed up on a chair, and peeped out of this window, what a wonderful view lay spread out before him! The Chateau St. Louis stood on the very verge of the cliff. So closely beneath were the buildings on the strand, that Stephen thought,

"If I had a stone, I could easily drop it down on that roof below!"

Beyond the strand was the great St. Lawrence, sweeping on, wide and majestic, bearing all the waters of the great lakes to the Atlantic. A French ship lay at anchor by the wharf of the fur magazine, and many batteaux and canoes were coming and going. Beyond the river stretched a densely wooded country, broken only by a thin fringe of log houses and cleared land, along the shore. In the southern distance rose blue mountains.

Stephen felt homesick and forlorn, in these new surroundings, so vast and strange.

"It doesn't look much like my ever getting home, or seeing father again either," he thought despairingly. The servants felt sorry for him, and at least he was well fed and kindly treated. He soon discovered too, that he was not kept confined as a prisoner, but allowed to go about the city somewhat. So the little boy from Deerfield rambled about Quebec, looking with open-eyed wonder on many sights novel to him; the massive stone buildings of the great church of Notre Dame, and of the Jesuit's College; the priests coming and going in their long black robes ; now and then a nun gliding past, her eyes fixed modestly on the ground ; the pupils of Laval Seminary, who looked strange to Stephen, clad in their long robes, belted with green sashes, and coming to their feet. The Seminary boys, for their part, gazed in wonder on this almost naked child, who looked so timid and forlorn, shrinking into himself if spoken to, evidently not understanding French.

Tuesday and Friday were the market days at Quebec, when the *habitans* from the surrounding country, for a great distance, brought into the city for sale their garden truck, their butter, cheese, and other produce. The first Tuesday after his arrival, Stephen was standing on one side of the market place watching the bustle and stir, and the people whose language and dress were equally strange to him, when to his surprise he heard a familiar voice cry out,

"Stephen Williams, as true as I live!"

Turning quickly, there stood Jonathan Hoyt, his brother Sam's friend, who had slept under his father's roof! Yes, it was unmistakably Jonathan, though dressed like an Indian.

"Oh, Jonathan," cried Stephen, "is it really you? I am so glad to see you, to see someone I know from Deerfield. I thought I was all alone here."

"And I am glad to see you, Stephen, and know that you are alive," said Jonathan. "No one knew where you were for a long time, and we feared you had perished among the Indians. You have had a hard enough time of it, I judge by your looks. Are you still living with your Indian master?"

Stephen briefly told Jonathan something of his experiences, and that he was now in the governor's hands, uncertain what next awaited him.

"I pray he may restore you and that speedily to your father, for it will be like medicine to a sick heart if good Parson Williams can get back even one of his children. He has suffered sorely," said Jonathan. He then told Stephen that he was living with an Indian master at the Indian village of Lorette, nine miles out of Quebec, on the St. Charles

River, and that Nanageskung, his master, treated him kindly; also that he often came to market in Quebec, bringing Jonathan with him, as he had done to-day.

"'Tis plain he means to keep me always, even as a son," said Jonathan. "But Stephen, you well know how I feel about that. No matter how kindly one may be treated, it is no life for an English boy, born and bred in the Massachusetts Bay Colony. If I ever see a chance to escape and get back home, I shall certainly jump at it, you may be sure of that. Though I've nothing against old Nanageskung save that he is an Indian and wants me to be one too."

Jonathan also told Stephen that Ebenezer Nims had been adopted in place of a dead son by one of the Huron squaws, and was living at Lorette, as was Ebenezer Warner, another Deerfield captive, and that his sister, Sarah Hoyt, was in or near Quebec.

"I sometimes see Sarah, which is a comfort to us both," said Jonathan. "And Ebenezer Nims manages to see Sarah now and then, too."

Here Stephen saw a tall Indian approaching. It was Nanageskung. Naturally good tempered, he looked particularly pleasant now, having sold all his bear's oil, wild honey and other wares at good prices. He said to Jonathan,

"Wawanosh, come now. Come to the wigwam. Nanageskung trade his bear's oil for sugar and flour. Get heap. Big feast tonight. See," he added, patting a sack thrown over his shoulder, and handing Jonathan a smaller one to carry. Then, looking at Stephen, he said,

"The paleface boy come too. Nanageskung have two sons."

Stephen shook his head and stepped back in alarm at this invitation.

"Goodbye, Stephen," said Jonathan, as he followed Nanageskung down the path to the point on the bank of the St. Charles, where his canoe was drawn up. "May God send you good luck and help us both."

Stephen was much cheered by this meeting with an old friend, and to learn that others of his Deerfield friends and acquaintance were nearby. He might possibly meet with Ebenezer Nims in the market someday.

"I will always go to the market place every Tuesday and Friday after this," he thought.

As he walked on, deep in these thoughts, he was startled by a hand laid on his naked shoulder, startled, because after all his sad experiences, any new incident might mean fresh trouble. Perhaps Waneton or Sagamore George had come to claim him! Looking fearfully up, he saw, not the red face of an Indian, but that of an Englishman, a stranger, who looked kindly down on the friendless child. Stephen's face brightened even before the stranger said,

"My boy, 'tis plain to me that you are an Indian captive. You look in sorry plight. Tell me your story. Perhaps I can help you. I will gladly do so if I can."

When he had heard Stephen's story, and learned that he was the little son of Deerfield's minister, for whose safety such deep anxiety had been felt, Mr. Hill (for this was the name of Stephen's new friend) was greatly interested.

"I know your good father well," he said. "His ministrations have greatly refreshed the spirits of the captive English here in Montreal, whenever he has been allowed to speak to them. But he stands so steadfast to the true faith, and so urgently exhorts his fellow prisoners and old parishioners to do the same, and holds such valiant disputations with the Jesuits, that he has been banished to some place down the St. Lawrence, and we no longer have the benefits of his ministry. I will try to see if I cannot procure some decent clothing for you, my boy. 'Tis a crying shame to see the son of Deerfield's godly minister roaming the streets of this city, almost naked, like a wild Indian."

Ebenezer Hill, with his brother Samuel and other friends, had been captured by the Indians, in the attack on Wells, Maine, August 10, 1703. Having known all the miseries of Indian captivity, though now living among the French in Quebec, he was full of sympathy for Stephen. From some kind-hearted Frenchwomen he secured secondhand clothing and came to the chateau ere long to see Stephen, bringing him a shirt, a pair of stockings, a jacket, and trousers. Stephen had a good pair of moccasins, which would answer as shoes. Indeed, many of the Canadians wore moccasins from preference.

"Now, Stephen," said Mr. Hill, "let me cut your hair into Christian shape. I'm not much of a barber, but I guess I can hack off your locks after a fashion, so you will look less like a little Indian, and more like a civilized Christian child."

When Stephen's hair was cut, and he was dressed again like a white child, he not only looked, but felt, like another boy. He glanced brightly up at Mr. Hill, at the same time pulling off his jacket, saying,

"If you do not mind, Mr. Hill, I'll not wear the jacket now. It feels so heavy. But after sundown I am often cold, and then I shall like it.

I thank you ever so much. I wish I could stay with you," he added, looking wistfully at his new friend. "I am so lonely here."

"Perhaps you can. I will see if I can so arrange it," said Mr. Hill.

Mr. Hill succeeded in obtaining the care of Stephen during the rest of his stay in Quebec, on condition that he kept careful watch of the boy, neither allowing his escape, nor his recapture by the Indians, should either of his former masters chance upon him. This was a happy change for Stephen. He was not, however, to remain long with Mr. Hill, for at last the governor, moved perhaps by some natural sympathy with the father's longings and sorrows, decided to send Stephen to his father.

It was an ideal spring morning, the 11th of May, when Stephen, all happy excitement, bade an affectionate Goodbye to his friend, Mr. Hill, who stood on the shore looking almost as happy as Stephen himself, from sympathy, and stepped into the canoe, rowed by two soldiers, that was to take him to his father. Yes, at last, after these weary fourteen months of separation, he was again to see his father! How often, in the dreary days spent among the Indians, had this seemed an impossibility, too absolutely hopeless even to be dreamed of! And now, God, in his great mercy, had wrought the miracle, as it seemed to Stephen, and in spite of what had seemed such insuperable obstacles was bringing father and child together again.

Stephen's heart was full of gladness and thankfulness. Happily he saw the high promontory of Cape Diamond, with its massive structures grow fainter and sink lower, as the boat went steadily on downstream, farther and farther from it, until they passed the Falls of Montmorenci. Far away, above the splashing of the paddles, Stephen heard the roar of this cataract, wondering much what it was, but unable to ask, as his companions spoke only French. Then he saw a cloud of white spray rising, irradiated with shifting rainbow tints in the sunshine, and, when nearer still, he saw the Montmorenci River making its great leap of two hundred and fifty feet down the face of the rocky precipice into the St. Lawrence. Never had he seen anything so wonderful.

The canoe glided swiftly on, keeping near the shore, passing the Cote de Beaupre, then, as now, one of the fairest parts of Canada. It was one of the earliest sections settled, having been occupied soon after the arrival of Champlain. It had long been the special property of Laval Seminary, and at this time it was the most thriving and well-ordered part of Canada. Rich meadows, whose grass was of a peculiarly soft, deep green, bordered the shore, where the thrifty *habitans* were seen at work, planting their crops. The meadows ran back into wooded slopes, in terrace after terrace, ending in the foothills of the Laurentian Mountains seen beyond, blue in the distance. Among the woods were frequent clearings, with scattered log houses, and occasionally a low, one-story cottage of stone, with high, sharp-pitched roof, curving at the eaves. Not far below the Falls of Montmorenci, Stephen saw a cluster of houses, gathered around a chapel standing among trees high up on the river's bank. He wondered if this could be Chateau Richer, which he had heard was the name of the place where his father was staying.

"Chateau Richer?" he asked, pointing to the village.

"Non, non," said the soldiers, shaking their heads. "C'est L'Ange Gardien."

At the right of the voyagers now rose the bold cliffs of a large island, covered with luxuriant forest, lovely now in the soft hues of spring foliage, the Isle of Orleans. Although the river was divided by this island, it was still a broad stream. The beauty of the scenery was great. They passed several more fine waterfalls, where streams, wearing the rock for centuries, had cut a deep rift, down which they plunged into the St. Lawrence. As the voyagers paddled on, they saw many wild duck, and one of the soldiers succeeded in shooting one. As he flung it aboard, he said something about the "cure."

When they had paddled about twelve or fifteen miles, as nearly as Stephen could judge, he saw that they were approaching another village, a group of small cottages, clustered around a stone chapel which bore aloft a cross, and which stood in a commanding position, high above the river.

"Chateau Richer," said one of the soldiers, pointing ahead, and nodding kindly to Stephen.

Soon then Stephen would see his father! His heart beat fast, and he closely watched everyone along the shore, often, in fancy, seeing his father in some distant *habitant*, working on his land, or trudging along the fields. The canoe was run ashore on a sandy beach. Stephen, jacket in hand, walked behind the soldiers, one of whom carried the fat duck by its legs, a gift for the priest. Up the bank they went, directing their steps towards the chapel, and climbing the steep street. Small houses bordered close upon the road, the front doors opening directly upon the street. As they ascended the hill, Stephen, looking up the street, saw the tall form of a man pacing slowly up and down beside a high stone wall, his hands clasped behind him, his head dropped on his breast, as if lost in meditation. He was poorly clad in beggarly garments, yet bore himself with unmistakable dignity. No one would have mistaken him for a mean person or one of low degree.

"It is my father!" cried Stephen, running towards him. "Father! Father!"

The tall form turned; the pale, sad face looked up, startled, then brightened with the light of joy unspeakable.

"My son! My little Stephen! Do my eyes not deceive me? Is it verily you at last?" cried the minister, trembling with emotion, as he again clasped the little son, so long lost, who had suffered so much since they parted, long weary months ago, at the mouth of the White River.

19

AT CHATEAU RICHER

MR. WILLIAMS was living with the priest of the parish, at the priest's residence near the church, and here also Stephen stayed. Oh, the comfort to the boy, after the long months of wandering with Indians in the wilderness, living as they lived, a savage in all outward circumstances, to be once more with his father!

"It seems almost like home, father, to be with you again," he said one day.

"God has shown me great favor, Stephen, in granting my petitions that you be restored to me," said his father. "His loving kindness to me in this particular, quickens my hopes that I shall yet live to witness the redemption of all my children. Yet I pray always for grace to be willing that he should dispose of me and mine as he pleases, and as is most for his glory."

Of course, Stephen and his father had much to talk over and tell each other. Mr. Williams told Stephen that in the previous October (eight months after his capture),[10] he had received letters from New

10 Eight months may seem a long time to my young readers for such important news to wait to be conveyed. They must remember that there were no mails in those days. If the Governor of Canada wished to write to the Governor of New York, he sent his letter by a special post, or messenger, and private individuals eagerly embraced this opportunity to dispatch letters to friends. Much later, mail in New England was carried by special messengers, and travelers were always asked and expected to oblige friends and acquaintances, by carrying and

England, informing him that many of their old neighbors had escaped with their lives in the destruction of the fort at Deerfield, and that the body of his dear wife had been recovered by them, taken back to Deerfield, and given decent burial; also that Eleazer, his oldest son, who was so fortunate as to be in Hadley at the time Deerfield was assaulted, had been provided for by kind friends and sent to Harvard College.

"All these mercies," said Mr. Williams, "caused my heart to swell with thanksgiving to God, even in the midst of afflictions."

Stephen told his father the long story of all his hard experiences, not omitting the story of the whipping received from the Jesuit priest.

"That this Jesuit should take upon himself to whip you, at the complaint of a squaw!" exclaimed Mr. Williams, with darkening face. "They use many crafty designs to ensnare our young ones, and turn them from the simplicity of the gospel to Romish superstition. Sometimes they try flattery, sometimes severity. The Jesuits have even told me that it was a great mercy that so many of our children had been brought to Canada, for now there is hope of their being brought over to the Romish faith. Certainly they will spare no effort to that end. I praise God, Stephen, that you have been strengthened to stand fast in the faith of your fathers. I tremble for your brother Samuel. He is, I fear, exposed to sore temptations."

"Have you seen Sam since you reached Canada, father?" asked Stephen.

"No, I was separated from all my children and parishioners, while on my way with my Indian masters," said Mr. Williams, "and knew not where they were, or how faring. But after I reached Montreal, the last of April, the governor redeemed me from the Indians, took me to his own house, and was most kind and courteous to me in all relating to my outward man. He sent for Warham and Esther, who were in the city, that I might see them."

"I saw Esther at Sorel, father, and she told me about herself and Warham. But she knew little about Sam."

"One Monsieur Jacques Le Ber, a rich merchant, redeemed Samuel, and took him to his own abode. There he is now, two hundred miles away from me, and I have no means of knowing how it fares with him. My fears are not so much for his body as for his soul, for the family

---

delivering private letters.

of Sieur Le Ber are notedly rigid Catholics. I pray for him, day and night, with groanings that cannot be uttered."

"Esther said she feared that little Eunice was still with the Macquas."

"Yes, poor child, it is even so. When I think of that tender lamb among wolves, soul and body both exposed to death, 'tis hard for me to be resigned to God's sovereign will."

Then Mr. Williams told Stephen of all his efforts to see and redeem little Eunice. The governor had done everything possible to aid him, finally going with Mr. Williams in person to Caughnawaga, where he succeeded in procuring an interview between the father and his little daughter. The child of but seven years was brought into the room in the fort where her father was.

"I discoursed with her for nearly an hour," said Mr. Williams. "She had not forgotten her Catechism and could read very well. She was most desirous to be redeemed out of the hands of the Macquas, and bemoaned her state among them, poor child. I told her she must pray to God for His grace every day. She said she did, as she was able, and God helped her. I charged her to be careful not to forget her Catechism and the Scriptures she had learned by heart. At last I had to come away and leave the child, my heart rent within me. I saw her once more, for a short time only, a few days after, when her master brought her to Montreal, and I improved the time to give her the best advice I could."

"What a shame for our little Eunice to be living among the Indians!" exclaimed Stephen. "Will not the governor get her away?"

"He has done his utmost, I will say that for him," said Mr. Williams. "He labored much with the Indians for her redemption. At last they promised to give up Eunice, if the governor would procure for them an Indian girl in her stead. Accordingly, the governor sent up the river some hundreds of leagues for one, but when she came, the Indians refused to exchange Eunice for her. He then offered one hundred pieces of gold for her redemption, but even this they re-fused. The governor's lady was most kind. She even went to the Indians herself to beg Eunice from them, but all in vain. The poor child is still with her captors, and I am told, has forgotten how to speak English."

And the father heaved a heavy sigh.

"I wonder "—said Stephen, hesitating, with tears in his eyes. "Don't you think it strange, father, God allows such a thing to happen?"

"We must lie low at the feet of God, my son. These sore chastenings are no doubt meant in mercy, even tokens of his love, could we see all as he sees. Shall not the Judge of all the earth do right? Yet I confess to sore wrestlings of the spirit over the case of your poor little sister. I pray that God may yet see fit to intervene for her redemption, but also, whatever happens, that I may have grace to resign all to his holy will."

Mr. Williams then related something of his own experiences. After being some weeks at Montreal, he was sent down to Quebec, in company with Governor de Ramsey, the Governor of Montreal, and the Superior of the Jesuits, and was lodged with one of the Council for seven weeks, from whom he received many favors. Indeed, his troubles were rather of the soul and heart than of the body, for he was kindly and courteously treated. But the efforts of the Jesuits to convert him to Catholicism were most distasteful to the Deerfield minister.

The Jesuits, from their point of view, felt it their plainest duty to spare no effort to win to the true faith the souls of the heretics, providentially brought within the sphere of their influence. Could the shepherd of the flock be won, it would be easy, they felt, to draw the stray sheep into the true fold. Offers were made to Mr. Williams of an honorable pension from the King, and the restoration of all his children to him, would he recant his religious errors, to all of which Mr. Williams sturdily replied,

"If I thought your religion to be true, I would embrace it freely, without any such offer; but so long as I believe it to be what it is, the offer of the whole world is no more to me than a blackberry. My children are dearer to me than all the world, but I would not deny Christ and his truths for the having them with me. I still put my trust in God, who can perform all things for me."

Mr. Williams proved such a sturdy controversialist that the priests, fearing his influence over the other English captives, not many days after this caused him to be removed down the river, to the little parish of Chateau Richer, where he was the only captive. The priest of this parish was one of the most learned men in the country, universally respected, a man of kindly heart and courteous nature.

"I have been most courteously treated by him ever since I came here," said Mr. Williams, "and by his people, too. The priest is indeed most friendly and sympathetic. He told me frankly that he abhorred the course of his government in sending the heathen down to commit ravages against the English people, and said it was more like committing murders than managing a war. He loans me books, and I have undisturbed opportunities for prayer, for reading the Scriptures, (I have an English Bible given me by Captain de Beauville) and for meditation. Nor does he make attempts to proselyte me. Others who come to his house try to shake my faith, but the priest sees it to be useless, I think, and so spares both himself and me vain controversy."

The good priest was very kind to Stephen, having a natural fondness for children, and being also moved to pity for the motherless child, whose face, still thin and pale, showed so plainly the hardships he had undergone. Like his father, too, Stephen met with only courteous treatment from the kind-hearted French at Chateau Richer. There being slight danger that a boy of his age would try to escape, especially when with his father, he was allowed entire freedom, and roamed about at will with the French boys, with whom he soon became well acquainted. He had learned some words of French since his arrival in Canada, and the French children thought it vastly amusing to ask Stephen the names of various objects in the strange, outlandish tongue of the "Anglois," and to try to repeat them after him.

"Listen, Francois. Stefen calls cheval 'horse,' and oiseau, 'bird,' and mere, 'mother!'"

Only three days after Stephen's arrival at Chateau Richer, came his twelfth birthday. He was but ten when captured. His eleventh birthday had occurred, unknown to him, while he roamed the wilds of Northern Vermont with Waneton and Kewakcum. But now he could know the day of the month and the year, and Stephen realized that he was twelve. After breakfast, he and his father were working in the garden, Mr. Williams trying thus partly to repay the priest for his kindness, and also feeling the need of bodily exercise.

"Father," said Stephen, "it is the fourteenth of May today. I am twelve years old today."

"True, my son. God grant you grow in grace, as you increase in years."

"Somehow I feel a great deal older than I did yesterday. Twelve seems a great deal older than eleven. Next year I shall be in my teens."

"Yes, the years slip away fast, my son. And the older we grow, the faster they go."

After a pause, while both hoed steadily on, Stephen spoke again.

"By and by, after we have finished hoeing, father, do you care if I go off with Pierre Binet and his brother, Henri, down the river a little ways?"

"Are the boys going fishing?"

"No father," said Stephen, hoping his father would ask no more questions.

"What is their business then?" asked his father, for even in Canada boys were not expected to be idly paddling about in working hours, merely for pleasure.

"They go to St. Anne, on an errand for their mother."

"Hump, St. Anne! Well, you may go, Stephen," said his father, after some hesitation, while Stephen stood anxiously by. "But do not countenance, or mingle in any of the Popish superstitions, such as I am told are greatly practiced at St. Anne."

"No, father," said Stephen, delighted at receiving the permission he had feared would be refused.

The hoeing done, Stephen hurried down the hill to the riverside, where Pierre and Henri, two boys with sparkling, black eyes and vivacious faces, were standing by the canoe, impatiently waiting for Stephen.

"Come on, then," cried Pierre. "We should have been gone an hour ago."

Stephen jumped in and took up one of the paddles. The canoe looked but an atom, tossing on the wide, surging St. Lawrence. But the French boys were as much at home on the water as on the land, and their mother felt no uneasiness in sending them on this errand.

Although it was only May, the sun shone down with summer heat on the broad river, on the green woods of the Isle of Orleans at the boys' right, and on the rich green meadows and marshes of the Cote de Beaupre at their left, as they paddled past. The sun shines in Canada in summer with an intense heat, as if to atone for the shortness of the season. But the frequent fogs along the river keep the meadows green with a thick, velvety grass, like that of Ireland. So, it was a lovely world upon which Stephen gazed on his birthday morning. The boys paddled on for about five miles, when Stephen saw a chapel among a cluster of houses nestled among trees under a sheltering hill, called the Petit Cap.

"Behold," said Pierre, "the shrine of La Bonne St. Anne de Beaupre, the mother of the Blessed Virgin!"

"Are you going to the shrine?" asked Stephen.

"Yes, we come for that. Our baby sister is sick, and my mother has sent us for a bottle of water from the shrine of St. Anne, that she may be cured."

"You do not really believe that can cure her, do you?" asked Stephen.

"Truly I do," said Pierre, with a look of surprise that Stephen could doubt such a fact.

"Stephen is but a heretic," said Henri. "He knows nought. Wait, Stephen, until you see."

As the boys landed, they noticed beyond them a poor old Indian, sick and lame, hobbling up the bank on rude crutches. He had nearly reached the chapel, while yet another, weak from illness, was crawling painfully on hands and knees from the canoe which had brought him, up the hill towards the shrine.

St. Anne was a pretty village. The roads were marked with stiff Normandy poplars, some of them having been brought over in Champlain's time. Before many of the houses were bright flower gardens, the seeds or roots having also originally been brought from France, by the flower-loving French settlers.

The boys entered the chapel. The French boys knelt devoutly, repeating a silent prayer. Stephen stood looking around with much interest and curiosity, though also with an uneasy feeling.

"I wonder if father will mind my coming in here just once, to see it all," he thought.

Over the altar hung a picture such as Stephen had never before seen, and would never see again; the magnificent painting of St. Anne and the Virgin, by LeBrun, presented the chapel in 1666 by the Viceroy Tracy. Before the altar was piled a great heap of crutches, bandages, trusses, splints and spectacles, which filled Stephen with wonder. In spite of himself, a feeling of awe and reverence stole over him, in the dim light of the sacred edifice, so filled with an atmosphere of devotion, and with holy symbols.

The shrines of the saints! Cannot even Protestants view them reverently? Do we not each bear in our soul the memory of some pure saint, at whose sacred shrine we worship, entering whose presence for the time we dimly foreknow the peace of heaven?

Pierre rose, and whispered to Stephen,

"Do you see yonder vast pile of crutches and canes?"

"Yes, I wondered much how they came here," replied Stephen, also in a whisper.

"They have been left as votive offerings by the poor sufferers who have been miraculously cured by La Bonne St. Anne, and therefore needed such supports no longer."

Stephen felt like saying, "Pooh, I don't believe it." But there were the crutches; there was no disputing that fact. The lame Indian whom they had seen entering, was now on his knees before the shrine, praying devoutly.

The boys slipped quietly out, and next went to a rough grotto in the rock beside the church. In a rude niche, above the grotto, was set an image of the saint, over which was a cross. Down over the stones, below the image, flowed the clear waters of a spring, the sacred spring of St. Anne.

Pierre filled his bottle from the waters of the spring. Hardly had he done this, when Stephen saw the lame Indian coming from the church without his crutches, able to walk very well, his face lighted with gladness, as he approached the spring.

"Behold, Stephen, now you see for yourself," said Henri. "Can you longer doubt?"

"'Tis very strange. I know not what to think of it," said Stephen. "But of course I cannot think he was really cured by St. Anne."

"What did cure him, then?" asked Henri.

Stephen made no reply. He did not believe, yet what could he say? He took refuge in a discreet silence.

"The Christian Hurons and Algonquins have a special devotion for St. Anne, the mother of the Blessed Virgin," said Henri. "You should be here in October. They flock to her shrine by the hundreds and the shore is covered with their wigwams. La Bonne St. Anne is truly a saint of wondrous power. I doubt not that this water will speedily cure my little sister."

Again Stephen made no reply.

"Come," said Pierre, "before we start home, let us show Stephen the falls of St. Anne."

The boys followed the River St. Anne upstream, climbing along the edge of the picturesque ravine, down which the river had cut its way to the St. Lawrence, until they came to a beautiful waterfall, where the stream dashed down many feet in white spray.

"There are other falls beyond, as wonderful as these," said Pierre.

"Behold our beautiful New France!" cried Henri, pointing off at the glorious view spread out beneath them, as they stood on the hillside.

Below them lay the pretty village, the broad river shining in the sun, the whole northern shore of the green Isle of Orleans. Down the St. Lawrence to the east rose a height crowned with large buildings, and beyond it loomed a steep, bold mountain.

"What buildings are those?" asked Stephen, surprised to see such imposing structures so far away from any city. "And what is yonder mountain?"

"That is Cap Tourmente, and the buildings belong to Laval's Seminary. It is a farm school where the pupils from Quebec come to learn trades and farming."

Far up the St. Lawrence a dim, gray height showed, which Stephen knew to be Cape Diamond and Quebec. There was a sense of exhilaration in standing thus high above the world, as it were, and looking down on so far and wide an extent of its surface. But soon Pierre said,

"The sun wanes. And we must paddle five miles against the current. 'Tis time we were starting."

"Are you not glad, Stephen," said Henri, as the boys scrambled through bushes and ferns down the side of the ravine, "that we brought you to see the shrine of St. Anne?"

"Yes, I am glad to have seen it," answered Stephen.

"Have you aught like it in your Guerfiel?" asked Pierre.

"No, indeed," said Stephen warmly, resenting even the implication that Deerfield might cherish a saint's shrine.

"I should think you would much rather remain here in King Louis' goodly domain, than go far away into that heathenish land of the Bostonnais to dwell," said Pierre.

"Yes, I wonder at you, Stephen," said Henri. "When you might dwell here in our good land, and become one of the true faith, saving your soul, to choose to turn your back on it all, and return to that far away country—it is a marvel to me."

"You boys don't know what you are saying Deerfield is no heathenish land. We have the true gospel there. And it is not Deerfield that is far away, but Canada! But there, let us not talk of it more. There is no use in disputing."

The boys amiably consented to let the argument fall to the ground, each being decidedly in the state of mind described by Hudibras,

> "A man convinced against his will
> Is of the same opinion still."

They sought their canoe, and paddled homewards, preceded by the sick Indian, whom they had seen crawling up the hill to the shrine, whose paddles now swept the water with a vigor and quickness speaking well for his improved strength. The good priest was pleased when he learned that Stephen had visited the shrine of La Bonne St. Anne. Not so Mr. Williams, who took much pains that night to expound at length to Stephen the fact that the so-called miracles he had seen were, no doubt, delusions wrought by Satan himself, for the undoing of poor mortals. But when Stephen went to bed that night, the vision of the picture and the shrine, so different from anything he had ever before seen, so beautiful, still rose before him, and he thought,

"I shall always remember my twelfth birthday."

20

A PERILOUS ESCAPE

EVENTS were occurring at Montreal on Stephen's birthday that would have intensely interested him and his father, but which they did not learn until long after. The captives taken at Deerfield in the raid of 1704, were delighted to find in Montreal young John Nims, who, with his stepbrother, Zebediah Williams, had been captured by the Indians in October, 1703, when out on the North Meadow in search of lost cattle. Nothing had been heard of the young men since their disappearance that night. Their friends were, therefore, rejoiced to find them in Canada, alive and well. Zebediah was in or near Quebec, John at Montreal.

To both the young men it had meant much to see again their pastor, Mr. Williams, and the familiar faces of many old friends. John Nims, with mingled feelings, found Elizabeth Hull among the captives. Elizabeth was a bright, pretty young girl of fifteen, his stepmother's daughter, and one of the home circle. Between her and John was a warm attachment.

As John clasped the girl's hand, and looked into her sweet face, worn and thin from her sufferings on the toilsome march to Canada, but suffused now with a sweet blush as she met him again so unexpectedly, and after such long anxiety, John said,

"I'm sorry enough, Betsey, to find you here, and to have you suffer such hardships. Surely 'tis of God's mercy only that any of you lived to reach Canada. I know full well what that journey is. But, since you must be taken, I cannot help rejoicing to see you."

"And I to see you again, John," said Elizabeth. "It is so long since you were captured, and we thought you must be dead."

"It's no thanks to the Indians if I am not," said John. "I hope, Betsey, you will be kept here, where we may perhaps meet now and then."

This hope was realized, for Elizabeth was taken by a French family living near Montreal. But John's baby sister, little Abigail, only two years old, was supposed to be still with the Indians, and no one knew where she was living.

Among others captured in the raid on Deerfield were three young men, Thomas Baker, Joseph Petty[11] and Martin Kellogg. The family of Kelloggs, living a little north of the stockade, were among the severest sufferers on that terrible night. A little son was killed, and the father, Martin Kellogg, with four children, Martin aged seventeen, Joseph aged twelve, Johanna aged eleven, and Rebecca aged eight, were all carried off to Canada. Only the wife and mother escaped. These children were scattered about among the Indians near Montreal.

The young men, Nims, Petty, Baker and Kellogg, had cherished strong hopes of being redeemed by Captain Livingstone and Sheldon, and being taken home by them. To this end they had bent every energy. When these hopes failed, the cruel disappointment made them more restless than ever in captivity. Joseph Petty, the oldest of the four, finally made up his mind to escape at all hazards, and, under a quiet exterior that made his French owner think him quite contented, was constantly brewing over plans to that end.

On Thursday, May 10th, 1705, came a Catholic holiday and "the great procession day" at Montreal. Petty, who was living about nine miles from the city, was allowed to go there for this occasion. He stood on the Place d' Armes, watching the procession bright with banners and emblems of strange device to the Deerfield Protestant, as it wound across the square and into Notre Dame Street. Suddenly, in the mixed crowd of *habitans*, soldiers and Indians, he saw a familiar face, that of John Nims.

---

11 Joseph Petty was assigned land on Petty's Plain, in Greenfield, named for him.

"Well met, John!" cried Petty. "So you too were allowed to visit the city to witness these performances?"

"Yes. My Indian master and his squaw brought me in with them rather than leave me at home alone. I tell you, Joseph, it does my heart good to see white faces, but above all, that of an old Deerfield friend and fellow captive like yourself. I'm sick enough of this Indian life. It passes my patience to stand it longer. I'm willing to do anything to get away."

"Don't speak so loud, John," said Petty, looking anxiously around. "Step apart here with me, where we shall not be overheard. I have something I want to tell you."

When they were in a quiet nook, withdrawn from the crowd, Petty continued in a low tone,

"I have made up my mind to endure this bondage no longer. I mean to escape."

"Good!" burst in Nims.

"This wretched slavery is so unbearable to me, that I had rather die in trying to get home than endure it longer."

"So had I," said Nims. "I feel exactly as you do. You know I have had a year longer of captivity than you, and I am forced to serve an Indian master too. I would go with you in a minute, but—there are Elizabeth, and little Abigail. Ought I to desert them, escape myself, and leave them in captivity?"

"I cannot wonder you feel so," said Petty. "But you can do nothing to help them here. If you succeed in getting back home, then you can work for their redemption."

"Yes, that is true," said Nims. "Have you made any plans?"

As the two were deep in talk, Petty unfolding his plans, and Nims absorbed in listening, suddenly Petty exclaimed:

"I declare, John, there go Martin Kellogg and Thomas Baker yonder. It seems as if they were sent here purposely to join us."

He hailed the young men, who, like the others, had been allowed to come into the city to view the procession. They felt it indeed a happy chance that had thrown them and these old Deerfield friends together, and listened with eager interest to Petty's plans.

"I am certain I can secure guns and some provisions to take with us, from my master's house," said Petty. "They are kept in a room next mine, where no one sleeps, and I can easily slip in there and take enough to aid us greatly on the long journey that lies before us. If you three can manage to escape and come down there, we will start from that point."

The young men now separated, lest this conference of four captives should happen to be noticed by French or Indian masters and excite suspicions of their schemes.

"We must try to get off by Sunday night," said Petty, as they parted.

"The quicker the better," said Nims.

"I will be up again next Sunday, to conclude with you further about our escape," said Petty. "If possible, meet me here again on the Place d'Armes, corner of Notre Dame Street, about noon, Sunday."

Petty returned to the house of his French master. Great was his dismay to find that, during his absence, a bed with a sick person in it had been placed in the room where were stored the guns and provision he had hoped to secure I Without these essentials, it would hardly be possible to preserve life in the vast wilderness which he and his friends must needs traverse to reach home. Petty was greatly cast down.

"I am afraid we shall have to give it all up," he thought, dejectedly. "It is impossible for us to make the trip without guns and food. Evidently Providence is against us in the matter."

But at night, when he came in from work in the field, to his relief and surprise, he found that not only had the sick person been removed to another room, but his own bed had been placed in the room with the guns.

"It is as if planned for us! Nothing could be better. Providence does mean us to escape," he thought, his spirits reacting to as great a height as they had been depressed. He was so bright and full of talk at night, that his French master said,

"The Anglois grows content. He is as one of us now."

He went up to Montreal Sunday, and managed to see his three friends. He arranged to set up a sign by the river before his master's house, as a guide to them. He also directed them how to know the window of his room.

"Well, Goodbye, boys," he said as they parted, after having arranged these details as quickly as possible. "Keep up good heart. Everything seems to favor our undertaking. If you succeed in getting off and down to my house undetected, tap lightly on my window, and I'll not be long in joining you."

Petty returned home, devoured with inward excitement, which he tried to conceal under a quiet, cheerful bearing. But he found, to his dismay, that, this day of all others, the son of his master had arrived on a visit and was to lodge that night with Petty! Petty's hopes now sunk to low ebb. How was it possible for him to escape, unknown to his unwelcome bedfellow? And if he and his comrades did not get off now, they might never again be able to meet and arrange plans for an escape. It seemed now or never to him as he mused with downcast face, in the gathering darkness, saying over and over to himself,

"What shall I do? How can I contrive to get off?"

Remembering that he had promised to set up a sign by the river, to guide his friends, he went out under cover of the darkness to fulfill his promise.

"I know not what to do," he thought. "I have no means of warning the others not to set out. They will certainly come, if they manage to get off unobserved, and then—I cannot join them! Oh God," he prayed, "help me now, I beseech thee. Open the door of deliverance, if it be thy good pleasure!"

As he returned towards the house, a light streamed out from the open door, where stood a horse, and the whole family were out chattering wildly around the son, who seemed about to mount.

"What! Can it be he is going?" thought Petty.

Such was the fact. The son had suddenly changed his mind and although it was night, and in spite of the persuasions of his parents, he was determined to set off then and there. Nothing would induce him to stay, and off he galloped, every stroke of his horse's hoofs sending Petty's heart bounding higher with relief and joy. Never was there, in his opinion, a kinder Providence. He went to bed, but not to sleep. Many a time did he spring from his bed at some slight noise, and peep anxiously out his window to see only the stars shining solemnly down, in the unbroken silence of the dark night.

At last, in the small hours of the morning, he heard a faint tap on his window. Three dark forms stood silently beneath. Cautiously Petty handed out the guns and such provision as he could seize in his haste, and then climbed out and dropped down. He led the way to the shore of the St. Lawrence, where lay a canoe, in which the four embarked, paddling across the wide river and reaching the opposite shore just as the sun was rising. They succeeded in passing the houses nearby on the shore, unperceived, and plunged into the woods to the southeast. This was Monday morning, May 14, Stephen's birthday. By Wednesday afternoon, two hours before sundown, they reached the Richelieu River, about nine miles below Fort Chambly. Here they made a raft and crossed the Richelieu. The few provisions they had been able to bring with them were exhausted, and it was absolutely necessary to forage for food.

Thursday morning, they worked their way cautiously up towards the settlement around Fort Chambly, in their quest of food. Spying a calf which, unluckily for itself, had strayed away towards the edge of the wood where they lay concealed, they shot it, and carried the body into a safe retreat in the depths of the thick woods, where they spent the rest of the day drying all the meat possible, in the manner they had learned among the Indians.

They intended to push on southwards the first thing next day. But Friday morning, alas, they woke to find a heavy rain soaking them, as they lay unprotected on the ground. All Friday and Saturday a drenching rain fell, making it impossible to travel or do anything but lurk in the dripping woods, wet to the skin, gnawing bits of dried meat. They ate barely enough to sustain life, for their slender store must be used carefully to make it last as long as possible. Dark and dreary days were those, full of despair. Providence was against them, they felt. How could they possibly succeed, with such a setback at the very beginning of their desperate attempt?

Later, they learned, as people often do, that their seeming ill fortune was really the best possible good fortune, for the pursuers from Montreal, who were hot on their trail, and might have recaptured them had the weather been fine, gave up the pursuit discouraged, and returned home.

Sunday morning the four fugitives started down the Richelieu, walking through the forest towards Lake Champlain, guided by the sun, and by their knowledge of woodcraft. They reached the lake Wednesday. Drawn up on the lake's shore, partly concealed by brush, Nim's quick eyes spied from afar two canoes.

"Here's a stroke of good luck at last," he cried. "Could anything be handier for us?"

"We will borrow one," said Petty. "Our need is so sore, that even the owner could hardly grudge it to us. He would do the same in like strait, I doubt not."

The young men paddled this canoe not only all that day, but all night too, not daring to rest, lest they be overtaken and recaptured. Their one feverish desire was to get on. Every stroke of the paddle put another, bit of space between them and Canada. All the next day too they paddled along the east side of the lake, rounding the point of a large island, and by night reaching the mouth of the Mississquoi River. Some among them recognized this stream, having camped here with the Indians on their way to Canada.

"It is some encouragement to be thus far on our way home," said Baker, like the others already worn and haggard from their terrible exertions and exposure. Again they paddled all night, up the Mississquoi, and in the morning going down one of the outlet branches, through which that river seeks Lake Champlain. They kept wearily on all day, not' daring to stop until night, when, feeling themselves reasonably safe from pursuit, they ventured to land, and seek much needed sleep on the shore.

They threw themselves on the hard ground, and without blankets or any covering, slept soundly, so utterly exhausted were they. The next morning Petty, who woke first, found the sky shrouded in dark clouds, and a fierce gale blowing across the lake. As he stood looking at the dark, threatening waves running high, and dashing up on the desolate shore, the others awoke, and, stiff and sore, limped down to join him.

"Hard luck again," said Petty. "We cannot venture on the lake today. Nor can we afford to lose a minute of time. We must press on, while we have strength left to travel. We must abandon the canoe, and travel along shore afoot."

"It cannot be more than twenty or thirty miles at the most, down to the Winooski," said Baker, "as I remember the road we traveled coming up"

"I think we shall strike it today," said Petty, as he set off, followed by the others, weak and feeble, yet animated by a dogged will and desperate resolve to push ahead. On they plodded all day, wading streams, leaping from tuft to tuft of solid land in marshes, climbing over rocks and fallen trunks of trees, and pushing through tangled thickets of undergrowth, where the Indians had not burned it away. That night they again slept on the ground.

The next day, guided by Petty and Baker, they struck across country, traveling steadily on all that day and most of the night. About nine o'clock Sunday morning, May 27, they came out of the woods at the falls of a stream which they thought they recognized.

"Praise and thanks be to God!" exclaimed Petty, as he gazed on the clear, brown water, tumbling down over the rocks in the solitude. "These are the falls of the Winooski, if I mistake not."

"Yes, this is the Winooski River, I am certain," said Baker. "Now our way is plain before us."

"Yes," said Martin Kellogg, "if our strength only holds out to get through. I feel rather dubious about ever seeing Deerfield again myself."

"And if we do not have the ill luck to fall in with a band of Indians," said Nims.

"I am holding some of our ammunition to be ready for such an encounter," said Baker. "We will not be taken again without a fight."

"And a hot one too," said Nims.

The young men followed up the Winooski for two or three days, through its wild gorges, into the heart of the Green Mountains, and then struck across for the branches of the White River. They reached that stream about nine o'clock, as they judged by the sun, on the morning of Sunday, June 3. It was three weeks since they had started, and their meager provision, although so carefully used, was now entirely gone, save a few poor bits they had saved for bait.

Being now reasonably safe from pursuit, they ventured to halt and try to get food. Improvising hooks and lines from parts of their clothing, they spent the day fishing in White River, but succeeded in catching only enough fish to satisfy present hunger. One small fish was left, after the hungry boys had finished their hasty meal, cooked in fear lest some wandering band of Indians should spy the smoke of their fire.

"We had better take this fish along with us," said Petty.

"We certainly cannot afford to throw away anything eatable," said Baker, as he pocketed the fish, wrapped up in leaves.

This proved a prudent precaution. Later someone caught a little land turtle. This, and the fish, were divided among the four, Petty's part of the turtle being one leg, and this was all the young men had to eat for the rest of their hard journey.

They followed down White River all day Monday. Gradually the hills grew less high, and receded farther from the river. At last, just as the sun was sinking behind them, John Nims, who was in advance, gave a wild shout.

"What's the matter, John?" asked Petty anxiously. Was John's brain crazed by the hardships they had endured?

"Do you not see?" cried John, pointing east, where in the distance the White River was seen entering a broad stream, bounded by blue hills beyond. "'Tis the Connecticut! Our own river, the Connecticut! We are as good as home now."

"Yes. If we can live to get there," said Martin Kellogg. The boy of seventeen was already nearly at the point of utter exhaustion.

"We *must* get there now," said Petty.

They soon reached the mouth of the White River.[12] Here they ventured to build a fire, and intended to rest for the night. Baker went down to the Connecticut to try to catch some fish. But it was a sultry June night, and the hungry swarms of flies and mosquitoes in the woods along shore, seemed to regard Baker's arrival as a special festival prepared for them. After enduring the torment as long as humanly possible, Baker was forced to give up. He came back to the fire, swinging his hands around his head to drive off his swarming tormentors, saying,

"A man would need Goliath's coat of mail to sit down out there, if he would not be eaten up alive."

"Give me the line," said Petty. "I am going down to the river for a drink, and perhaps I can stand the pests long enough to catch something, our need is so great."

As he threaded the forest towards the shore, suddenly in the dusk he spied an object on the opposite shore of the Connecticut that made his heart give a great leap. It was an Indian also coming down to the river. Jumping behind a tree, and peeping cautiously out from time to time, Petty waited until he saw the Indian come down to the river for a drink, and then disappear again in the woods. Then he ran back to the fire, around which the exhausted men had thrown themselves, this being almost the first rest they had ventured to take. In upon the group burst Petty, crying,

"We must up and on boys, for our lives! It's hard, but I've just seen an Indian across the river!"

"I don't believe I can take another step," said Martin, despairingly.

"We have no choice," said Petty. "If we stay here tonight, the chances are that we shall be either slain, or captured, before morning. That

12 In Hartford, Vt.

Indian is not alone, you may depend. The Indians will quickly spy the smoke of our fire. They may be starting for us even now!"

The disheartened boys dragged themselves wearily up, and followed feebly after Petty, as he set off to the South, forcing his way through the wild forest along the Connecticut's western shore. Sometime the next day, finding their strength so reduced by hunger and fatigue that it was impossible to struggle farther on foot, they contrived to build a rude raft that would carry four. On this they drifted all that day and night down the Connecticut, and still another day, until on Thursday, June 7, about nine or ten in the morning, they reached "ye great falls."[13]

Here they were forced to let their raft go, being unable to get it over or around the falls. When they had traversed the thicket in the woods to a point below the falls, they again fell to work with the strength given by desperation to build another raft. Their wild and desolate surroundings, the roar of the river as it boiled and tumbled down over the rocks, the great mountain looming up almost over their heads, the dense forest around, the eagle flying high above to its eyrie on the mountain's summit, all conspired to make them feel forlorn and hopeless. But still they worked on with dogged determination, wasting little strength on words. Once Martin broke the dreary silence, saying to John,

"John, see that old buzzard, roosting up on that dead pine? I believe he is waiting to pick our bones."

"He will not pick mine, so long as I have skin enough to hold them together, and to carry them on," said John, with a grim look of determination.

He thought of Elizabeth, so young, so pretty, alone among French and Indians, a helpless captive in faraway Canada.

"Those priests will be trying to marry her to some Frenchman, I don't doubt," he thought. "I *will* get home, God helping me, and then I will raise heaven and earth, but Betsey shall be redeemed."

That day, Thursday, they floated downstream to the "Great Meadows."[14] There at last they ventured to go ashore and sleep, being indeed forced to do so by their utter inability to travel farther without rest.

---

13 Bellows Falls, Vt.

14 In Putney, Vt.

The next morning, they floated down the river, until they reached other meadows known to them.[15] Here they left the raft and struck off across the wilderness for Deerfield. So weak and exhausted were they, that only a sort of dumb instinct kept them mechanically moving on, along the path they had traveled when captured. They crossed Green River,[16] and followed the Indian path at the base of the Shelburne mountains southwards towards Deerfield.

Friday night, June 8, one of the scouts from Deerfield (whence scouts were constantly kept out reconnoitering the country around for Indians), happened to be in West Deerfield, over in the woods near the foot of Shelburne mountain. His keen ear, alert for the least sound, suddenly heard in the woods what seemed like stumbling footsteps, and breaking twigs. He sprang behind a tree, instantly on guard for danger.

Out of the woods in the dim twilight, he saw four men, seemingly white men, coming, staggering and wandering aimlessly as if insane, not knowing where they went. At a glance he knew them to be escaped captives. Joyfully did he aid and guide them into the Deerfield palisade. Great as was the delight to welcome them there, yet tears rolled down many a bronzed cheek at sight of the poor fellows, reduced now to almost imbecile condition.

Some of the older men, who had undergone starvation in former campaigns, directed broth to be made, and given the young men only in small quantities, as they were able to bear it. But often they begged and even fought for more, a hard sight, impossible for their friends to resist. The friends would have weakly yielded, and only the firmness of the wiser heads prevented the re-turned captives from being literally killed with kindness. Gradually they were allowed more substantial food. But it was long before the cravings begotten by their long fast were overcome. "After having eaten all they could, they still felt as hungry as ever."[17]

But all lived, and were destined to do good service for their country later. And all, with devout gratitude, realized that their own unaided efforts might have proved in vain, but for help from a higher power. Long years afterwards, Joseph Petty wrote,

15 In Brattleboro or So. Vernon, Vt.

16 At the point in Greenfield where Mrs. Eunice Williams was slain.

17 Sheldon's History of Deerfield, p. 352.

"Thro the good hand of divine Providence (which watched over us all the way) we safely arrived to our own native land again, and were joyfully received, and well taken care of by our friends, upon which cannot but say that we have reason to praise God for our deliverance."

21

THE RETURN

ONE August afternoon near the close of a very warm day, Stephen and his father seated themselves in the shadow of the church to enjoy the evening breeze and the view. The church stood on a commanding elevation, high above the little village and the river.

"Truly a goodly land and a desirable one, if only it might be brought to the true faith," said Mr. Williams, as he looked off toward Quebec, up the broad river, bright in the sunset. Stephen, meantime, was looking down the river, watching intently a vessel which he saw in the distance, sailing rapidly upstream, with a favoring southeast breeze. She was a larger vessel than the ordinary river craft.

"Father," said Stephen, "see yonder large brig. She must be from France. Why, no, that is the English flag flying at her mast head! Isn't it, father?"

"It is indeed. She must be from Boston," said Mr. Williams in an excited tone.

The sight of his own flag in this foreign country would alone have thrilled him. But what tidings, what letters, what changes in the lot of many in Canada, might not that little vessel be bringing! It was growing late in the season, and probably the brig brought the only tidings to be had from Boston and New England, until the river's ice broke up the next spring. Her coming, therefore, was of vital importance to all the captives. No wonder that Mr. Williams was excited.

Father and son eagerly watched the brigantine, as she sailed between them and the Isle of Orleans upstream, growing smaller and at last disappearing in the evening dusk. Then, from the far distance, came the boom of guns.

"She is firing her salute. She is approaching Quebec!" cried Stephen. "Oh, I wonder how soon we shall hear what tidings she brings from home! I can hardly wait to know."

"We must have patience, my son, and bide the Lord's time," said Mr. Williams, not without a heavy sigh, for he too shared his son's feeling, and often had to fight down the restless impatience in his captivity rising in his heart.

The English vessel which the Williamses had seen was Captain Vetch's brigantine from Boston, bringing home Captain Courtemanche, who had escorted Captain Livingstone and company home to the Massachusetts Bay Colony. On board was also young Mr. William Dudley, son of Governor Dudley, who brought new proposals to Governor de Vaudreuil for an exchange of captives. History tells us, "The arrival of an English vessel in the St. Lawrence made a great stir. De Vaudreuil at first ordered her anchored fifteen leagues down the river, but finally had her brought up to Quebec, her sails removed, and a guard put on board."[18]

On his journey to Boston, in the previous spring, with the five returning captives, Captain Courtemanche had left Captain Livingstone at Albany, and taken Esther Williams, Hannah Sheldon and the other captives to Springfield,[19] though some may have been taken to Boston, where went Captain Courtemanche and Deacon Sheldon. Deerfield was still but little more than a garrison post. Home living was not yet resumed there, and it was no place for women. Hannah Sheldon returned to the house of her father, Japhet Chapin, in the north part of Springfield, which she had left as a bride not so many months ago, eventful months for her and hers. Esther Williams went to live with her grandmother, Mrs. Stoddard, at Northampton.

A few days of anxious waiting and expectation on the part of Stephen and his father, were followed by the arrival of a batteau manned with

18 "True Stories of New England Captives," page 184.

19 Now Chicopee.

soldiers at Chateau Richer, sent by Governor de Vaudreuil at the earnest solicitation of young Dudley, to bring Mr. Williams and his son to Quebec. Dudley was anxious to confer with Mr. Williams.

So, Stephen bade farewell to the kind priest, and his other friends at Chateau Richer, and left that place, never to return. At Quebec he and his father were handsomely entertained by Captain Courtemanche, who had himself received much kindness during his stay in Boston. So were the asperities of war sometimes softened by acts of genuine human kindness on both sides.

Mr. Williams, however, only enjoyed Captain Courtemanche's hospitality and the pleasure of young Dudley's society, and of meeting his fellow captives, for about a month. He fell into a religious controversy with a mendicant friar, a converted Englishman, sent out from France especially to labor for the conversion of the English at Quebec and, through the influence of the priests, was ordered back to Chateau Richer, lest he prevent the friar's success among the captives. "But," says Mr. Williams in his narration, "God showed his dislike of such a persecuting spirit, for the very next day the Seminary, a very famous building, was burned down. The chapel in the priest's garden, and the great cross were burnt, and the library of the priests burned up."

This was Laval's Seminary. Stephen was out in the crowd that thronged to the fire. He saw the flames rising to heaven from the great rock of Quebec, lighting up the river and the whole country round for miles with its red glare, and heard the wild cries of the excited people as they ran here and there in the vain attempts to check the devouring conflagration. It was a scene he never forgot.

Though again separated from his father, he was not unhappy, for he was full of excitement over the immediate prospect of returning home.

"It is fully settled with the governor that you go home with me, Stephen," young Dudley had said. And he had further cheered Stephen by adding,

"Governor de Vaudreuil gives me great encouragement to hope for an exchange of all the remaining captives next spring. God so willing, I have strong hopes of then securing the release of your father, your brothers and sister, and all these poor doleful captives."

Stephen was sent on board the brigantine to await the day of sailing. To the boy's impatience, the days were long, and it seemed as if the vessel would never start. He could not help an uneasy feeling that something might yet happen to prevent his actually going.

"I shall not feel safe until we are really under weigh," he often thought.

One day Stephen was hanging over the side of the brigantine, watching some French sailors who were loading a batteau nearby for a long voyage through the Ottawa to the great lakes. But presently his attention was attracted in another direction, for he saw Mr. Dudley coming down the hill towards the landing, accompanied by a young Indian. Stephen, looking at the Indian suspiciously, felt sure he was a white boy and, as the two drew nearer, he recognized his friend, Jonathan Hoyt. Joyfully he flew to meet Jonathan as he came aboard.

"Oh, Jonathan," he cried, "Are you going home too?"

"Yes, I am, though I can hardly realize my good fortune yet," said Jonathan.

"How glad I am!" said Stephen. "Glad for you, and for myself too, because I shall have your company on the long voyage."

"Sam isn't on board, is he?" asked Jonathan, looking around for his old friend.

"No," said Stephen, shaking his head sadly. "We know nothing about Sam. I wish he were going with us, and the rest too. But Mr. Dudley hopes to redeem all next spring. Now tell me how you happened to get away, Jonathan."

Jonathan was nothing loath to relate the story of his good fortune to his sympathizing listener. It seemed that young Mr. Dudley had chanced to be in the market place, it being market day, watching with interest the many Indians there, who had, as usual, come in from the country to sell their vegetables and other produce. Among these Indians, Dudley was struck with the face and bearing of a boy, whom he could not help fancying to be English, although he was dressed and painted like an Indian, an Indian in all outward guise. This was Jonathan Hoyt. Approaching the boy, Dudley asked,

"Am I mistaken? Are you not an English boy?"

"Yes, I am," said Hoyt, looking with anxious heart at his questioner. Like all the captives, he was always watching for the slightest possibility of release.

"Do you not wish to go home to your friends?" asked Dudley.

"Indeed I do," answered Hoyt earnestly.

"Where is your master?" asked Dudley.

"Somewhere in the city," answered Jonathan, his face lighted with new hope.

"Bring him to me," said Dudley. "I will await your coming here."

Jonathan rushed away, full of excitement, found Nanageskung, and brought him to Dudley, though he felt it best not to tell the Indian what Dudley desired.

"I want to buy this boy of you. I will give you this in exchange for him," said Dudley, holding up a purse, through whose netted meshes gleamed temptingly twenty gold dollars.

This was more than Nanageskung could resist. He took the money and went away pleased, so absorbed in this unexpected gain of wealth that he almost overlooked the fact that he was parting with Jonathan.

Mr. Dudley hurried Jonathan on board the brigantine, directing him to remain closely on shipboard, while he returned to the city.

"Unless I mistake your master," said Mr. Dudley, "he will repent of his bargain ere long, and try to get you back."

Jonathan, rejoiced to find himself safely on board the vessel, actually bound for home, was careful not to go ashore, nor to show himself.

Mr. Dudley's surmise proved correct. No sooner had Nanageskung reached his home at Lorette, than he felt that he had made a sad mistake in parting with the boy, of whom he was very fond, regarding him as a son. He hurried the nine miles to Quebec, and sought out Dudley, wishing to give up the money and take back the boy. Dudley told him it was impossible; it was too late. The boy had gone out of reach. Poor old Nanageskung departed mournfully, saying to himself,

"Nanageskung big fool. Give up his son Wawanosh for a few dollars. Dollars no talk, no fish, no hunt, like Wawanosh. Nanageskung heap big fool."

To the impatient boys, fearing possible disappointment, it seemed as if the brigantine would never sail. Daily they asked Captain Vetch,

"Do we sail today, Captain?"

"I'm afraid not. No such luck," the good-natured captain was forced to reply.

But at last, on October 12, 1705, the French guard was withdrawn, the sails were returned and raised, and, amid much bustle and excitement on board, especially among the returning captives, the brigantine weighed anchor, and started off down the St. Lawrence for Boston, at that time a long and hazardous voyage.

"I wonder if I shall ever see Quebec again," said Stephen, as, looking back, he saw that city set upon a hill already fading away in the distance.

"I hope we shall not, as captives," said Jonathan. "Although I have been kindly treated, I never want to live among the Indians again."

As the brigantine passed Chateau Richer, Stephen strained his eyes for a possible glimpse of his father.

"Poor father!" he thought. "He must still stay here. How hard it is! Yet I know he will be glad because I am released and going home, and he is willing to stay while he has three children still in captivity. But I wish I could see him."

At that moment Jonathan cried,

"Look, Stephen, I believe that is your father now! See, that man in a long black coat standing on the hill near the church."

"Yes, it is, it is! Goodbye, father!" shouted Stephen, waving his hand, while Jonathan also tried to make Mr. Williams see that he too was aboard. Mr. Williams evidently saw them, for he waved his hand in return, and Stephen felt happier for this glimpse of his father, and because certain now that his father knew his boy had at last started on the homeward trip.

"Father will pray for me," he thought, "that I may be kept on this long voyage and reach home safely."

Knowing that the brigantine must soon sail, Mr. Williams had watched daily for its passing and was rewarded at last by the assurance that his happy boy was on the way home, after all his hardships. The voyage was tedious, lasting forty days; days of tossing on stormy seas, of seasickness, of cold and discomfort and danger. But the brigantine weathered all storms and perils successfully, and on November 21, 1705, entered Boston harbor, and at last came to anchor at Long Wharf. Stephen's feet, after all their weary wanderings, stood again on the soil of New England. Kind friends were not wanting to welcome the almost orphaned boy, homeless and motherless. He was taken directly to the home of his father's brother, Park Williams, probably living on the old Williams place in Roxbury, the home of his father's boyhood. Here, at the grandmother's house, was doubtless kept a real Thanksgiving, full of rejoicing over the return of the little boy, after so many strange adventures, though it was a thanksgiving necessarily tempered by sadness and anxiety for the fate of those still in captivity.

Stephen had been a captive for twenty months. He had travelled, mostly on foot, the three hundred miles, through the wilderness to Canada. He had lived almost a year, alone with the Indians, to all outward seeming an Indian boy, knowing starvation and peril, and weariness almost unto death. In Canada, he had encountered new ideas, foreign characters and experiences, seen and known many things that would never have come into his life, but for his captivity. The little boy from Deerfield had experienced much, the influence of which could not but be felt, during all his after years. Through it all, his one support had been his unwavering trust in God.

In the library of Memorial Hall in Deerfield is framed a time-stained letter, written to Stephen in the spring of 1706, on the 21st of the March after his return, by his grandmother, his mother's mother. She, after the death of her first husband, Rev. Eleazer Mather, had married Rev. Solomon Stoddard of Northampton, the father of young John Stoddard, one of the soldiers quartered in Mr. Williams' house on the night of the assault. The fact that Mrs. Stoddard did not know of her grandson's return in November until the following March, shows how completely cut off from the outside world, during the winter season, were the remote settlements on the Connecticut. No post could travel to or from the Bay in winter. The letter follows, and brings us vividly in touch with the experiences and feelings of the time.

"Northampton, March 21, 1706

"Loving Son,

"Yours of March II came to hand and glad I am that you are alive after so many appearances of death and now you have an oppertunity to secure eternal Life oh do not let it slip Let not the temptations of vain companions divert you from seeking god pray every day read the scripture meditate on what you read and hear god loves the young ones should remember him as it is said in holy writ Remember thy creator in the days of thy youth &c many have bewailed ye not doing it but I never heard of any that repented of serving god betimes; such tho father and mother be gone ye Lord will take them up godliness hath ye promise of ye life that now is and that which is to come; but I

> hope god will bring back your father and brothers and Eunice out of their doleful captivity: I have sent you a pair of stockings by John Warner I must break of abruptly least the oppertunity of sending these lines be gone give my love to your unkle and aunt and your brother and sister, and I remain
>
> "your afflicted
> "granmother
> "Esther Stoddard."

Sewall's Diary gives us another glimpse of this good woman. He says, on occasion of his visit to Northampton to hold court, "Madam Stoddard, though lame of sciatica, spins at the linen wheel." She was then aged seventy-two.

22

SAMUEL WILLIAMS' EXPERIENCES

SAMUEL WILLIAMS, the minister's second son, was fifteen years old when captured. As has been told, he had been redeemed from the Indians by the chief merchant of Montreal, wealthy and prominent, Monsieur Jacques Le Ber, who had recently, by the payment of six thousand livres, succeeded in being ennobled by King Louis. Another captive, little Freedom French, aged eleven, the child of Deerfield's town clerk, Thomas French, was also taken by the family of Le Ber.

Samuel was sent to school to learn to read and write French, and in many ways kindly treated. But the son of the Deerfield minister found himself in an atmosphere of thought and belief strange to him and surrounded by powerful influences almost impossible to resist. He had not been long in the family before he heard much of the surpassing virtues of Mademoiselle Jeanne, the favorite daughter of Sieur Le Ber, who was venerated as a saint throughout Canada. Samuel was told her story by various members of the family, all proud to claim kinship with such an one.

As a young girl, Jeanne was ardent, loving, sensitive, and full of religious fervor and aspirations. Her devotion to religion constantly grew. Gradually she abandoned all the interests of her young life, refused all suitors, and finally at the age of twenty-two, shut herself up in her chamber, refusing to see anyone but her confessor, and the maid who brought her food, passing her time in devotions. Only once did she come forth from her retreat, when her brother, slain in battle by the English, lay dead in an adjoining room. She startled her sisters by appearing suddenly like a vision, standing for a few moments in silent prayer by the body of her brother, and then vanishing as suddenly as she had come.

About eleven years before Samuel's capture, she had left her home, to dwell in a cell built expressly for her, directly behind the altar of the recently erected church of the Congregation. Through a narrow opening food was passed to her. She lay on a bed of straw, her head against the partition that separated her from the Host on the altar.

"Here she lay, wearing only a garment of coarse gray serge, worn, tattered, and unwashed. An old blanket, a stool, a spinning wheel, a belt and shirt of hair cloth, a scourge, and a pair of shoes made by herself of the husks of Indian corn, appear to have formed the sum of her furniture and wardrobe."[20]

She passed her time in prayer, and in spinning and embroidering for the churches, usually, we are told, "in a state of profound depression." In this way she lived until her death in 1714. Her mother and father died, but no entreaties could draw the recluse from her cell. Miraculous interventions were attributed to her prayers, and she was held in the highest reverence.

As may be supposed, the family of such a devotee felt themselves bound to be strict in religious matters above all others. A kind Providence had, as they felt, placed among them a Protestant boy, the son of a heretic minister, as if meaning his conversion. Their first and most obvious duty was plain to the Le Bers; this boy must be converted, his soul saved. How pleased would the saintly Jeanne be, could they report to her this soul won to the true faith, saved by their pious efforts! Her prayers were no doubt joined with those of her family for the boy's conversion.

Sieur Le Ber, seeing in Samuel a bright boy, with the refined instincts and intelligence inherent in one descended from an educated ancestry, may have intended to adopt him as a son, feeling the time drawing near when he himself must resign his weighty business cares, and looking

20 "Old Regime in Canada." Parkman.

about for a capable successor. At all events, the strongest possible pressure was brought to bear on Samuel, to induce him to change his religion. He was told he would be given back to the Indians again, unless he changed. The priests sometimes spent whole days reasoning with him, anxious to please the Le Ber family; and his schoolmaster, whip in hand, at last obliged Samuel to make the sign of the cross.

"You are afraid you shall be changed if you do it," said the master, "but you will not. You will be the same. Your fingers will not be changed."

Later, when he recited his lesson, not crossing himself, his master said, "Have you forgotten what I bid you do?"

"No, sir," said Samuel.

"Down on your knees," said the master.

In this position Samuel was obliged to remain for an hour and a half, until school was done, and this was continued for a week. One morning when Samuel refused to go to church, four of the biggest boys in school were sent to drag him by force to mass. Boy human nature is the same the world over, and we can imagine the fervor of religious devotion in the four boys to have been mingled with considerable genuine enjoyment of the fracas as they pulled along, inch by inch, this stubborn descendant of the Puritans, all the blood of all his ancestors making him sturdily hang back.

At home also, every possible influence, argument and persuasion were brought to bear on Samuel. Under all this pressure, the fifteen-year-old boy at last yielded. Miss C. Alice Baker, in her researches in Canada, found in the ancient church records, in the handwriting of Father Meriel, this account of Samuel's baptism into the Catholic church:

> "On Monday, the 21st day of December, in the year 1705, the rites of baptism were by me, the undersigned priest, administered in the chapel of the Sisters of the Congregation, with the permission of Monsieur Francois le Vachon de Belmont, Grand Vicar of mv Lord, the Bishop of Quebec, to Samuel Williams, upon his abjuration of the Independent religion; who, born in Dearfielde in New England, the 24th of Jan. O. S. (3d of Feb.) in the year 1690, of the marriage of Mr. John Williams, minister of the said place, and his 'wife, Eunice Mather, having been taken the 29th of Feb. O. S. (11th of March) in the year 1704, and brought to Canada,

> lives with Mr. Jacques Le Ber, Esquire, Sieur de Senneville. His godfather was Jacques Le Ber. His godmother, Marguerite Bouat, wife of Antoine Pascaud, who have signed with me."

"Then follow," says Miss Baker, "the signatures of Senneville, Marguerite Bouat Pascaud, and the unformed and tremulous autograph of Samuel himself."[21] How little could the boy imagine that, after the lapse of almost two hundred years, a descendant of some among the Deerfield captives would be poring over that signature!

On the other side of the partition, behind the altar where this scene was taking place, Jeanne Le Ber in her cell was no doubt thanking God fervently for the mercy of this young heretic's conversion. Mr. Williams, two hundred miles away, with no means of communication with his son, knew nothing of all this, though full of grave anxiety for the boy. Not until January 11,1706, ten months after Samuel's conversion, did Mr. Williams have a chance to send his son a letter, happening to learn that someone from Chateau Richer was going to Montreal. On this traveler's return, he brought Mr. Williams a strange letter from Samuel, dated January 23, 1706, beginning,

> "Honored Father:—
>
> "I have received your letter bearing date January 11th, 1705-6, for which I give you my thanks, with my duty and my brother's.[22] I am sorry you have not received all the letters I have wrote you; as I have not received all yours. According to your good counsel, I do almost every day read something of the Bible, and so strengthen my faith. As to the captives newly brought, Lancaster is the place of two of them, and Marlborough that of the third; the Governor of Montreal has them all three. There is other news that will seem more strange to you—that two Englishwomen, who in their lifetime were dreadfully set against the Catholic religion did on their death bed embrace it; the one Abigail Turbot, the other of them Esther Jones, both of them known to you."

---

21 "True Story of New England Captives"—Baker, p. 195.

22 Warham.

The letter then goes on to relate edifying details of the deathbed scenes and sayings of these two Englishwomen, and ends abruptly, with no word about Samuel himself.

As may be supposed, this letter was calculated to stir Mr. Williams deeply. Moreover, the bearer of the letter told Mr. Williams that his son had embraced the Catholic faith. The sorrow of Mr. Williams was so great that some feared it would cause his death. Many blamed the messenger for telling him of Samuel's conversion, "but the messenger," says Mr. Williams, "told me he thought with himself, that, if he was in my case, he should be willing to know the worst, and therefore told me as he would have desired to have known in my place. I thanked him," continues Mr. Williams, "but the news was ready to overwhelm me with grief and sorrow. I made my complaint to God and mourned before him; sorrow and anguish took hold upon me."

Mr. Williams wrote an agonized letter to his son saying,

"Oh, why have you neglected a father's advice in an affair of so great importance as a change of religion?" In closing, he warns Samuel "not to be instrumental to ensnare your poor brother Warham, or any other, and so add sin to sin. Accept of my love, and don't forsake a father's advice, who above all things desires that your soul may be saved in the day of the Lord."

Weeks passed, and Mr. Williams received no answer to this letter. Thanks to Miss Baker, we have one little glimpse of Samuel during this interval. On February 3, 1706, one of the Deerfield captives, Elizabeth Stevens, was married to a Frenchman, Jean Fourneau, in the church of Notre Dame at Montreal by "Meriel Pretre," and among the signatures of the witnesses is that of Samuel Williams. The boyish handwriting seems to make the boy of two hundred years ago and all his experiences very real to us.[23]

Mr. Williams, still not hearing from his son, believed that his letters were intercepted. Finally, on March 22, 1706, he wrote Samuel a powerful epistle, covering fourteen pages of his narrative, which, he says, "I sent by a faithful hand." In it he said, "I long for your recovery, and will not cease to pray for it. I am now a man of a sorrowful spirit and look upon your fall as the most aggravating circumstance of my afflictions," and he ends, "My prayers are daily to God for you and your brother and sister, yea, and for all my children and fellow prisoners. I

23 "True Stories of New England Captives," p. 207.

am your afflicted and sorrowful father, John Williams. Chateauviche, March 22, 1706."

At last, in May, Mr. Williams's heart was gladdened by a short and guardedly written letter, beginning,

> "Montreal, May 12, 1706.
>
> "Honored Father,
>
> "I received your letter which was sent by------- , which good letter I thank you for; and for the good advice which you gave me; I desire to be thankful for it, and hope it will be for the benefit of my soul. As for what you ask me about making an abjuration of the Protestant faith for the Romish, I durst not write so plain to you as I would but hope to see and discourse with you. I am sorry for the sin I have committed in changing of religion, for which I am greatly to blame. You may know that Mr. Meriel, the schoolmaster, and others, were continually at me about it. At last I gave over to it, for which I am very sorry." The letter ends, "I am your dutiful son, ready to take your counsel.
>
> "Samuel Williams."

Here we must leave Samuel for the present, returning to others among the captives.

Zebediah Williams, the stepson of Godfrey Nims, had been for about two months living on the Island of Orleans in the St. Lawrence, only two miles from Chateau Richer, and it had been a great pleasure and consolation to both the pastor and Zebediah, to be able to see each other often. But one day Zebediah appeared looking very feeble. To Mr. Williams' anxious inquiries he said,

"I can but fear this is the beginning of a long sickness; it may be my last sickness. I go to the hospital at Quebec to-morrow. Pray for me, Mr. Williams, that whatever the outcome of this illness, be it life or death, God will sustain and strengthen me to do his will. And, should it be so, that you go home without me—" here Zebediah's voice faltered and broke, but with an effort he continued, "give my love to my dear young wife, Sarah. Tell her I never forgot her through it all."

"I will, I will," said Mr. Williams, looking sadly on Zebediah's face, where the pallor of death seemed already to rest.

Zebediah had been one of the most "hopeful, pious young men" in his flock. Since coming to Canada, he had won the respect of the French who pronounced him "a good man." He was intelligent, pleasant, studious and devout. In April, Mr. Williams' heart was filled with grief to hear that this young man, whose life seemed so full of promise, had died at the hospital in Quebec.

January 20, 1706, Deacon John Sheldon again set out for Canada in a second attempt to redeem the captives, accompanied by Joseph Bradley of Haverhill, and John Wells of Deerfield, going by the usual land route, via Albany and Lake Champlain. Early in March they reached Quebec, where Mr. Williams was staying, but only for a few days. Mr. Sheldon and his minister were glad to meet again and had many matters to discuss. After Mr. Williams' return to Chateau Richer, Mr. Sheldon went there to confer with him, one item on his expense account being, "For a cannoe and men to go from Quebec to visit Mr. Williams, 6 livres."

Mr. Sheldon may have hoped to take his minister home with him, but perhaps Mr. Williams was in no haste to leave, while three of his children yet remained in captivity, their souls, as he felt, in sad peril. Mr. Sheldon reached Boston on his return August 2,1706, on the French vessel "La Marie," with forty-four English captives. Among them were his two sons, Remembrance and Ebenezer, Thomas French, and Benjamin Burt and wife of Deerfield. Mrs. Burt had one child, Christopher, born April 4, 1704, while on the march to Canada, and a second, named Seaborn, born on the return voyage.

Mehuman Hinsdale, the first white child born in Deerfield,[24] and his wife, Mary, had been among the captives, their only child, an infant son, having been slain by the Indians during the assault.[25] Mrs. Hinsdale also gave birth to a son, named Ebenezer,[26] during the homeward voyage. Soon after the returned captives landed in Boston, the little ones born under such strange circumstances were baptized by Rev. Samuel Willard, president of Harvard College.

24 "Young Puritans in King Philip's War," p. 26.

25 Mehuman Hinsdale's house stood on the site now owned by the Misses Whiting.

26 Ebenezer Hinsdale became a prominent man, being the founder of Hinsdale, N.H. He married Abigail, eldest child of Rev. John Williams by his second wife.

Mr. Williams, unable to return with, or even see this large company of his returning flock, followed them with his prayers, and wrote them a pastoral letter to be read on shipboard. It was sent on board, says Sheldon, addressed "Per Samuel Scammon Q. D. C. Present with Care I Pray."

The end of September came. The autumn was of unusual severity. Mr. Williams and the captives still unredeemed were bracing themselves to endure another winter of Canadian exile, feeling, on account of the season's lateness, that any hope of their return before winter was faint indeed. But on October 1, up the St. Lawrence came sailing an English brigantine, bearing the appropriate name of "Hope," and the French vessel "La Marie," from Boston, with the French prisoners. The vessel also brought Captain Samuel Appleton, an agent of the Massachusetts Bay Colony, empowered to arrange a final exchange of prisoners.

Great efforts were made by the priests to induce the captives to remain in Canada. Especial pressure was brought to bear on Samuel Williams. He was promised, if he would stay, that he should receive a yearly pension from the king, and was told that his master, Sieur Le Ber, now an old man, and the richest in Canada, would leave him a fortune.

"If you return," urged the priest, "what have you to expect? Nothing. Your father is poor, has lost all his estate. It was all burnt. He can do nothing for you. It is far better for you to remain here, where your prospects are so bright."

But Samuel steadfastly resisted all these allurements and went down to Quebec to join the returning party. Miss Baker's researches show that Samuel and Warham joined their father at Quebec October 28. It seems somehow cheerful and human to learn that one of the boys, little Warham, we may presume, was charged on the innkeeper's bill "with breaking a glass."

On the last day of October, 1706, the Hope sailed away from Quebec, bearing Mr. Williams, his two sons, and fifty-five other captives. Mr. Williams' long and trying captivity was ended. But, even amidst his heartfelt thanksgiving to God for these mercies, the father's heart was saddened as he sailed away, by the thought of leaving behind the little girl who bore her mother's name. Eunice was still living with the Indians and had forgotten her native language. The father's oft renewed efforts for her redemption had been in vain. He hoped, however, that once at home, he could bring influence to bear through the government that would be effectual.

The homeward-bound ship encountered great storms, and narrowly escaped shipwreck, but finally reached Boston, November 21, 1706. Immediately on landing, the returned captives were sent for to appear before the General Court, where their wretched plight excited such sympathy that it was voted that "twenty shillings be allowed each prisoner this day returned from captivity."

Probably Mr. Williams and his sons went directly out to his father's old home at Roxbury. Two weeks after his return, Mr. Williams was invited "to preach the Boston lecture." Rev. Thomas Prince speaks thus of this service: "Mr. Williams returning from captivity and arriving at Boston November 21, 1706, to the great joy of the people; and being informed that he was to preach the public lecture there on December 6, I, with many others, went down, and in an auditory exceedingly crowded and affected, I heard the sermon herewith reported."

As soon as the glad tidings of their loved pastor's arrival reached Deerfield, prompt action was taken to secure his return. At a town meeting held November 30, 1706, Captain Jonathan Wells, John Sheldon and Thomas French were appointed a committee to "go down to the bay" and treat with Mr. Williams about his resettlement.

We can but admire the love for his people, and the entire consecration to his Master's service which induced Mr. Williams, after all his heart-rending experiences, declining several fine offers of settlement near Boston, again to resume life in the exposed frontier post of Deerfield. A state of war still existed there. Military orders of the time show that men of Deerfield were often impressed to do military duty, or to pilot scouting parties sent out "up the river and adjacent woods" under Captain Jonathan Wells, and Captain John Stoddard. On September 25, 1706, Captain Stoddard had orders to impress at Deerfield men, horses, and provision "to be imployed in her Majesties service" in scouting.

Mr. Williams' home in Deerfield was as effectually wiped out as if it had never been. The remnant of his family was scattered far and wide among various friends. Eleazer was in Harvard College, Samuel and Warham were with their uncle, Experience Porter of Hadley; Stephen was still at his Uncle Williams's, in Roxbury; Esther with her Grandmother Stoddard at Northampton; little Eunice a captive in faraway Canada.

Mr. Williams returned to Deerfield the last of December, 1706, probably boarding or staying with some friend. It was at best a forlorn homecoming for him. During the winter he wrote the narrative of his experiences, called "The Redeemed Captive," which was published in Boston in March, 1707.

Deerfield, since the memorable 29th of February, 1704, had been only a military outpost, but now the people felt encouraged by the return of their pastor to resume home living. At a town meeting held January 9, 1707, the town voted to build a new house for Mr. Williams on the site of his former abode. It was "agreed and voted that the Towne would build a house for Mr. John Williams, as big as Ensign John Sheldon's,[27] a back room as big as may be thought convenient." In May a petition was sent to the General Court for aid in "Rebuilding the Forts there so as to take in Mr. Williams his house." In October another petition was sent to the General Court from Deerfield, which gives us an inside view of the condition of Deerfield at that time.

A letter from Esther Williams, preserved at Memorial Hall in Deerfield, tells the next event in the Williams family. The letter is addressed

"For Stuen Williams living at Mr. Parck Williams at Roxbury."

> "Dear brother
>
> "I received your leters with joy and would pray you to excuse my not wrighting to you sooner I have so many leters to wright that I am hurried aboute them O let us be improving all opertunity now while the day lasts for when the night comes no man can work let us make choice [?] of that beter part which will stand us in stead in a dying our so that we may meet in that glorious place never to part I would pray you to learn them verses that I sent Cousin Elizabeth them was the verses that my dear mother youse to singe. I pray you to send me a pencil of selen waxe; and Ant Sarah would be very glad if you would send them verses [?] in print about the King of France; but now for who and what the gentlewoman's name is" [A line here is illegible]. "All friends are well and give their love to you and to all our relations except

27 The "Old Indian House."

> br Samuel who has got a bad cold. My duty to granmother and respects to unkels, and ants of that name except of my love to your self and to all cousens as those named I think I shall go up to Dearfeald before you have an opertunity to wright pray tell cousens of it no more at present but ascke your prayers for me so I remaine
>
> "Your loving
> "Sister till death
> "Esther Williams
>
> "Northampton
> "September 1707 father is to be mared next week."

As in most letters of the period, the important news was reserved for the postscript.

The new house being now done or nearly so, Mr. Williams wished once more to gather his children in a home and felt the need of a kind and loving woman, to be not only a helpmeet for himself, but a second mother for his children. On September 16, 1707, he married the cousin of his first wife, Mrs. Abigail Bissell, of Hartford, who was, like Eunice Williams, a granddaughter of Rev. John Warham of Windsor. Thus, after almost three years of distress and desolation, the Williams family were again reunited, and back in the town of Deerfield.

The house built for Mr. Williams occupied the site of that burnt during the assault by the Indians, on the corner of the common and the road leading West past the burying ground, still known as the "Albany Road." In 1877, when Dickinson Academy was to be erected on this site, the Williams house had a narrow escape from destruction. It was to be ruthlessly torn down, had not Mr. George Sheldon, the antiquarian to whose active interest Deerfield owes the preservation of so many historic relics, intervened, and succeeded in having the house preserved and moved west on the Albany Road, where it now stands, a most interesting link with other days. After the terrible experiences undergone by Mr. Williams and his people, it is not strange that a narrow, secret staircase was built, close to the great chimney, leading from attic to cellar, with concealed openings on each floor, to facilitate escape in case of Indian attack. A portion of this staircase, between the first and second stories, still remains.

The picture of the front door, given on the opposite page, recalls many scenes. In and out of this door passed Mr. Williams and his family. Here was heartily welcomed many an honored guest from down the valley, for we are told that Mr. Williams "cared not to eat his Morsel alone. How often did he invite persons from other Towns (occasionally there) to rest and repose under his Roof." His Honor, Judge Sewall, on his visit to Deerfield in September, 1716, raised this knocker and entered this friendly door with all the stateliness becoming his rank and character. Here the body of Lieut. Samuel Williams was carried out, when he died in the bloom of his young manhood, but twenty-one, after having returned once to Canada, when nineteen years old, as escort for a party of returning prisoners. Sewall recorded in his diary, "July 4, 1713. 'Tis known that Lt. Samuel Williams died at Derefield last Tuesday night to the great grief of his Father."

Forth from this door went Esther Williams that June morning when she left her father's home forever, as the bride of Rev. Joseph Meacham of Coventry, Conn. Up to this door rode Stephen Williams more than once from Longmeadow, with his fair and loving wife Abigail on the pillion behind him. Would that the old door could speak and tell us all it saw and remembers!

On another June morning, in 1729, through this door walked a sad company, the family and friends of Rev. John Williams, following his body to the church and burying ground. He died suddenly of apoplexy, at the comparatively early age of sixty-four, after an eventful ministry of forty-three years, as pastor of Deerfield. His life was undoubtedly shortened by the hardships and heavy anguish he had borne. Said Rev. Isaac Chauncey, of Hadley, in his funeral sermon:

> "His Captivity was a Complicated affliction, and his Conduct under it a considerable passage in the Scene of his life. It was a stumbling block to some that such a Religious Family should meet with so much Adversity."

The whole sermon, under the quaint phraseology of the time, pictures a conscientious, devout, and lovable character. Not only was Mr. Williams faithful to every home and parish duty, but he rendered public service, serving as chaplain for expeditions fitted out against Canada in 1709, in 1710 and 1711, and in 1714 he was sent to Canada as commissioner with Colonel John Stoddard, accompanied by Captain Thomas Baker and Captain Martin Kellogg, to arrange the release of captives. Every May he rode down to Boston, to attend the General Convention of Ministers. He is affectionately mentioned by Sewall, Prince, and other writers of the period. His body lies beside that of his wife Eunice, in the old burying ground in Deerfield.

23

THE OTHER CAPTIVES

MUCH might be written about the experiences of others among the Deerfield captives, which were full of romance and picturesqueness. Only a brief account can be given here, enough to gratify the invariable desire of young readers to know "what became of them."

Twenty-eight of the captives from Deerfield never returned, and their fate was unknown until 1896, when Miss C. Alice Baker, herself a descendant of some among the captives, went to Canada, resolved to solve if possible the mystery of their fate. By her painstaking researches among ancient parish records in Canada, records written in antiquated French, in minute handwriting, on time-stained pages with faded ink, often almost undecipherable, she succeeded in ascertaining the fate of eighteen captives, told in her "True Stories of New England Captives," to which volume frequent reference is here made.

It is difficult to realize the entire destruction that befell some families, on that night of February 29, 1704. Godfrey Nims had everything swept from him. The previous October, his son John, and stepson, Zebediah, as has been related, had been carried off into captivity. Now his house and barn with their contents were burned, five children, his wife's mother, his grandchild and other friends slain, and his wife and remaining children, (except his daughter, Thankful, wife of Benjamin

Munn, who, in their temporary cellar refuge on the Hinsdale place, escaped the Indians' notice), carried off into captivity. His wife was slain on the march northward. Nims was probably out the night of the assault fighting the enemy, being an old soldier, one who bore his part in the Battle of Turners Falls. Whether wounded or not in the North Meadow fight history does not say; but probably the strain of agony and excitement undergone that night hastened his end, for he died soon after the assault.

A desolate homecoming was that of John Nims, when he staggered into Deerfield, half dead, that night of June 8,1705, to find his father dead, and his family almost extinct in Deerfield. Elizabeth Hull was later redeemed and returned to Deerfield. She and John Nims were married by Rev. John Williams, December 19, 1707, and settled in the house which John had built after his return, on the site of his father's old homestead.[28]

Ebenezer Nims remained in Canada some years longer. He and Sarah Hoyt at least had the comfort of living in the same locality, where they occasionally met. The priests, anxious to induce as many captives as possible to settle permanently in Canada, urged Sarah to marry a certain young Frenchman. They insisted that it was her duty to marry. Finally Sarah (probably with slight doubt who would volunteer), consented, provided some one among her fellow captives would be her husband. Ebenezer Nims promptly stepped forward, and the lovers were married then and there. A little son, Ebenezer, was born to them in Canada, while they were still captives.

In November, 1713, Captain John Stoddard and Rev. John Williams, guided by Captain Thomas Baker and Captain Martin Kellogg, set out for Canada to endeavor to redeem Eunice Williams and as many other captives as possible. Detained in Albany by a thaw, which made the river impassable, they were finally able to continue their journey over land and lake, and reached Quebec January 16, 1714. All efforts to secure Eunice Williams were vain. Ebenezer Nims and his wife were living with Indian masters, at Lorette. There was much difficulty in gaining access to them, their owners being very reluctant to part with them. Stoddard insisted that they be sent for. After much delay and repeated urging by Stoddard and Williams, Nims was at last brought into Quebec, accompanied by several Indians. The Indians said that his

28 On the corner of Academy Lane, now owned by the Misses Miller.

wife, Sarah, was unable to travel. Disbelieving this, Captain Stoddard sent his own physician to Lorette to investigate and learn Sarah's actual condition. On his return he reported her perfectly well, and very soon she proved that fact by walking the nine miles into Quebec. Both Nims and his wife said they were anxious to return home and were sent on board ship. Effort was made to retain baby Ebenezer in Canada, but Nims refused to part with his child. Even after the Nimses had gone on ship board, the Lorette Indians came and tried to entice them to return.

Stoddard and Mr. Williams set sail for home July 24, 1714, bringing only twenty-six captives after their nine months' efforts. Ebenezer and family lived awhile with John on the old homestead, and then removed to that part of Deerfield known as Wapping. In 1737, Parson Ashley of Deerfield records that "Ebenezer Nims Jr, who was Baptized in the romish chh. being dissatisfied with his Baptism, consented to the articles of ye Xtian faith, entered into Covenant, was Baptized and admitted to ye fellowship of ye chh. to day." Two sermons were preached on the occasion.

Little Abigail Nims, Godfrey's youngest child, but four years old when captured, never returned, and her fate was unknown until Miss Baker at last succeeded in tracing the long-lost girl. Abigail was brought up as an Indian by the squaw, Ganastaria. She was baptized in the Catholic church and her name changed to Marie Elizabeth. At the time of the assault on Deerfield, Josiah Rising, a little boy of nine, who was visiting his father's cousin, Mehuman Hinsdale, was captured and carried away. Later he also was baptized in Canada under the name of Ignace Raizenne.

In 1712, young Samuel Williams, now Lieutenant Williams, "on account of his having the French tongue," was sent to Canada as commissioner to procure the release of more captives. With him went John Nims and others, Nims no doubt bent on the rescue of his brother Ebenezer, then still held captive, and his sister Abigail. Abigail was now thirteen years old. She had grown up in Canada as a Catholic, educated by the nuns, and resisted all her brother's entreaties that she would return home with him, saying that she would rather be a poor captive among Catholics, than return to become the rich heiress of a Protestant family.

In July, 1715, the two captives, Josiah and Abigail, or rather Ignace and Elizabeth, were married. Father Quere recorded on the parish register that they "wish to remain with the Christian Indians, not only renouncing their nation, but even wishing to live *en sauvages*." The children and descendants of this couple stood high in the Catholic church. Their eldest son became a priest. Their youngest son was a devotee and philanthropist, and their daughter Marie became the Mother Superior of the Nuns of the Congregation. In Abigail's last illness she persisted in wearing to the end a hair shirt, which she had always worn in penance. Under the Catholic guise, we detect the stern religious devotion of her Puritan ancestors.

The family of Martin Kellogg was another which was almost wholly destroyed in the capture of Deerfield. Only the wife escaped. The father and children (except one married daughter) were slain or carried away captive. When the father returned from captivity, it is little wonder that he removed to Connecticut. The story of the escape of his son Martin has been told. In 1707 young Martin was granted a home lot in the "Green River,"[29] section of Deerfield, but in 1708 he was again captured by Indians, while on a scouting expedition up the river. This time he remained several years in Canada, becoming so expert in both the Indian and French languages that, after his return, he was often employed by the Massachusetts government as an interpreter. He taught in the school for Indians at Stockbridge, and for some years had charge of the Hollis school for educating Indian boys in Connecticut. Eleazer Wheelock, in his "Narrative" of the work among the Indians says, "Captain Martin Kellogg complain'd of this as his great discouragement in the school at Stockbridge (the dislike of the Indians for rules and regularity) notwithstanding he understood as well as any man the disposition of Indians, and had the advantage of knowing their language and customs, having been so long a captive among them, and was high in their affection and esteem; yet he was obliged to take the children home to Weathersfield with him quite away from their parents, before he could exercise that government which was necessary to their profiting at school." Sheldon says of him, "Captain Kellogg was a valuable frontier officer, saw much service, and was a man of note in his day, remarkable for strength of body

29 Now Greenfield.

and mind." He lived in Wethersfield, and later in Newington, Conn., where he died.

Joanna Kellogg, eleven years old when captured, grew up as an Indian, married a Caughnawaga Indian chief, and never returned. Joseph Kellogg, aged thirteen when captured, remained in Canada thirteen years, learning both the French and Indian languages perfectly, living a free life, trading in furs, etc., with the Indians, and supported himself handsomely. When Captain Stoddard and Mr. Williams were in Canada, Martin was sent to hunt up Joseph, and make him good offers from the Massachusetts government if he would return. He accepted, and he and Martin struck off home together by the land route, not awaiting the sailing of the ship. Captain Joseph Kellogg was afterward military commander at Northfield, Mass., and at Fort Dummer, Vt. He was general interpreter to the Indians during his life, aiding in the school at Stockbridge, Mass., for the Indians, and succeeding his brother, Martin, in the Hollis school for Indians in Connecticut. Sheldon says, "He died at Schenectady in 1756, while with Governor Shirley on his unfortunate Oswego expedition."

Rebecca Kellogg, eight years old when captured, was probably redeemed by Stoddard and Williams. She married Captain Benjamin Ashley of Westfield. Both she and her husband were employed as teachers at the Stockbridge school for Indian children. Like her brothers, she was often called upon to act as interpreter for the government, and finally died while thus employed by the colony, on a mission to the Susquehanna Indians.

Another family wholly swept away on that February night was that of Samuel Carter. His barn was burned and the house rifled, but not burned. Three of his little children were killed, his wife and the other children dragged away, the wife slain on the march. He lived on the site of the old Willard house, its gambrel roofed ell being his residence. In "The Story of the Willard House," Mrs. Yale wrote: "Scared faces at midnight, looking through these small window panes at the rising, spreading flames of the burning houses, and, with wild dismay, suddenly seeing among the moving figures Indians nearing the house. It is all soon over; the house has been rifled of property, the wife and all the children are captives on their way to Canada. Hearthstone and roof remain, we see them today."

Ebenezer Carter, the only child of this family who returned, was redeemed through the efforts of Colonel Schuyler of Albany in 1707. He came home by way of Albany, and joined his father in Norwalk, Conn., where the desolate father had moved. Stoddard and Williams saw John Carter, another son, when in Canada. At first John said he wished to return home, but, overawed by strong influence brought to bear, finally decided to remain. Mercy Carter, ten years old when captured, married an Indian, and became practically an Indian squaw.

Deacon Thomas French, the town clerk, with his whole family were swept away by the assault. Mrs. French and her infant were killed on the march to Canada. Thomas French and two children were redeemed, but three little daughters never returned. Sheldon says, "In 1751 two Frenchmen came down from Canada, who said their mother was old Mr. Thomas French's daughter, taken in 1704." Again are we indebted to Miss Baker's researches for knowledge of the after fate of these three captive children. Freedom lived with Sieur Jacques Le Ber in Montreal. When baptized in the Catholic church, her name was changed to Marie Francoise, and later she was married to Jean Davelny. Martha French was given by her captors to the Sisters of the Congregation at Montreal, and was baptized under the name of Marthe Marguerite, and later married to Jacques Roi. A grandson of Martha, and great grandson of Deacon Thomas French, by name Joseph Octave Plessis,[30] was eminent in the Catholic church, becoming Archbishop of Quebec.

The fate of Abigail French is thus told by Miss Baker. "Archbishop Plessis used to relate that when he went to the Iroquois village near Montreal (Caughnawaga) he watched from the sacristy the Indians, as they stole noiselessly into the church and sat down, the men on one side and the women on the other. Though the women's faces were hidden by their blankets, he could always recognize his aunt by her tall figure and European gait.[31] This was his grandmother's sister, Abigail French, daughter of Thomas French of Deerfield, taken captive at the age of six, and since lost sight of, until now found among the Saint Louis Indians, where, adopting the language and habits of her captors, she lived and died unmarried."

John Stebbins, his wife and five children, were all captured and carried to Canada. Of this family, three children, Thankful, Ebenezer and

30 "True Stories of Now England Captives," Baker, p. 284.

31 An argument for the strength of heredity.

Joseph, never returned. Miss Baker traced the Stebbinses, finding that they married and dwelt in Canada. Thankful Stebbins was apparently taken by Hertel de Rouville, or one of his brothers, to the fort at Chambly. She was baptized at Chambly in 1707, under the name of Therese Louise Steben, her godfather being Hertel de Rouville, her godmother, Madame de Perigny, wife of the commandant of Fort Chambly. In 1711 she married Adrian le Gain, *habitant* soldier of Chambly. She had nine children, dying at the early age of thirty-eight. Almost by accident, Miss Baker, in her researches, happened upon her grave, in the ancient burying ground near Fort Chambly. The inscription over it read simply

"Therese Steben
1729."

Miss Baker says, "The spirit of the unredeemed captive, ransomed at last and safe in its eternal home, her dust lies there with that of the old noblesse, her friends and protectors. Gentle breezes whisper softly among the grass that waves above the sod; the rapids of the Richelieu cease their angry roaring as they draw near the spot; and the beautiful river sings its sweetest cadence, as it flows by the place where Thankful Stebbins sleeps."

Abigail Stebbins, oldest daughter of John Stebbins, but twenty-six days before the assault had married a young Frenchman, one Jacques de Noyon, who had happened to stray to Deerfield. She and her husband went to Canada with the army and lived with his relatives at Boucherville. She was baptized in the Catholic church as Marguerite and never returned to Deerfield; but her little son, Rene de Noyon, when ten years old, came to Deerfield with a band of Indians to visit his relations. His grandfather, John Stebbins, persuaded him to stay, and when the Indians departed, Rene could not be found. He grew up in Deerfield, his name becoming in plain Yankee parlance Aaron Denio. He became a noted tavern keeper in Greenfield, was prominent in public affairs, and a soldier in the later wars. Many anecdotes are told of his French vivacity and impulsiveness. Some of his descendants are still living in Greenfield.

Deacon John Sheldon, after three difficult journeys to Canada in pursuit of captives, moved to Hartford soon after the return of

Rev. John Williams to Deerfield. Remembrance went with his father. Ebenezer Sheldon lived in his father's house. Here he was frequently visited by old friends among the Caughnawaga Indians whom he had known while in captivity, and in 1735 the General Court granted to him and his sister Mary three hundred acres of land as recompense for their expenses in entertaining Indian guests.

Mary Sheldon returned from captivity to find that her lover, Jonathan Strong of Northampton, despairing perhaps of her return, had married another. In 1708 Mary married Samuel Clapp of Northampton. The Clapps lived across Mill River on South Street. In 1761, her husband and Jonathan Strong's wife both having died, the old lovers were married. During Mary's captivity, she was adopted by a squaw, and the Indians were very fond of her. In after years these Indian friends were wont often to visit her at Northampton. They always came when Mr. Clapp's corn was green, and devoured it in large quantities, roasting the ears at a fire under an apple tree. Once two squaws came to visit her. "Leaving their pappooses under the bushes on Pancake Plain, they came into Northampton Street, and found the Clapp's house by means of the step stones which had been described to them. They asked permission to bring their children, which was readily given."[32]

Thomas Baker was serving as a garrison soldier at Deerfield, from Northampton, when captured. After his escape and return he was actively employed as a soldier on the scouts to the North which were constantly maintained. In 1712, he was made a lieutenant, and led thirty-two men North on a scouting expedition. In returning from this scout, at the junction of a small stream with the Merrimac (since known as Baker's River), he came upon a band of Indians, and killed one Wattanamon,[33] the captor of Stephen Williams. Tradition says that Baker and Wattanamon levelled their guns at each other at the same instant, firing simultaneously. The Indian's bullet grazed Baker's eyebrow, but the chief was slain. On the bank of the river was found a wigwam filled with beaver skins. Baker and his men took all they could carry and burned the rest. They brought home "the weapons and ornaments of a chief," no doubt those of Wattanamon.

Baker was soon promoted to the rank of captain and went with Captain Kellogg as escort for Captain Stoddard and Mr. Williams to

32 "History of Northampton," J. R. Trumbull.

33 "Boy Captive of Old Deerfield," p. 185.

Canada in 1713. Here he fell in love with a young widow, Madame Le Beau, who, as Christine Otis, had been captured at Dover, Maine, in 1689, and, growing up in Canada, had married a Frenchman. Miss Baker tells the romantic story of Christine's escape.[34] A grant of land was made Christine by the government, on condition that she did not return to Canada, but "tarries in this province and marries Captain Baker," which conditions she willingly fulfilled. She and the captain were married at Northampton and lived on Elm Street, on the present site of the Methodist church. In 1717 the Bakers removed to Brookfield, where the wife's grant of land was located.

John Catlin, on reaching Canada, was given to a Jesuit priest, with whom he lived two years. The priest naturally tried to induce him to become a Catholic. Finding it impossible to persuade John to change his religious views, the Father told him he might go home on the first opportunity. When he went, the priest kindly provided all necessities for the journey, and also gave him a sum of money when they parted. Ruth Catlin returned from captivity in 1707, the year in which Mr. Williams's house was built.

Jonathan Hoyt was always very fond of the Indians. He never forgot their language to the day of his death, though he lived to the age of ninety-one years. Soon after he returned to Deerfield, his old Indian master came down to visit Jonathan. He was kindly welcomed by Hoyt and treated with great respect. Sheldon says of Jonathan, "He did good service as a brave and skillful woodsman, scout and officer; was a lieutenant in command of the town at the time of the Bars fight, 1746, and was at the head of the party which went to the relief of Shattuck's fort in 1747."

Young readers sometimes ask the fate of Jonathan Wells, the boy hero of Turners Falls, and military commander of Deerfield at the time of the assault, and long after. Sheldon says "He was to his death a leading spirit in civil and military affairs." He was a representative to the General Court, the first justice of the peace in the town, serving in that office twenty-six years, and as selectman thirteen years. In 1713 Deerfield "granted to Captain Wells ye Green River stream to set a corn mill upon;" the town also voted to "build a darn for Capt. Wells on ye place above mentioned," and a road was ordered to be laid out from Deerfield River to the mill site. This was practically the beginning

34 "True Stories of New England Captives," p. 28.

of Greenfield, and from that day to this a gristmill has stood on Mill Street, and the waters of Green River still pour over a dam, on the same site first occupied by Jonathan Wells. He died in 1738, aged eighty.

In 1901, during the observance of Old Home Week, the children of Deerfield erected a granite tablet to his memory, in front of the site of his fortified house, where so many terrified fugitives fled for refuge on the night of the assault. The dedication was a pleasant and memorable occasion. The "Dedication Ode" sung to the tune of America, written for the occasion by Hon. George Sheldon, the venerable historian of Deerfield, was as follows:

"Hero of tender age,
High on historic page
Thy name we write.
Of old when through the land
Ran dread of torch and brand,
With Turner's valiant band
Dared thou the fight.

"Wisdom beyond thy years,
On storied page appears,
Attained by few.
In manhood's prime, thy fame
Glows like a brilliant flame,
And gilds a noble name
With honors due.

"As slowly furled life's sails,
Stood thou with balanced scales
To justice wed.
With civic honors crowned,
Rest at four score was found
In our old Burial Ground
With kindred dead.

"We come to mark the site,
Where on that fatal night,
The helpless fled;

Home of a hero brave,
Strong were thy gates to save,
Thy name which here we grave
For aye be read."

The inscription on the tablet was as follows:

"Here stood the Palisaded House
of
Captain Jonathan Wells
To Which Those
Escaping the Fury of the Savages
Fled for Safety, Feb. 29, 1703-4.
Jonathan was the
'Boy Hero of the Connecticut Valley'
1676, and
Commanded in the Meadow Fight
1704.
Erected by
The Children of Deerfield
1901."

24

STEPHEN WILLIAMS' AFTER LIFE

SOON after Stephen's return from captivity, kind friends arranged that he should study for Harvard College. Was it hard for the boy again to apply himself to study, after his long sojourn in the wilderness far from books? Or did he fall eagerly upon books again, with the hunger of the intellectually starved? Knowing Stephen's ancestry, we may believe that he felt the real joy of a student in this opportunity to fit himself for an honorable and useful career.

A letter written to him after he entered college gives us an interesting glimpse, not only of him, but of the times. Stephen's youth (for he was but sixteen when he entered Harvard), makes us realize the respect already felt for his character, even at that early age. The letter is addressed

> "To Mr. Stephen Williams att Harvard College in Cambridge.
>
> "Mr. Williams—
>
> "When I saw you last att the Colledge I was so Transported with the sight of so many of my old Acquaintance that I put all business together with good part of my Brains in my Pocket, and by that means forgot to mention something which upon more sober thought I can't Choose but concern myself about. Sir, my

business is to enquire of you (tho' not in the name of Elder—) whether you are unprovided of A Chamber mate. If so I must tell you that Captain Moody's son my Pupil takes as great a fancy to you as Brown did to—you know what. His father also is very desirous to get him settled with some senior schollar who will speak kindly to him and encourage him in his studies, and he has heard A Great Character of yourself. He'll maintain him like A Gentle man and suffer him to want for nothing and no doubt will make particular acknowledgements to any Gentleman that shows his son any favor. The Lad is good humored, and for good words will do anything, but is apt to be discouraged with harsh language which makes me the more concerned who he lives with. If you'l please to do him the favour of taking him into your Chamber and take some Peculiar care of him and encourage him in his Learning you will exceedingly oblige me who having heretofore had the care of him cannot but interest myself in his welfare.

Sir, I should be glad of A Correspondence with you to Barter East Countrey for West Countrey News. If you'l Please to favour me with a line att any time Leave it att Cap't Edward Winslows in Boston and it will come safe to me.

"I am your Honest Neighbor and Humble Servant,

"E. W.

"Newcastle on Piscataqua, July the 30th, 1712."

Stephen remained at school in Roxbury until his father's marriage, and then went home. In a brief autobiographical sketch written for his descendants he says:

"I studied some time at Deerfield, but the town being but as a Garrison full of soldiers, and two families in my Father's house, I could not prosecute my studies; so that I was sent to live with my Uncle Williams at Hatfield,[35] and from thence I went to Cambridge College in July, 1709, and was admitted a member of the College."

He graduated in 1713, in a class of five, at the age of twenty. He kept school for a while in Hadley. Among his ancestors were many godly divines, and it was natural that he should be attracted to the ministry as his profession. In his diary he says:

35 Rev. Wm. Williams of Hatfield was cousin to Rev. John Williams, and became Stephen's uncle by his marriage with Christian Stoddard of Northampton, half-sister to Stephen's mother.

"I was awakened by the Spirit of the Lord when I was young (even before I was taken captive) and was put upon the practice of secret prayer. I was remarkably preserved when a captive and restored to my native country." A boy of his training and nature could but feel that the life thus providentially shielded and preserved should be especially devoted to the service of God.

He began preaching at Longmeadow, Mass., in the fall of 1714, and was ordained and settled there October 17, 1716, when only twenty-three years old. This "Longe meddowe called Massacksick lying in the way to Dorchester from Springfield," had been until recently a part of Springfield. Being now a separate precinct, the town had built its first church and had called this young man to be its first pastor. The ordination was an important occasion, the town voting money and making extra provision for the entertainment of strangers, who, no doubt, flocked to the occasion from far and near.

The town had voted the young minister a fine lot, fronting on Longmeadow's broad, beautiful street, on the corner of the eastern street on which lies the town burying ground. The minister at once proceeded to build himself a house of such generous dimensions that some of the parish began to be "uneasy because my house is so stately," probably feeling that the minister's youth made him in need of counsel and oversight.

But Stephen was preparing for marriage. On July 3, 1718, when he was twenty-five, he was married to Abigail, daughter of Rev. John Davenport of Stamford, Conn. The ceremony was performed by the bride's father, assisted by Rev. John Williams of Deerfield, in the Stamford meeting house, which was crowded for the occasion. The young bridegroom recorded "Being before so great an assembly, it made the case look very solemn to me."

The modest, even reverential letter of the bride, written not long before the wedding, well illustrates the change in spirit and customs between 1718 and 1905. The bridal couple probably travelled on horseback to Longmeadow, escorted by a party of friends and relatives, and entertained by friends on the way, to receive a royal welcome on reaching Longmeadow. A feast had been prepared, and anagrams and acrostics were written to celebrate the joyful occasion. Here is a bit of one poem, "On the happy marriage of Rev. Stephen Williams with that virtuous gentlewoman, Madam Abigail Davenport."

"How happily two names are mett,
Two names of note and of Renown;
The foremost here in order sett
Is Stephen which denotes a crown.
The other name is Abigail,
A Father's joy it signifies;
Which Twain conjoyning will not fail
Of sounding forth sweet harmonies."

The bride's furniture and outfit were brought up later from Stamford, among them the case of drawers bearing her initials "A. D." painted on one end. This piece of furniture is still owned by her descendant in Longmeadow.[36]

When Warham Williams returned with his father from Canada, he had entirely forgotten English, but spoke French fluently. In 1719, the year after Stephen's marriage, Warham graduated at Harvard College, in a class of twenty-three, the college having grown in numbers since Stephen's time. He was settled as minister at Waltham, Mass., in 1723, when twenty-four years old, and remained there until his death in 1751, at the age of fifty-two.

Stephen Williams now settled down for his life-long ministry at Longmeadow. He had eight children. Of his six sons, three became ministers, and one died in the army in 1758. Mr. Williams says of himself, "I was weakly when I First Set out in the world; but have been remarkably favored; so that, when I have been at Home (for I was dangerously Sick when at Louisbourg in the year 1745) I have not been kept from the publick worship but one day and a half in fifty-two years."

In 1735 he was employed by Governor Belcher to treat with the Housatonic Indians about receiving the gospel, his efforts resulting in the settlement of Rev. Mr. Sergeant among these Indians, and the gathering a church there. He went as chaplain of a regiment to Louisburg, in 1745. Again, in 1755, he went as chaplain in the expedition against Crown Point, and was at Lake George when the American camp was attacked by the French and Indians September 8, 1755. Vivid must have been the recollections of his boyhood's experiences, recalled by

36 Miss Sarah W. Storrs.

this event! He went again later as chaplain to Lake George, but ill health obliged him to return home.

The many months spent as a child among the Indians left a deep impress on his life. We have hints that he never forgot the knowledge of woodcraft then learned. In his diary on September 6,1754, he records that "the Bears are about in great numbers," killing the Longmeadow hogs and sheep, and the next day he goes forth into the woods with his neighbors to hunt the bears. A pair of snowshoes belonging to him are still to be seen in Longmeadow.[37] The anniversary of his being taken captive never passed without his noticing the day. He wrote in his diary, March 11, 1755, "Fifty-one years ago I was taken prisoner and carried to Canada. Oh, that God would affect me with his dealing towards me, in preserving me from among ye Barbarous Heathen; in returning me and continuing me to this day." On March 30, 1755, he records: "This day I begin to read the Scriptures publickly in the Congregation." This step was a great innovation, requiring courage on the minister's part to inaugurate and maintain.

Eunice Williams was never redeemed. She wholly forgot the English tongue and became as completely a savage as if born one of them. Her case has always been a sad puzzle to the believers in heredity. In 1713 she married a Caughnawaga Indian. The government of Massachusetts made repeated efforts to redeem her, but all were in vain. After her marriage, in 1713, Colonel John Schuyler of Albany went to Canada, to try to bring her back. He thus describes her. She looked "very poor in body, bashful in the face, but proved harder than Steel in her breast." Through an interpreter Colonel Schuyler implored her to return to New England, if only to see her old father, promising her a safe conduct home. After he had talked two hours to her, she replied with only these words, "Jahte oghte," meaning "maybe not," in Indian parlance an emphatic refusal. Her husband then explained that she would have gone and seen her father had he not married again. Colonel Schuyler thus ends the story: "I Being very Sorrowfull that I could not prevail upon nor get one word more from her, I took her by the hand, and left her at the priest's house," where the interview had taken place.

In 1740, however, Rev. Stephen Williams received word that his sister Eunice and her husband were at Albany and wished to meet him. Accompanied by his brother, Rev. Eleazer Williams of Mansfield, Conn.,

37 At Miss Storrs'.

and his sister Esther's husband, Rev. Joseph Meacham of Coventry, Conn., he set forth on horseback for Albany by the Westfield road, the journey consuming three days. In his diary he speaks of "the joyfull Sorrowfull meeting of my poor sister that we had been separated from above thirty-six years." Mr. Williams succeeded in persuading Eunice and her husband to return with him to Longmeadow. We can imagine the interest and excitement in that village, when it was noised about that the minister's Indian sister was in town. Mr. Williams says, "the whole place seemed to be greatly moved at our coming." Captain Joseph Kellogg, the former captive, was sent for to act as interpreter.

Relatives and friends came from far and near to see Eunice, among them her uncle, Colonel John Stoddard of Northampton, who remembered her as a pretty little girl of seven, playing about her father's house when he was quartered there as a young soldier. He and Mr. Williams used every effort to persuade Eunice and husband to remain in New England, but only succeeded in obtaining a promise that they would return for another visit. The General Court offered Eunice and husband a large tract of land if they would remain. But all was in vain. On Monday, more friends came, and a feast was held at Mr. Williams' spacious house.[38] Mr. Williams says,

"Our sister and family dined in the room with the Company. Sister M.[39] and I sat at the table with them. At evening our young people sang melodiously that was very Grateful to my sister and company and I hope we are something endeared to her. She says 'twill hurt her to part with us."

The next day Eunice and husband left, Mr. Williams riding with them beyond Westfield, and his oldest son John escorting them to Albany.

The following year Eunice came again on a visit, bringing her husband and two children. From Longmeadow they went to Mansfield and Coventry, Conn., to visit Eunice's brother Eleazer and sister Esther. On their return to Longmeadow, Rev. Warham Williams came up from Waltham to visit his sister. Stephen Williams' heart never ceased to yearn over this poor sister. He writes, "'Tis pleasant to See her, but

38 The house built by Rev. Stephen Williams was unfortunately burned in 1845, after having stood 129 years. With it were destroyed most of his belongings, including part of his diary. His inkstand and desk are still treasured in the Longmeadow church.

39 Esther Meacham

Grievous to part with her. The Lord mercifully overrule that she may yet Return and dwell with us."

Eunice made another visit in 1743, and in June 1761, she came again with her husband, her daughter Katherine and the daughter's husband, Francois Xavier Onosategen, the great chief of Caughnawaga, and several other Indians. They refused to lodge in the house but camped in a wigwam which they erected in the orchard back of the house, across the street from the burying ground. Mr. Williams says,

"After meeting, people came in great numbers to see my Sister. I am fearful it may not be agreeable to be gazed upon. I am sending here and there to my children and friends, and I pray God to bring them together that we may have a comfortable and profitable meeting."

At the Longmeadow Centennial, the venerable Mrs. Schauffer, a great granddaughter of Rev. Stephen Williams, gave this reminiscence of Eunice's visit, which she had from her grandmother, who was Stephen's daughter Martha. "One day my grandmother and her sisters got their Aunt Eunice into the house and dressed her up in our fashion. Meantime the Indians outside were very uneasy, and when Aunt Eunice went out in her new dress, they were much displeased, and she soon went into the house, begging to have her blanket again."

Mr. Williams records: "I had a Sad discourse with my Sister and her Husband and find that they are not at all disposed to come and settle in the Country." He thus describes the final parting. "When I took leave of my sister and her daughter in the parlor, they both shed tears and seemed affected. Oh, that God would touch their hearts and incline them to turn to their Friends, and to embrace the religion of Jesus Christ."

This was Eunice's last visit to her native country. A glimpse of her in old age is given in a letter from James Dean to Rev. Stephen Williams. Sheldon says, "Dean had spent several years at Caughnawaga, and knew Eunice intimately." The letter says,

"She has two daughters and one grandson which are all the Descendants she has. Both her daughters are married. But one has no children. Your sister lives Comfortably & well & considering her advanced age enjoyed a good state of health when I left the Country. She retains still an affectionate remembrance of her friends in New England; but tells me she never expects to see them again; the fatigues of so long a journey would be too much for herself to undergo."

Stephen Williams never lost his interest in the Indians. At one time an Indian named John Wau-waum-pe-quun-naunt lived with Mr. Williams, and was instructed by him, and later was supported by Mr. Williams at the Hollis Indian school. Jonathan Edwards calls him "an ingenious young Indian." He was afterwards associated with David Brainerd in his work among the Indians. In 1773 Rev. Stephen Williams received the degree of Doctor of Divinity from Dartmouth College, then a new college, grown out of the Indian school from Lebanon, Conn., which was removed to Hanover, N.H., in 1770.

In 1837 one of the oldest members of the Longmeadow church gave his personal recollections of Dr. Stephen Williams in his old age. He said: "He wore a large wig, and his appearance was very venerable and imposing," adding that in his boyhood "it used to be said that the people of Longmeadow regarded Dr. Williams as their Maker; with the exception of one sceptical fellow who alone questioned it."

In Dr. Williams' will, made in 1771, after disposing of his property, he said:

"But principally and above all, I give and bequeath as my last legacy, to all my dear children, my serious and solemn advice, that they choose the Lord Jehovah for their God. He hath been my Father's God, and I trust and humbly hope, mine also. He hath been with me in great difficulties and troubles. He has remarkably helped, delivered, and saved me."

Such was his testimony when nearing the end of his long, useful life, and in his autobiography he also wrote:

"I have seen abundance of the Goodness, mercy, and Kindness of God in the course of my life, for which I desire to render praise to Almighty God, the Giver of Every Good Gift."

On October 16,1775, Rev. Robert Breck, pastor at Springfield, Mass., preached a sermon commemorating the centennial of the burning of Spring-field by the Indians. In it he said:

"I have lived with you longer than any minister in any part of the town except the Rev. Dr. Williams who is here present in the eighty-third year of his age, and has nearly completed the fifty-ninth year of his ministry. In a comfortable state of health and full possession of his intellectual powers, he promises to be useful for years to come."

Dr. Williams continued to preach for seven years longer, rounding out a devoted ministry of sixty-six years, which left an indelible impress on Longmeadow. His influence and usefulness increased to the end. In his historical address at the Longmeadow Centennial Rev. John W. Harding said of Dr. Williams:

"The last time he appears abroad, his loving and beloved deacons tenderly carry him in his armchair across the green, and help his tottering steps into the deacon's seat—for he cannot mount the pulpit stairs. They hear, with tearful eyes, his last address, bring to him three little ones for his parting blessing in the rite of holy baptism, and then carry him back to the home he builded in his youthful vigor, in a few days more to die in the ninetieth year of his age."

There was a great assembly at his funeral. The sermon was preached by Rev. Robert Breck of Springfield. In it he said to his fellow-ministers, many of whom were present:

"My brethren, it has pleased God to remove from us our father, who has been for many years at our head. I trust that we, his sons in the ministry, who in a body made him a visit when he was declining fast, will never forget with how much affection he committed us and our flocks to God; the advices he gave us; the fatherly blessing he bestowed upon us; and the tenderness with which he took his last leave of us. I could not help thinking that I had before my eyes the old prophet wrapped in his mantle, just stepping into his chariot, ready upon the wings of the wind to take his flight into heaven. My brethren, it is worthwhile to live as our Father Williams did, if it was only to die as he did."

His body was laid in the burying ground behind the church. The brown stone table covering his grave, bears this inscription:

"In Memory of
The Rev. Stephen Williams, D. D.
who was a prudent and Laborious Minister,
a sound and evangelical Preacher,
a pious and exemplary Christian,
a sincere and faithful Friend,
a tender and affectionate Father and
Consort, a polite and hospitable
Gentleman, and a real and disinterested
Lover of Mankind; departed this life
with humble and cheerful hope of a

better, June 10th, 1782, in the 90th year
of his age, and 66th of his ministry.

Softly his fainting head he lay,
His Maker kissed his soul away,
Upon his Maker's breast;
And laid his flesh to rest."

Thus ends the story of the Boy Captive.

Made in the USA
Middletown, DE
21 December 2019